Content warning:
strong language, suicide references,
violence, drug addiction

Also by P. C. Roscoe

How the Other Half Die

VANDENBURG RESORT, VAL D'AMER DOUX

CHALET GUESTS

Anike Dossongui
Minette Aillet
Chalet Host: Reilly Clarke

Noah Scarisbrick
James Scarisbrick
Janet Scarisbrick
Chalet Host: Tina Abbot

Jacob Arcilla
Mary Arcilla
Sandro Arcilla
Chalet Host: Marcus Johnson

Hugo Vandenburg
Mark Vandenburg
Chalet Host: Nils Schinz

THE VANDENBURG HOTEL

Charlotte Aillet
Head of Housekeeping: Lisolette Keller

PROLOGUE

Snow gleams in the moonlight, a strange otherworldly blue in the darkness. Overhead, the night sky is full of stars like diamonds — beautiful and cold — but nothing compared to the icy air slicing into my lungs.

It's agony every time I breathe, but I'm still sucking in great lungfuls of oxygen.

I'm going to hyperventilate if I don't stop, but the avalanche of panic burying me is so overwhelming that I'm not being rational. Hunching forward, I brace my hands on my knees, the ski suit thick and tight around me, as the rapidly cooling sweat slides down my back making me shiver.

Even my hands are sweaty, and I can't stop myself from tearing off my gloves. I want to strip off my jacket and undress right here on the side of the snow-topped mountain, but self-preservation is real.

I know that now, more than I have ever done before.

I start to shake.

Out of the corner of my eye, I see the arc of blood slashed across the snow.

They can't still be alive, can they? They just can't.

They must be dead. No one could have survived that.

I plunge my hands into pure white snow, grab fistfuls and rub it on my face. It's a different kind of shock, one I need. But when I pull my hands back and see that they are covered in blood. I watch the snow melt on my skin, turning red, bleeding down my wrist and slipping beneath the cuff of my jacket, and I scream, shaking my hands furiously trying to stop it.

It's not my blood. I don't want it on me. I have to get it off!

It's below zero, but I don't care. I can't have it touch me. I'm tearing at the zip of my jacket, my fingers numb.

I need to wash it off. My skin itches and I realise that I'll never be clean, not from this.

My heart starts to pound and I hear a scream, feral and desperate. I try to block my ears from the sound, but it's only then that I realise it's coming from me.

The swish of skis cuts through the thundering pulse in my ear, getting closer and closer.

I'm going to be sick.

I turn in the direction of the sound, bracing myself, but I catch sight of the body.

Dirty hair spattered with blood and bits of something that could quite possibly be brain matter.

Blood has soaked into the snow and all I can think of is Slush Puppies.

And then I think I might start to laugh.

Oh god.

The skier breaks through the dark tree-line on the side of the slope.

Their shock is nothing compared to mine. But seeing it makes me angry. Furious. The same kind of fury that ties me back to what just happened.

There's a moment of silence. Everything is still. Breaths held, hearts stopped; the two of us gathered in some bizarre tableau, as if it's possible that this isn't real. That none of the last twelve days actually happened.

And then that silence is broken by a question.

'What did you do?'

CHAPTER ONE
MINETTE

Minette jumped up and down trying to get warm. Her heavy boots crunched on the thick wedge of snow lining the driveway. She'd only been out here for, like, three minutes and was already freezing. She should have grabbed her coat. Blowing a stream of foggy breath into her hands, she rubbed the prickles out of her fingertips and tried to settle the flutter of excited nerves that danced in her chest. She almost couldn't believe that Anike had convinced her dad to let her join them. She pulled out her phone and reread the messages.

> Be there in five!
> So excited to see you!

Anike might be excited, but Minette was ecstatic. Not only did she get to spend the next twelve days with her dorm mate from college, but they were going to be staying in ultra luxury. Usually, she and Maman stayed in the hotel, just a little further down the hill.

Located not too far from Verbier, the Swiss village of Val D'Amer Doux also bordered France, but was even more exclusive than the better-known ski hub. And the reason? The Vandenburgs.

Their hotel was *incredible*. It was a beautiful building of warm wood and pale stone with huge expansive windows that glinted in the afternoon sun. It was 'the' place to be in Mont Blanc. Rooms were booked out nearly eighteen months in advance, and their Michelin-starred restaurant welcomed celebrity chefs as often as it did guests. But this year, Minette was staying in one of the chalets in the Vandenburg Resort. Reserved exclusively for a very select few, most people didn't even know about them.

Maman could have hired one of these on any of their previous visits if she had wanted, but her mother always insisted on staying in the Vandenburg Hotel. Minette had never understood why. Not that she would have dared ask, nor would Charlotte Aillet ever have explained herself. Maman hadn't become a diplomat by being nice.

But *this* year Minette was staying in one of the four chalets. And of course she was looking forward to the kind of luxury most people didn't even hear about. But what she was most excited about was being so close to the chalet where Noah and his family were staying.

Minette's heart fluttered. She hadn't seen her boyfriend much in the last three months since they'd both started college. She was in Paris studying at *la Sorbonne* and he was in England at Cambridge. It had been a huge change from spending all their time together at the Swiss boarding school where they'd met. One she hadn't been sure that their relationship would survive – despite being voted 'most likely to get married' by their school friends. But they *had* made it, she thought with a sense of unfurling satisfaction in her chest, and tonight she'd get to see him again.

Minette peered down the hill to see if she could spot Anike's car on the road that wound through the large skiing village and passed the Vandenburg hotel where, right about now, her mother would probably be sunk into one of their world-famous steam baths.

It made her wonder what her father was doing. Papa usually worked during the Christmas period. Last year it had been Zurich, which was close by, but this year he was in Hong Kong, which felt a million miles away.

Business never stops, ma chérie.

It was *always* about business.

'Business' was why Anike's father had thrown a fit when he'd got wind of what had happened when Anike had caught her boyfriend Jacques cheating on her with her best friend, two weeks ago. Some might have found it funny that Anike had tracked Jacques down at the hottest club in the Ivory Coast, identified his Bugatti Veyron, graffitied a swear word on the side and smashed in the passenger window with a tyre iron. The press certainly had. But her father? One of the wealthiest men in the Ivory Coast, on the brink of a hugely important business deal? *Pas du tout.*

He'd been furious that his daughter's dating life had jeopardised his company's interests and had threatened to put Anike under house arrest, but she'd convinced him that a few weeks in Val D'Amer Doux with her college dorm mate would achieve the same ends – get her away from Jacques *and* the press.

His agreement had been conditional: a bodyguard and the exorbitant cost of securing a private chalet at the Vandenburgs' resort. It wasn't as if she or Anike were complaining; they were about to have the best Christmas ever!

Each dwelling was nestled in an *extremely* private cul-de-sac set back from a private road that accessed the four chalets on the mountainside that overlooked Val D'Amer Doux. And each chalet had a host, servicing the lodge twenty-four hours a day. A car with a private driver was also on hand to take any guest wherever they needed to go.

Not that they would need to go anywhere. Everything they could ever dream of was immediately on hand. Like the spa centre! She'd visited that in past years with Hugo Vandenburg – the owners' son – and Noah and their friends. It had the most incredible sauna, a scented steam room, a treatment suite and a heated swimming pool that started inside, looped outside to look out over the mountain and slopes and then came back in again. And if that wasn't enough, there was an outdoor hot tub large enough for twelve people.

There was also access to the private ski track that cut through the woods and led directly on to the slopes that criss-crossed the mountains linking Switzerland, Italy and France. But since Minette had absolutely no intention of squeezing her feet into the torture traps known as ski boots and strapping on a pair of skis, she'd be using the car to get around the resort. *A lot.*

Her phone vibrated in her hand and she looked at the screen.

> URGH. This driver is SLOW. Send me a pic.
> I want to see it. Pleeeaaassseee!

Minette turned and snapped a couple of pictures of the chalet behind her. It jutted out of the side of the mountain on three levels, fronted in that same rich yellow wood and stone that was used for the Vandenburg Hotel. Balconies emerged from each large floor-to-ceiling window, ensuring views of the incredible mountain from every possible angle. Behind it, snow-covered fir trees reached towards a denim-blue, cloudless sky and Minette didn't think it could be more perfect.

> BORING! I want saunas and hot tubs and champagne.

Minette laughed, selecting the other pictures she'd taken twenty minutes ago from her photo library and sending them to Anike.

While she waited for the three dots beside Anike's name to turn into a message, she quickly flicked over to her last chat with Noah.

> Can't wait to see you, love.

> Me too. It's been so long!

> What are the chances of us getting your chalet to ourselves??!!

Minette bit her lip. The Scarisbricks had never allowed her to stay over, even though they were adults now. But as one of Europe's richest families, appearances were everything. But the possibility of spending time with Noah on her own? With no one else about? A twinge of guilt pinged in her chest as she realised that Anike wasn't even here yet and she was trying to figure out a way to get rid of her.

Her phone vibrated again, drawing her out of her thoughts.

> Yay! Just what I need after that bastard Jacques.

It vibrated again before she could reply.

> Nearly there!

Minette jumped up and down again trying to shake off the cold and decided she didn't have time to run back in and get her coat. She could probably message the chalet girl from here and get her to bring it out to her. In an ideal world, they wouldn't be sharing the chalet with anyone, let alone some English girl their age. But it would be nice having all their meals prepared for them, and someone to keep the chalet clean and to organise days out if they wanted them.

Just then, Minette heard the sound of wheels crunching over the grit-covered snow as a car turned into the cul-de-sac. It pulled up in front of her, the door pushed open and Minette was swept up into a hug that almost suffocated her. Wrapped in an oversized faux-fur coat, Anike Dossongui embraced Minette as if she'd just saved her from drowning.

'I needed this,' Anike whispered into her ear.

'I know,' Minette replied.

'I *really* needed this,' Anike insisted.

'I know,' Minette repeated with a laugh and a squeeze for good measure.

Finally releasing her, Anike pulled back, allowing Minette to take her in properly. The dark smudges beneath her eyes, which had not been there once during the entire semester at the Sorbonne, were enough to tell Minette how much Jacques had actually hurt her. But despite being jetlagged from her flight and emotionally reeling, Anike was still gloriously beautiful. At the beginning of December, Anike had styled her hair into two-strand twists that hung all the way to her elbows. Today she had tied half of those locs back from her face, showcasing her enviably high cheekbones and large brown eyes that sparkled with excitement.

'We're going straight to the spa that you told me about,' Anike announced.

'Of course we are,' Minette laughed.

A man dressed head to toe in black military style gear climbed out of the car and Anike rolled her eyes.

'Papa's guard dog,' Anike complained. 'He's going to be watching our every move.'

'We'll work something out,' Minette insisted in a whisper.

Anike didn't look so sure.

'Take my things to the chalet,' Anike ordered the bodyguard, before turning back to Minette. 'Now where is that champagne you showed me?'

REILLY

Reilly looked in the mirror and tucked a blonde tendril of hair behind her ear. She was just about getting used to the change in colour. She hadn't expected it to impact her appearance so much. And the slight touch of colour on her skin from the few days of glorious sunshine she'd experienced in Val D'Amer Doux had given her the kind of healthy glow she hadn't seen in a while. Reilly had considered coloured contact lenses, and even tried them, but they'd made her eyes water so they'd been thrown straight in the bin.

She'd even thought about changing her name, but had decided against it. The only two people she needed to not recognise her were unlikely to remember the quiet, unassuming girl she'd once been.

Reilly pulled on the Vandenburg polo she had to wear as part of the 'house' uniform, and smoothed it down over her stomach. It had been nearly seven years since her family had lost the kind of fortune that would have seen her come to a place like this as a guest rather than a staff member, but still she remembered what it had been like. What *they* could be like.

The rich.

She rolled her shoulders back and thrust her chest out proud and determined. She wasn't embarrassed by her lack of money or access. It had made her stronger. Strong enough to do what she needed to do.

Reilly's phone beeped. She picked it up and read the message from Lisolette.

Have they arrived yet?

'They' being her chalet's guests.

Minette had left the chalet to wait for her friend, Anike, daughter of Ivorian billionaire businessman N'Guessan Dossongui. The dossier provided to her by Savannah Coates, the stern Vandenburg Resort manager had detailed both pertinent and non-pertinent information about her 'guests'. Likes, dislikes, favourite foods, allergies, preferences and favoured pasttimes, as well as a worrying amount of information about their personal lives, had been provided, making her wonder what information would have been provided about herself had she been a guest here.

Reilly Clarke, nineteen years old. Parents: Mike and Emma. Once considered for the USA Olympic skiing team before a change in circumstances removed her from the slopes. Deferred place to study criminology at Berkley on a scholarship. No extracurricular activities. No life. After losing his housing development company, father is now working in sales and miserable. Mother working as a dental hygienist and resentful. Likes: skiing, hot chocolate and podcasts. Dislikes: bullies, arrogance and cold showers.

Reilly laughed at herself in the mirror. Even at the height of her father's success before the recession hit too hard and he was forced to declare bankruptcy, they'd never have been able to afford a place like this. The Vandenburg Hotel further down the mountain, maybe, but not the chalets, not the Resort. Her best friend's family might have, once, but that was in a different lifetime.

Returning to the message, she typed out her reply.

> A just arrived. M outside to meet her.

Good.

> I'm not sure when I'm going to be
> able to get away.

Don't worry about me.
You do what you need to do and
I'll help any way I can.

> You've already done so much.

And she really had. When Reilly had first met Lisolette Keller, she hadn't been where she was now – Head of Housekeeping at the Vandenburg Hotel. But it was Lisolette's role here in Val D'Amer Doux that had enabled Reilly to get in front of Savannah Coates. Without Lisolette, she'd never have got her CV read, let alone got an interview.

It had taken nearly two months of vetting and four separate interviews, three of which had been online, before she had been flown out for the last meeting in person. But Reilly understood. Access to the people who vacationed here – the Aillets, the Dossonguis, the Scarisbricks, who might not be royal in title but far outstripped royal wealth – was restricted for a reason.

Leaving the small room tucked away in the basement of the ultra-luxurious private chalet, Reilly made her way out into the rest of the building.

In the three days since she'd arrived, she'd familiarised herself with every inch of the three-storeyed chalet, undergone a two-day induction as well as being thoroughly tested by Ms Coates. She'd grappled with cooking, cleaning and a series of scenario-based role plays – which, frankly, she'd been relieved to pass – and finally she had been given a one-to-one with the owner.

Mark Vandenburg was as welcoming as Savannah Coates was intimidating, but no matter how approachable he appeared, Reilly wasn't naive enough to let that fool her. The man was a billionaire several times over, and while she'd heard rumours of a split with his husband, there was nothing distracted or weak about him. His son, Hugo, was a year older than Reilly, and from their very brief interaction, seemed polite and easy-going.

Neither one of them had displayed anything so much as a hint of what was rumoured to have happened over the summer on their private Caribbean Island resort. Given that it could impact her time here, Reilly had done as much research on it as she could. Information was scarce and speculation was rife.

A guest had died on Mokani Island, the son of a wealthy family had been arrested for murder and authorities were seeking extradition from the small South American island that the father, Dennis Devereux, had been rumoured to have fled to. But Reilly hadn't heard even a whisper about it since arriving in Val D'Amer Doux under the employ of the Vandenburgs. Not that she was surprised. Reilly knew better than most that rumours didn't mean a thing.

Proof was king in this world. Proof was *power*. Proof was what she needed.

Without it, she'd never get justice.

Reilly's phone vibrated with the reminder for the drinks reception scheduled that evening and the staff meeting set to follow it. There were only two events that she was required to 'work' at outside of her obligations as a chalet host. That evening's drink reception and the Christmas Eve party. Not only did the double-up of duties give the 'family' impression, which was a significant part of the Vandenburg brand, but also served to limit the number of staff that could sell their stories to a very well-paying press.

Making her way out of her small room and into the living areas of the chalet. Reilly found her eyes drawn to the impossibly large floor-to-ceiling window that stretched the entire length of the wall. On one side of the space was a sunken sofa suite that could easily accommodate twelve people. Fur throws were draped over buttery caramel-coloured leather. A huge coffee table, hand-carved from a single piece of oak, stood proudly opposite a sleek black fireplace with a chimney breast that was nearly as tall as she was. It should have dominated the room, but nothing could distract from the incredible view.

Wide slopes crisscrossed the mountainside dotted with small patches of trees and lined by button lifts on the lower sections and chair lifts from the middle, ready to take you not only higher up the valley but also across country borders.

The first time she'd skied here she'd thought she was in heaven. The challenge of it had thrilled her, the speeds she'd reached, incredible. It had been her and the mountain, nothing but the snow beneath her skis and the wind rushing in her ears. She'd loved it. And she'd been good at it. Damn near perfect.

Her memories tangled with hopes and snagged on losses and spun around the sound of her best friend's laughter. The best friend who had brought her on vacations to ski slopes around the world long after Reilly had been forced to move schools because they could no longer afford the exorbitant fees. Reilly clenched her jaw, for the first time not quite seeing the glorious white-capped mountains and blue sky.

She'd been forced to leave her best friend behind and Reilly knew that if she hadn't left, things would have been different. So very different.

A squeal from outside cut through her thoughts and jolted her nerves. So much depended on this first meet. They were more than just her first guests as a Vandenburg employee. If she did this right, if her plan succeeded, then they would also be her last.

She arrived just in time to greet them as they crossed the threshold, their laughter drying up when they caught sight of her standing there.

'Hi,' Reilly said, with a broad smile to cover the train of her previous thoughts. 'Welcome to your home for the next twelve days. My name is Reilly, and I'll be hosting you. It's really lovely to meet you both. Is English OK?' she asked. 'Or I can speak French if—'

Anike waved her off before Reilly could offer any more languages. 'English is fine, I need the practice anyway,' she said, word perfectly, before tossing a glare at the man Reilly recognised from the dossier as Anike's bodyguard, Karel, busy unloading bags from the car.

'Wonderful!' Reilly exclaimed. 'Now, would you like some champagne while I give you the tour of the chalet, or just the tour? Or just the champagne?' Reilly pointed to the ice bucket she'd prepared with flutes of champagne, the rim of which was punctured with a chunk of strawberry.

'Oooh, we're going to get on *well*,' Anike replied, with a wagging finger. 'Champagne while we tour and then . . .'

'The sauna at the spa centre? Surely that's the *only* way to start a ski holiday,' Reilly dangled.

'Yes! Yes, and yes,' Anike agreed, passing the glass Reilly offered her to Minette and taking the second one for herself. 'Let's go, girls.'

CHAPTER TWO

JACOB

Blowing out a breath that turned white in the frigid air, Jacob paused on the private road that led to the chalet at the top of the hill. Christ, this was something else. He'd been skiing before, but the places he'd gone to – Breckenridge, Vail, Telluride – had nothing on this. The mountains stretched out before him like a picture from a magazine; so perfect, they didn't seem real. He couldn't take his eyes off them.

The cold nipped at his cheeks, and his heart – working a little harder to get him up the sharp incline – thumped strongly in his chest. The snow cracked and shifted around him. The trees either side of the road groaned beneath the weight of last night's snowfall, trembling when birds landed delicately on their branches.

Peaceful. Serene. A gift.

A *literal* gift.

'Why don't you come for Christmas?' Hugo had asked about a month ago.

Yeah right. As if, just like that, he and his parents could fly over to Europe for twelve days.

'Honestly, you'd be doing me – *us* – a favour. It's not going to be the same this year without Darian, but Mark will try and it'll just be messed up. So please come. Dad has already said it's fine. It won't cost you a thing, promise.'

Hugo's parents were taking things slowly after Darian's affair nearly blew their marriage apart, and all three of them were trying really hard to get past the events of the summer just gone.

So, Jacob had hesitantly asked his father. Three years ago it wouldn't have been much of a stretch. They had been doing well financially for themselves – great actually. But that had been before his mother's accident. And before the medical bills that exceeded health insurance had eaten into their savings, so Jacob genuinely hadn't known if his dad would say yes. But his parents had agreed that it would be nice to get away for a bit.

They'd arrived late last night and stepped straight into the most out-of-this-world-level luxury they could ever imagine. His parents' master suite had its own living room, an en suite bathroom and a balcony with a hot tub on the decking that looked out over the forest behind the chalet. There was a media room, which was a posh name for what turned out to be a mini cinema, a games room and a boot room in the garage that had every type of ski equipment that Jacob could dream of, not to mention direct access to the private ski road that would take him directly to the bottom of the central slope.

He and his father had grinned like they'd just won the lottery. Marcus – the guy acting as chalet host – seemed cool and easy-going and had made them dinner on their arrival despite them saying that it was too late for him to be working. And that morning Jacob had woken up in a super king size bed in a room with a view out over the mountains, a small living area with a wood burner and an en suite bathroom complete with a claw-foot tub. Jacob had decided that the only real way forward was to just enjoy it. So that's what he was going to do.

Hit the slopes, hang out with Hugo and his rich friends and enjoy it all.

With that in mind, Jacob hurried up to the top of the private road and tried not to gasp when he saw the ginormous lodge masquerading as a 'chalet'. When Hugo yanked the door open, Jacob yelled out 'Bro!', which was met with an answering 'Bro!' They laughed at each other and Jacob found himself pulled into a hug.

The three strong slaps on his back made Jacob smile – familiar and strong – physically grounding him here and not back at the chalet with his parents. Hugo leaned back to give him an assessing look before hauling him across the threshold and into the awe-inspiring place that Hugo and his father Mark were staying for the next twelve days.

'A little place in Switzerland?' Jacob asked, parroting the description Hugo had first given him of his dads' resort in Val D'Amer Doux.

Hugo shrugged affably and grinned. 'I mean, compared to the place in Italy, this is pretty little.'

Hugo laughed when Jacob playfully shoved him in the shoulder.

A dark-haired guy, a few years older than them, appeared behind Hugo wearing a Vandenburg-branded polo, and Hugo introduced him as Nils.

'Mr Arcilla, please allow me,' he said, holding out his hands for Jacob's coat.

'Thank you,' Jacob smiled awkwardly at the formality, shrugging out of the thick-lined coat and passing it to him.

A blonde woman in her early fifties passed behind them, and Hugo smiled.

'That's Savannah. She likes to pretend she's a vampire, always lurking in shady corners. But without her none of the chalets would run even half as smoothly, would they, Sav?' Hugo asked, flashing her a cheeky grin.

She rolled her eyes, even though Jacob saw affection there, and disappeared into the bowels of the, quite frankly, freaking amazing chalet.

Shrugging his shoulders so that the dark suit he'd worn for that evening sat properly and he didn't stick out like a sore thumb, Jacob walked further into Hugo's chalet.

'Dude,' he said, taking in the three-storey-high windows opposite him that looked out at a different view of the same mountainside he'd woken up to. Twisting his head to look around, Jacob took in the mezzanine second floor and the chandelier that was bigger than an SUV hanging from the ceiling. Without a doubt, it would kill him instantly if it fell.

'I know,' Hugo said, grinning.

'Do you? Like, do you *really* know how damn lucky you are to have all this? And I thought my chalet was impressive!' Jacob skirted the sunken living area that surrounded the biggest fireplace he'd ever seen. Sumptuous cream leather sofas, a pouffe big enough for an entire body to sink into, a reclining chair. The only thing that stopped it from looking like a magazine spread were the little personal items dotted around. A book face down, spine cracked. A pair of reading glasses. A glass of half-drunk wine.

'Yeah, I do,' Hugo said, his voice changing just enough to bring Jacob's attention back to him.

Then he saw it . . . what the others probably didn't see. Jacob knew as much as Hugo could tell him about what had happened in the summer on Mokani Island – the resort owned by Hugo's adoptive parents. But Jacob would never push for more, just like Hugo never did with him.

'Come on, let's get a drink and catch up before the others get here,' Hugo said, leading Jacob over to a fully stocked bar area with a granite countertop. Unable to stop himself, Jacob ran his fingers across the surface, his fingertips pressing into the dark fissures at the edge.

'Where's your dad?'

'Mark's getting ready for the dinner this evening.' Hugo groaned a little.

'Not up for it?'

'I'm just a little worried that he's clinging on to things we *used* to do.'

Hugo caught Jacob's questioning gaze.

'First night dinners, grand performance evenings, making

the effort,' Hugo said, bobbing his head between the various events. 'It feels as if that was Darian's thing.'

'Did you see him before you came out?' Jacob asked, and nodded to accept the bottle of beer Hugo tipped in his direction.

Hugo took a breath, and ran his hands through the blond hair that had grown longer since Jacob had first met him – *what* – only three months ago? Other members of the Harvard lacrosse team had given Hugo a wide berth after the coach had kicked him off the year before for fighting. Hugo wasn't quite back on the team yet, but the work that he'd been doing with the first-year students – helping with training and running drills, and being there at every team event – was going a long way to show how much he'd changed.

'Yeah. It was . . . tough. But good, in a really weird way. I . . . miss him, you know?'

Yeah, Jacob knew exactly what Hugo was talking about. But he also knew now wasn't the time to delve into it.

'So, who exactly is coming tonight? Anyone I know?' Jacob asked.

Hugo's face scrunched in concentration. 'Not sure. I mean, you won't know them personally, but you might have heard of them. Charlotte Aillet and her daughter Minette will be there. Mark has known Charlotte since way back. She's a French diplomat and her husband is a businessman. She's stayed down the hill in the Presidential Suite every Christmas since the hotel opened.'

Jacob might not have heard about Charlotte Aillet, but there wasn't anyone who took skiing seriously who hadn't heard of the

Vandenburg Hotel in Val D'Amer Doux; it had been rated one of Europe's best ski destinations for the last eleven years running.

'And then there's the Scarisbricks. English, not titled, but act like it, if you know what I mean.'

Jacob *didn't* really know what Hugo meant, but nodded just the same anyway.

'Noah, their son, your age, has been seeing Minette for ages. They met at school and his family has been coming to the chalets ever since they started dating. This year, though, Minette is staying with a friend. Anike Dossongui. Mini's mother is still down the hill though.'

Jacob let out a low whistle. 'Isn't Anike the one girl who destroyed the Bugatti out in the Ivory Coast?'

'Yup. Anike's father thought renting a chalet away from trouble was a good "punishment" for her,' Hugo said drily.

Jacob laughed. 'Wow. OK.'

'But basically, they're all about our age. I haven't really seen Mini and Noah since this time last year, but they're good fun. Hey, listen, can I add you to the group chat?'

'Sure, why?'

'It's just easier to meet up on the slopes and arrange going out and stuff,' Hugo explained as he pulled out his phone and tapped on the screen.

Seconds later, Jacob's phone pinged, alerting him to a new message from a group chat called SKI 26.

'You're literally standing next to each other and messaging?' Mark Vandenburg asked from behind them.

Jacob turned to see Hugo's father coming to join them. He was always struck by how, even though Hugo had been adopted, they shared mannerisms that clearly connected them as father and son. It made him wonder if anyone saw that between him and his father.

'Hey, Mr V,' Jacob said.

'Jacob, it's good to see you again. Did you get here OK? How are your parents?'

'The journey was great, and the chalet – seriously. We can't thank you enough.'

Mark Vandenburg waved away his thanks.

'My folks are back there getting ready for the drinks evening.'

Mark grinned. 'Excellent, it will be really lovely to meet them.'

Jacob anchored the smile in place on his face, before it could drop. He just hoped that his mother wouldn't cause a scene. Not here. Not somewhere like this.

After Christmas, fine. But he just wanted *this*. It was going to be a *good* Christmas.

MINETTE

'We could have walked, you know,' Anike groused at Karel, who had driven them the three minutes up the hill to the main Vandenburg chalet.

Minette tried to hide her smile as Karel raised an eyebrow until Anike said, 'But thank you!' in a voice that could cause teeth cavities.

'Thank you,' Minette added, but Karel was already getting out of the car to open the back passenger door for them. He'd wait until they were inside the Vandenburg chalet before leaving, she knew that from the close protection officers Maman used when she was working.

Karel held out his hand first for Anike and then for Minette. She stepped into the cold and shivered, secretly thankful that they hadn't had to struggle up the hill in the dark, in heels and their dresses. Anike met Minette's eyes, clearly thinking the same thing and they giggled to themselves as they walked up the steps to the large wooden front door.

'I think it's so cute that they do this,' Anike said, looking around at the picture-perfect view of forest and ski slopes.

'Do what?' Minette asked, checking her phone for a message from Noah.

'Bring everyone together like this for the first night. It's,' Anike shrugged, *'personal.'*

'Mmm,' Minette replied. She was distracted, wondering why Noah hadn't responded to her last message. For a brief second, she thought about messaging him to ask but then decided against it. She'd be seeing him soon enough.

Standing in the circle of light, as a gentle dusting of snow began to fall, Minette pulled at the side seam of her form-fitting midnight blue dress dotted with Swarovski crystals beneath her thick black cashmere coat.

'Tu est belle,' Anike whispered in her ear, making Minette smile.

'Maman likes me to look a certain way, that's all,' Minette explained.

'Well, your maman and my papa can both go—'

The door swung open, cutting off Anike mid-sentence. She quickly plastered on a picture-perfect socialite smile and Minette had to bite back a laugh.

There was no doubt about it. Anike was beautiful, but few would guess that she had the dirtiest laugh and the foulest mouth, and filled Minette with the kind of happiness she'd not expected to find at college. And she looked incredible tonight in an off-the-shoulder black fitted dress, her locs piled high in a tight bun, and a diamond necklace that glittered around her slim neck and shoulders.

'Mademoiselle Minette, Mademoiselle Dossongui,' greeted Savannah Coates.

'Bonjour, Madame Coates,' Minette said as Savannah stepped back to welcome them into the chalet.

Their coats were taken before they were led through to the brightly lit living area where the festivities were already under way. Despite her own family's considerable wealth, Minette was awed by the Vandenburg chalet. A row of staff who would service the chalets and guests over the next twelve days lined one side of the room. Reilly, who was at the far end of that line, had changed into a white shirt and black trousers to match the other staff members, and Minette found herself frowning. There was something about their chalet host that niggled in the back of her mind, but Minette couldn't put her finger on what it was.

The sound of laughter drew her gaze to the inconceivably large Christmas tree in the far corner of the room where her mother stood talking to Janet Scarisbrick, glass in hand, with what Minette liked to think of as her 'professional face'; a mask that made her appear interested, but not so much that she'd actually have to contribute to a conversation.

The two women couldn't be more different. Her mother, tall – almost willowy – while Janet was nearly two foot shorter. Mrs Scarisbrick's bone white, soft and round features belied a scalpel-sharp tongue and a meanness that bordered on aggressive. Mrs Scarisbrick terrified her. But she wasn't a child any more, Minette reminded herself. She was nineteen, at university, and was even staying at one of the chalets this time, not down the hill in the hotel with her mother.

On the other side of the room James Scarisbrick and Mark Vandenburg were talking to a couple Minette didn't recognise. The man – tall, dark-haired and probably the only man wearing a necktie rather than a bowtie – looked at ease, but the woman at his side seemed less comfortable. The fitted green dress she wore hung a little loose on her frame and was the wrong shade against her pale skin, making her look sallow. Her eyes roamed the room and landed on Minette for an awkward second before her gaze moved on.

'Who's that?' Anike asked nodding at the couple Minette had been looking at.

'Don't know,' Minette replied, as she swept two glasses from a passing waiter, trying to stifle the odd twist of nerves unspooling in her chest.

She knew her mother had registered her arrival because, despite all appearances to the contrary, her mother knew everything that happened around her. Minette was simply being ignored, 'punished by silence' for having the temerity to arrive late. And it didn't matter if that was because Minette had changed her dress three times to make sure Charlotte Aillet would be happy with it. The crime was tardiness and her mother disliked *anything* that could possibly reflect negatively back on to her.

If her mother had been only mildly annoyed, she would have at least raised a glass in her direction. But this? This was her mother at her most annoyed – like the summer five years ago when her mother had ignored her for fifteen whole days. Minette's crime? She had called a delegate by the wrong title. So no, it would not do to approach her now when she was in this mood.

'Mini,' hissed a familiar voice.

She turned to find Hugo behind her, a big cheesy grin on his face.

She felt an answering smile bloom across her face. 'Hugo!'

He swept her up in his strong arms and she only realised then how much she'd actually missed him.

Her arms tightened around him for just a second and then he let her go. They'd spent nearly every Christmas together for the last eight years and during that time, he'd become one of her favourite people. One of her *really* favourite people.

'I'm sorry about being a dick last year,' he whispered in her ear.

'You weren't,' she whispered back.

He had been.

'I'm so sorry about your dads,' she whispered back.

He squeezed her a little harder and pulled back so she could see his clear blue gaze. 'Thank you. It's been a . . . tough year.'

She opened her mouth to ask about Mokani Island, but the wariness in his eyes warned her against it.

'Later. In the meantime, let me introduce you to . . .' Hugo's words trailed off as he caught sight of Anike over Minette's shoulder.

'Jacob,' Hugo finished, eyes wide and slightly dumbstruck.

'No,' Anike replied, confused. 'I'm Anike. Nice to meet you,' she said with a small flirtatious smile on her lips.

Minette tried to contain her own smile. She should have known that these two would hit it off.

'And *I'm* Jacob,' the boy next to Hugo said. His American accent was familiar, which probably meant his family was from New York or Washington. Minette figured that the couple she hadn't recognised must be his parents. Jacob was tall like his father, his hair longer than usual for guys their age, falling forward to just below his high cut cheekbones. Dark brown eyes looked back at her and his smile was easy-going, softening the sharpness of his jawline. Handsome. *Very*. But he was not the person she had been looking for.

'Nice to meet you, Jacob,' Minette said with a small wave of her hand, before scanning the room for Noah.

If his parents were here, then surely . . .

A waiter passed in front of her and then there he was.

Noah Scarisbrick.

She felt something ease in her chest when she saw his charming grin. He looked divine in the dark suit and white shirt, open at the neck. He'd always appeared older, as if he were set apart from them all. Comfortable in his skin in a way that Minette wondered if she'd ever be.

'Hey, Mins,' he said easily and closed the distance between them. His lips against hers in a greeting she felt she'd been waiting on for months was both everything and not enough at the same time. The familiar scent of him drugged her senses and her fingers curled possessively into the chestnut hair at the back of his neck. She felt his hands pull her against him, his thumb skating perilously close to her breast, making her breath catch. When she pulled back, he looked at her with a wicked gleam in his eyes and she wanted him so much she almost felt sick with it.

Noah Scarisbrick. Her boyfriend.

Anike cleared her throat behind her and Minette tried to hide her embarrassment by pressing herself into Noah's jacket.

'Sorry,' Noah said, pulling her slightly into his side so he could greet the others. 'It's just been a while since we've been able to see each other.'

Noah held his hand out to Jacob, while Anike nudged her with her shoulder, laughing at the PDA.

'I'm Noah. I hear you're a friend of Hugo's and on the Harvard lacrosse team?' Noah asked.

'Yeah, do you play?' Jacob asked.

'Cricket and rugby, but not lacrosse,' Noah said, while reaching out to Hugo with one arm to pull him into a hug. 'Mate, how's it going?'

'Good thanks,' Hugo replied, having to tear his eyes away from Anike, who was biting her lip and holding Hugo's gaze.

Oh, this Christmas was going to be so much *fun*.

'So, you guys have all been here before?' Jacob asked.

Minette shook her head. 'Not Anike, but we,' she said pointing between herself, Noah and Hugo, 'have been coming here for years!'

Jacob smiled, looking around at the others. 'Cool, so you know the best places to go for fresh snow then?'

'Urgh, no,' Minette replied, leaving Jacob surprised and making Noah laugh.

'Minette hates the snow, don't you, love,' Noah said.

Oh, she'd *missed* hearing him call her that.

'You know I don't like being cold,' she pouted.

'What about you, Jacob?' Noah asked.

'This is my first time here, but I've skied before.'

'He's being modest,' Hugo said, slinging an arm around Jacob's shoulder. 'He's a demon on the slopes.'

'Well, I've never skied before. Not once. I'm having my first lesson tomorrow,' Anike announced.

'Ahh, you're in safe hands with Gustav,' Hugo said, clearly jumping on the chance to chat to Anike. 'He's not only a gold medallist, but I hear he taught Pedro Pascal.'

'Really?' Anike asked, the word sounding more like a gasp.

'No, I just made that up to make him sound impressive, but he really is a gold medallist and you're going to love it,' he announced with a little more conviction than was strictly necessary. 'But before then, we need to get this party started!'

And in that moment Minette couldn't think of any place she'd rather be than right here.

CHAPTER THREE
JACOB

Waiters carrying trays of Moët and caviar canapes with actual gold flakes wound through the guests Jacob tried to play it cool. But, seriously, this was the kind of money that he just wasn't used to.

If it didn't sparkle, it gleamed. And it wasn't cheap plastic glitter, but diamonds, sapphires, gold. The artwork wasn't reproduction, it was original. The interior wasn't mass-produced, but one-of-a-kind, handmade, to the highest specification. It almost didn't seem real. Thousands of tiny lights decorating the giant Christmas tree in the corner were reflected in the window, making Jacob feel like he was trapped inside a glass bauble, watching how the other half lived. Except it wasn't the 'other half'. The combined wealth in this room had to be in the top one percentile, *globally*.

He looked over to where his parents were talking to Mark and another man who, by facial features alone, was clearly Noah Scarisbrick's father. Concern wound tight around his gut and he prayed that his parents didn't do anything to embarrass him or themselves.

Please god.

Noah and Minette were whispering to each other and Hugo was trying to impress Anike so Jacob glanced over at the staff lined up on the opposite side of the room. There was something deeply uncomfortable – intimidating almost – in the way that they all looked stared straight ahead with the same approachable smile on their faces.

And for some reason, Jacob couldn't shake the feeling that he was on the wrong side of the line. But then he caught sight of a girl about his age at the end of the staff line. He couldn't tell what it was that had drawn his attention. But something had.

As if she'd noticed him looking, her gaze met his, and Jacob felt his entire body flush. There was no other way to describe it. As if fire had brushed over him from head to toe and then disappeared, leaving him a little shaken and confused.

Her blonde hair was pulled back from her face, eyes a near glacial shade of blue. Her features were fine and narrow, and undeniably beautiful but . . . it was the severity about her that struck him.

But then her gaze untangled from his and moved away. She probably hadn't even really seen him at all.

What an idiot.

She's working, for Christ's sake, and probably thinks you're one of these rich assholes . . .

Only they weren't assholes. Actually, they all seemed pretty decent.

Just then Jacob caught sight of Gustav Reinhardt. Tall, bearded, with an easy smile, the Olympic skiing champion made his way towards their group and Jacob had to struggle hard not to fan-girl.

'Hugo,' the man said, holding out his hand to shake and when Hugo took it, pulled him into a hug. 'How have you been?'

'I'm good, Gustav. Really good,' Hugo beamed, which clearly had everything to do with Anike Dossongui and very little to do with anything else. 'Let me introduce you to everyone.'

When Hugo got round to Jacob, Gustav said, 'Ahh, *you're* the skier.'

'What have you been telling everyone?' Jacob asked Hugo.

'Bigging you up, bro!' Hugo replied affably, before turning back to Anike and leaving him with Gustav.

Jacob shrugged. 'I'm *OK*,' he acknowledged.

'Mmm,' Gustav said, eyeing him with a grin. 'Humble. Fine. You keep your secrets. But I *will* get them out of you!'

'If anyone can, my money's on you,' Jacob replied, laughing.

Gustav turned to Anike. 'And we have a lesson tomorrow, I believe?'

She beamed and Jacob lost the thread of the conversation as he searched the line of staff for the girl who had intrigued him so much. He turned back to the group to see Gustav had followed Jacob's line of sight and seemed to be looking at the same girl with, at first a frown, and then a look of surprise as if he'd recognised her. But when Gustav caught Jacob's eye, he smiled and shrugged.

'So, tell me about your last ski,' he commanded.

Jacob started to tell Gustav about Breckenridge three years

ago, realising that this would probably be his last ski trip for a while. At least until he could pay his own way now that his parents were in the deep end with creditors.

Shoving that from his mind, they chatted away about the best places for different types of skiing. Gustav was clearly an expert both on and off-piste, but also very entertaining company.

The alcohol flowed at an alarmingly easy and high pace and when Jacob was coming back from the bathroom, he passed Mark and Mr and Mrs Scarisbrick chatting with his mother. He hovered, wondering whether he should check on her. He knew she didn't always feel comfortable in social situations without his dad, but she smiled and slightly shook her head as if to say that she was fine.

'Yes, it was a terrible business. Minette was roommates with her.'

'Really? I didn't know,' Mark said, sounding consolatory.

'She handled it in her stride, obviously. But it made a pretty big impact on the school. They held a memorial for the girl.'

'I thought she'd not been found,' Noah's father said sounding almost bored of the conversation.

'She wasn't, but the police clearly decided that there was no hope of finding her and declared her dead. Just imagine, taking a boat out by yourself in that kind of weather. So irresponsible. I mean, I feel absolutely dreadful for her parents.'

'And nothing came of the rumours after all that. As if bullying could even happen at that school. I mean, that's why we pay such ridiculous fees,' complained James Scarisbrick.

Jacob couldn't work out whether it was obtuse or just bad taste to be talking about the death of a schoolgirl in such a dismissive, unfeeling way, and wondered how close Minette and Noah had been with her. He glanced up and caught Mark giving his mother an uncomfortable smile.

'Jake! Over here,' Hugo called and beckoned him over to the fireplace where he was standing with the others.

James Scarisbrick looked his way as if surprised to see Jacob standing there, clearly in a position to have heard their conversation and, from the look of it, not exactly happy about it either.

'See you later, Mom?' Jacob said, passing his mother who smiled and nodded, as he made his way over to Hugo and the others.

'We were just talking about the next twelve days,' Hugo explained, catching him up on the plans.

'Excellent, fill me in,' Jacob said, passing on a glass of champagne offered by one of the staff circulating the room. He frowned and looked back to the line of staff, wondering what differentiated the ones lined up to the ones serving drinks.

'We're going to hit the slopes tomorrow—'

'*You* will,' Minette interrupted. 'I'll be taking full advantage of the *aprés* ski scene.'

'OK, while you do that, we'll be skiing,' Hugo continued.

'I'm going to join you on my board, if that's cool with you?' Noah asked Jacob.

'Sure,' Jacob replied.

'And then in the evening we'll head to a local place in town for some drinks.'

'*Some*,' Noah laughed.

'OK, a lot,' Hugo clarified. 'Dad wants to have dinner the next day but we'll all meet up at the spa centre after. And then the following day is the Christmas Eve drinks.'

'Oooh, your dad always does something *amazing* for Christmas Eve,' Minette exclaimed, her sleek brown bob swinging across her shoulders. 'Has he told you what we're doing this year?'

Hugo shook his head. 'It's a secret, even from me.'

Minette pouted, and Noah grinned as he pulled her against him again, Jacob seeing her catch his fingers in hers.

'We'll all do our Christmases, and then pretty much carry on as before. Skiing, drinking, having fun,' Hugo said, waggling his eyebrows at Anike. 'And then there's New Year's Eve.'

'Have we figured out what we're doing yet?' Noah asked.

Hugo's face scrunched a little. 'I've got a couple of options that don't involve the folks. I'll put them in the chat.'

'Sounds good,' Noah said, absently kissing the top of Minette's head.

The sound of a glass being tapped cut through the room.

'If I could have your attention?' Mark Vandenburg asked. 'I'd just like to take the opportunity to welcome you all to our resort this Christmas. It means so much to me and Hugo that you could all make it. I won't keep you long as I know you all have better things to do with your time than to listen to me drone on. But just a reminder that, as always, our staff are on hand twenty-four seven for whatever you might need, you only have to ask. My only wish is that you all truly enjoy yourselves as we celebrate the beginning of what will hopefully be a brilliant and bright new year.'

'Cheers!' everyone replied with their glasses raised in a toast.

As Jacob took a mouthful of his champagne he glanced across at the blonde, who continued to stare straight ahead.

REILLY

Reilly sank into a plastic chair at a table that reminded her of school lunches at her second high school – *not* the posh one. The other staff members who had been at the welcome drinks reception joined her, with a few still to come, having stayed behind to wait on the rest of the reception after the staff line had been dismissed.

They were in a building just a little out of the way – and a lot out of *sight* – of the chalets and guests, which the staff *un*affectionately called The Kicker. Reilly presumed the name was a crossover between a place to 'kick back', and a reference to the small slope-jumps made of snow called 'kickers'. It was where all the staff without 'onsite' accommodation slept. Reilly looked around and thanked her lucky stars that she and the other chalet hosts had their own apartments. The Kicker had a small kitchen and open living area but the entire get-up looked like an oversized youth hostel with cheap white paint and bright white lights.

Tapping her fingers on the table as she waited for the staff meeting to begin, Reilly's mind raced.

They hadn't recognised her.

Noah and Minette.

She was pretty sure that she'd been in the clear with Minette after Reilly had led her and Anike on a tour around the chalet, but when Noah hadn't even spared her a second glance, Reilly had finally been able to let out a breath of relief. The small changes she'd made to her appearance had been enough.

Though, perhaps it wasn't such a surprise. It had been at least five years since she'd been forced to leave the Institute – the nickname for the obscenely expensive Swiss boarding school, located in Laussanne, known around the world as Salis Institute D'Excellence. It was where she'd met Asma Chaudhury, her best friend. They'd all been in the same school year and a lot had happened since then.

A lot.

A glass of water was placed in front of her as Tina took a seat beside her and introduced herself as the person looking after the Scarisbricks.

'What are they like?' Reilly asked, curious.

'She won't tell you,' Savannah said, coming into the room, clearly having heard Reilly's question. 'And if she did, I'd fire her on the spot. Discretion is absolute. Understood?'

Savannah stared at Reilly, who blinked, probably more surprised than she should have been by the harshness of the Vandenburg Resort manager. Lisolette had warned her after all.

'Yes, ma'am.'

Savannah glared at every staff member in the room. 'You will all do well to remember that. The Vandenburg reputation has been tarnished by the events on Mokani Island, and I will allow nothing and no one to do any further harm. They pay us extremely well for our service and we honour that exchange by giving them *everything* we have in return.'

It sounded a little fanatical to Reilly's ears, but she'd learned her lesson and wouldn't dare say as much.

'Careful, Sav, or you'll scare them,' Gustav Reinhardt said, placing a kiss on the intimidating woman's cheek, before dropping into a chair on Reilly's right and turning to stare at her in a *very obvious way*.

'Fancy seeing you here,' Gustav said to Reilly, drawing a glare from Savannah, though whether that was because he'd spoken, or because he seemed to know her, Reilly couldn't tell.

'OK,' Savannah said, calling everyone to order. 'This is the one and only staff meeting we'll have in the next twelve days unless something awful happens. Which it won't. So I'll get on with things.'

Reilly tried to block out the weight of Gustav's attention on her as Savannah ran through the duties and health and safety protocols, but ignoring him was impossible. At first, she'd been able to keep a straight face, but the more obvious his attention, the harder it became.

'You all have your staff packs, which contain the relevant information and contact numbers you need. There will be no practice fire alarms, so if any fire alarm goes off in the next twelve days, it's a real situation, so act accordingly.'

Reilly thought about the information pack she had read through before Minette's arrival. There was also a section on the other guests, which had covered the Arcillas.

Jacob Arcilla.

She'd caught him staring at her. It hadn't been rude or intrusive, it had seemed . . . surprised.

As surprised as she'd felt when she locked her eyes with him.

Reilly frowned, remembering the feeling. Like someone had hit her with a jolt of electricity. It had been his eyes that she'd noticed first, a rich dark brown that reminded her of bitter chocolate. The rest of him was more impressions, because her gaze – as if knowing it would be dangerous – couldn't linger on a single feature for long. Sharp cheekbones, long hair tucked back behind his ear, broad lips nearly perfect in their shape, a cupid's bow she wanted to shockingly, *stupidly,* trace with her thumb. He looked like a younger version of his Filipino father, who Reilly had seen earlier.

He was handsome, but she'd seen hot guys before. There was something about him . . .

She'd forced her gaze away and had spent the rest of the evening trying to ignore him. She'd felt the touch of his attention a few times, but had resisted the urge to look his way, until she'd seen him leave with his parents, catching his mother's arm as she'd stumbled slightly on the way out. Reilly hadn't realised that Mrs Arcilla had had that much to drink.

'Lastly,' Savannah added, 'and most importantly, there will be no fraternisation with the guests.'

Reilly tried to fight the blush that began to creep over her cheeks, knowing that Gustav would notice just from how close he was sitting.

'You're all adults, so you know what I mean. If one of the guests becomes problematic, we understand – these things happen – you won't be held responsible and you won't be punished. But we do need to know about it so we can do something about it. Now does anyone have any questions?'

'Oh, I do,' Gustav said under his breath for Reilly's ears alone.

'No?' Savannah asked. 'OK, then. One last thing: Do. Not. Mess. This. Up. Do I make myself clear?'

'Yes, ma'am,' everyone answered together, before the others began to make their way out of the room.

'Why, Ms Clarke. I do declare,' Gustav said affecting an impressive Southern American accent. She tried to ignore him, but the way he fanned his cheek just made it harder.

Finally, a burst of laughter that she couldn't hold back erupted from her mouth.

'Reinhardt. I'd say it's good to see you but that would only make your ego bigger and it's already big enough.'

'That's what they tell me, *ma chérie*,' he replied without missing a beat.

'Still breaking hearts all over the slopes?' she asked.

'Absolutely. But that does lead me nicely to my question. Why aren't you?'

'I don't know what you mean,' Reilly evaded, feeling her pulse begin to quicken from the lie.

'What I mean is, why are you playing chalet girl instead of teaching these little shits how to ski? You know you're more than capable, and you'd certainly earn more money doing it, let alone get more slope time in.'

'But then what would *you* do?' she teased.

'Oh, darling, I'd be absolutely fine and you know that. What is it that you're not telling me?'

'Gustav, I imagine there's a lot I'm not telling you,' Reilly replied with a genuine smile. 'Besides, at least I'm in a chalet and not bunking down here,' she said, looking around at the soulless, bland staff accommodation.

Gustav barked out a laugh. 'Oh god, you don't think I'm staying *here*, do you? No, I have a little pad in town.'

Reilly rolled her eyes, and he laughed at her.

'Jealousy turns those baby blues bright green, Clarke. It gives you away.'

And she was. A little. Not of him, just for what *could* have been.

But she'd decided two years ago that this was her path and she would see it through to the very end. Even if it killed her.

'Come on. Walk me home and tell me all about what you've been up to since I last saw you eating my snow,' Gustav said, offering her his arm.

'I'd love to,' Reilly replied, surprised to find herself meaning it. She'd been so worried about Noah and Minette recognising her that she hadn't even thought that anyone from the old scene would remember her. 'But I have to be up in less than four hours to make breakfast for "the little shits",' she groaned.

Gustav half-growled, half-grumbled. 'Fine. But you owe me a drink and an explanation, and I want both,' he said, pointing a finger at her in warning.

'Fair,' Reilly replied, knowing that her ambiguous answer would only infuriate the Swiss ski star further. But she wasn't lying. Reilly really did have to get back to the girls' chalet, *and* be up at some ungodly hour in the morning to make breakfast and prepare the cakes for afternoon tea tomorrow.

It was all part of the Vandenburg 'experience'.

Gustav plucked her phone from her trouser pocket, and shoved it under her nose, indicating for her to open it.

Reilly raised an eyebrow, and Gustav raised his back.

'Urgh, fine. You're such a drama queen,' Reilly complained and pressed her finger to the phone's screen.

'Takes one to know one,' Gustav bit back.

He typed his number into her phone and added himself to her contacts.

'Message me when you get a free night.'

'What makes you think I'll get a free night?' Reilly scoffed.

'I know these "little shits". They party harder than their parents and they're going to want to give you the slip quicker than they ran out on their au pairs. You'll be free by lunchtime tomorrow,' he predicted, kissed her on the cheek and left her standing alone in The Kicker staff room.

Reilly ground her teeth together. She hoped he wasn't right. She needed to befriend them, not alienate them. Especially if she was going to get what she needed.

CHAPTER FOUR

MINETTE

Minette woke up to the smell of coffee and French toast sighing as the dreams of her and Noah mixed with the scents of sugar and caffeine in a near mouthwatering combination.

She covered her face with a pillow and squealed into it, delighted that she'd got to spend some time with Noah last night. She hadn't said anything – barely admitted it to herself – but she'd been really worried that they wouldn't last after the Institute. Oh, she wasn't naive, she knew that it was a brilliant match on paper. Two dynasties, Mrs Scarisbrick often said, in a way that curled Minette's stomach and made it seem like that was the only reason they were together.

And, *oui*, of course there was a part of her that imagined a fantastic wedding at Westminster Abbey; she with a train as long as the aisle and Noah standing at the altar in top hat and tails. But sometimes that dream got a little hazy. Especially when Noah would go quiet on her.

'Mini.'

Minette smiled at the whispered sound of her name.

'Yes, Ani,' she whispered back.

'Are you ready for breakfast?' Anike asked, still whispering.

Minette huffed out a laugh. 'Yes, but why didn't you go down?' she asked. Unlike her, Anike was a morning person.

'I was waiting for you.'

'Liar, you never wait for me at college.'

'OK, I didn't want to go down there on my own and have to make conversation with the chalet girl.'

'That's silly. You make friends with *everyone*,' Minette replied and then groaned. There was no way she'd get back to sleep now.

'Yes!' Anike cheered.

Minette threw back the gorgeously heavy duvet, in time to see Anike fist-pump the air with the hand clutching her vape.

'*Merde*, Ani. If this is just because you want to smoke—'

'No! I need coffee too. Come!' Anike said, beckoning her with rapid hand movements.

Holding back a smile, Minette shrugged into her dressing gown, paused at the mirror to run her hands through the bob and followed Anike to the small elevator that ran through the centre of the chalet and would take them down to the living room.

They got in side by side, Minette resting her head on Anike's shoulder and, sleepy-eyed and hungry, they emerged into the living area where they stopped at the large dining table. Their mouths fell open.

'Ohmygod,' they said in unison.

Large bowls heaped with every conceivable type of fruit, freshly baked pastries with cinnamon, chocolate and icing sugar, plates with pancakes and even bowls of steaming porridge, filled the table. Freshly squeezed orange juice, sausages, sliced meats, eggs, mushrooms, tomatoes, avocado, sourdough toast – it looked like an Instagram-worthy feast for twenty, not for two.

'I wasn't sure what you might want to eat, but I'm fairly sure you'd both need some coffee?'

They turned to find Reilly holding a pot of rich dark coffee, swirls of seductive steam rising from it.

'Reilly, this is amazing!' Anike said, as she reached across the table, snagged an almond croissant and moaned in delight. 'Will you marry me? We'd have beautiful babies.'

Minette laughed and slapped her on the arm

'Seriously,' Anike continued. 'Amazing things can be done with DNA these days.'

'Oh, god, it's too early in the morning, Ani, just sit down,' Minette ordered.

'But how can I when I'm about to go skiing? For the very first time!' Anike sang, swirling around the room like she was Julie Andrews.

'I still can't believe that you've never gone skiing before.'

'Father's business associates are all men who would rather meet in dingy male-only men's clubs than on the slopes. Did I say it right?' Anike asked, turning her chaotic attention on to Reilly. '*On the slopes?*'

'Yes,' Reilly said with a laugh.

'You'll get used to her, I promise,' Minette grumbled as she reached for a coffee.

'If there's anything you'd like that isn't on the table, I can get it for you.'

Minette shook her head. 'This is perfect, *merci*.'

Anike pulled out a chair and ushered Reilly into it, piling croissants and fruit on to a plate for her, even as Reilly tried to protest.

'Oh no, that's OK. I've eaten and I would never—'

'Can you ski, Reilly?' Anike asked, cutting off her protestations, seemingly having forgotten her earlier discomfort, Minette decided. 'Is it amazing?'

'I can and it *is* amazing,' Reilly said. 'You're in good hands with Gustav. He's excellent. And what about you, Minette?' she asked, turning to look at her with those arctic blue eyes. 'What are you going to do today?'

'Oh, my schedule is utterly full of nothing but pampering, shopping and cocktails,' she replied loftily.

'You don't like skiing?'

'I *hate* being cold. Hate it,' she replied with a shiver. That icy cold ache and the way that ski boots made her shins hurt . . . No. She *could* ski and actually she could ski well – Maman had seen to that. But given the choice? *Non, merci*.

'She's always getting me to turn up the temperature in our dorm room. I swear I could do a hot yoga class in there,' Anike added.

'Is that how you two know each other?' Reilly asked and Minette rolled her shoulders, not quite sure whether her discomfort was because she hadn't had enough coffee, or from Reilly's questions.

'Our eyes met across a messy dorm room, in Paris, three months ago, and my life has never been the same since,' Anike said dreamily and Minette snorted into her coffee. 'Ahh, there she is, finally coming round.'

Minette waved her off.

'I just need a little more time than you in the morning, that's all,' she said, putting down her coffee and reaching her arms into the air. She pulled on each wrist, the stretch pulling out the kinks in her back, and wiggled in the chair.

'*Ça va, ça va*, I'm here. I'm awake.'

'Mmm-hmm,' Anike hummed, sceptically, before turning her attention back to their chalet host. 'Are you at college, Reilly?'

'I'm going in the fall. I deferred for a year, but I'm going to study Criminology at Berkeley.'

'Really?' Minette asked, surprised in spite of herself.

'I got in on a scholarship, but yeah.'

'You got a scholarship to Berkeley? That must have been hard,' Anike said.

'A little. But it was worth it.'

'What do you want to do with that?' Anike asked.

Reilly smiled, but something about it felt a little off to Minette. 'Justice. I want to get justice.'

Minette and Anike's eyes met over the strange reply.

'Hugo's ex went to Berkeley,' Minette remembered. 'But she dropped out to go travelling with her new boyfriend.'

'Hugo's ex?' Anike asked, innocently and not fooling anyone. 'What was she like?'

Minette smiled. 'Nothing like you. In a *good* way.'

'And what about you?' Reilly asked Anike, which was strange, because Minette was pretty sure that she had been told everything about them in order to work here.

'I'm studying Business. Father says he wants me to take over when he steps down.'

'But . . . ?' Reilly let the question dangle.

'Father will never step down while there's breath in his lungs. And I don't really want to take over the business.'

'No?'

'She doesn't want to work,' Minette explained.

'*No?*' Reilly asked again, surprised.

'No. I don't,' Anike announced without a trace of embarrassment. 'I know it's grand and vain and self-indulgent. But I don't want to work. I like to look pretty; I like people liking me to look pretty. I like nice food, strong drinks and to laugh. To laugh and laugh and laugh and, honestly, I don't see why I should be ashamed of saying so,' Anike said with an elegant shrug of her shoulder.

Minette hid her smile. The look on Reilly's face was priceless and for the first time she seemed honestly lost for words. Ani had delivered her whole speech with a kind of wry honesty that made it seem utterly . . . *acceptable* that she didn't want to work a day in her life.

'*Oui*,' Minette said, smiling at Reilly. 'That was my response too. Stunned acceptance.'

'And what about you?' Reilly asked Minette.

'She's going to work for the UN,' Anike whispered as if confiding some great secret.

Minette laughed.

'What? You are!' Anike insisted. 'And she'll be great at it,' she said to Reilly, 'because she's absolutely the best!'

Something warm and lovely twisted in Minette's chest from

Anike's words. Her mother had always dismissed Minette's dream to work at the UN. She'd not be good enough. She'd not work hard enough. She'd not have earned it enough. Her mother would say that any job that Minette might be able to get there would be solely because of *her*, Charlotte Aillet. As if Minette wouldn't, couldn't, carve out a name for herself in her own right. She'd always be riding on the coat-tails of her mother . . . *Or Noah*, a small voice whispered in the back of her mind.

Thick, dark, twisting emotions filled Minette's empty stomach.

'So, I was thinking for dinner—'

'Oh, don't worry about that. We're going out,' Minette announced, interrupting Reilly.

'Where?' Anike asked.

'Le Cheval Noir,' Minette replied to Anike, before turning back to Reilly. 'So, you can have the night off.'

Reilly smiled, but once again Minette could have sworn there was something edgy to it. As if that wasn't what Reilly had wanted at all.

JACOB

The adrenaline rushing through Jacob's bloodstream was something else entirely. It felt like he'd not skied for years, but at the same time it was as if it was only yesterday.

Hugo whooped and hollered behind him as he kept pace. He didn't know it, but Jacob was holding himself back a little, not wanting to make Hugo feel bad. Hugo liked to think – and predominantly was *right* to think – that he was naturally gifted at all sports. But skiing? That was Jacob's thing.

It's like your body just reads the snow beneath it, one ski instructor had poetically said.

He'd probably been angling for a hefty tip, but hey. Jacob was happy to accept the compliment. It's not as if they were coming thick and fast at home. Maybe he'd come out here on his own one afternoon and really let go.

But for now, he didn't mind keeping pace for Hugo, and since it was the first day out on the slopes, it probably wasn't a bad idea to ease into things. Brush off the cobwebs and let his body remember all the muscles that only skiing used.

Looking up, he saw the perfect place to take a moment. He looked up at a baby-blue sky and thought *this* was what it was all about; that strange sensation of the sun heating his skin from above while the snow froze his body from below; the heart-pounding, breath-sucking, sharp *cold*-tasting air in his lungs and the dead quiet around him.

Below them were the graceful twists of slopes that led all the way down the mountain into the town, criss-crossed by ski lifts and chair lifts and, lower down on the easier green slopes, button lifts.

Yeah, he'd come back here one day on his own.

He heard the slice of Hugo's skis on the thick, powdery snow as he came to a stop just behind him.

'Glad you came?' Hugo asked, cheeks rosy, and his blond

hair shoved different ways by the wind and the band from the goggles.

'Yeah, dude. Seriously, this is amazing. Thank you,' Jacob replied.

'No thanks needed,' Hugo said easily, his gaze shifting from Jacob out to the incredible view.

Jacob used one ski to step on the clip of the fastening of his other ski and freed his boot, before punching down on the other fastening with his ski pole. Turning to face the dramatic sweep of the mountainscape he collapsed down into the raised snow-bank behind him. He rested his forearms on his knees and breathed in that crisp alpine air.

He *did* owe Hugo his thanks, though. Christmas at home would have been fraught and stressful. His dad watching his mom like a hawk, having to make excuses to family and friends about why they wouldn't, couldn't, attend various social functions.

Three years ago, after the accident, everyone had been completely understanding. At first, his mother had needed rest, to let the broken bones caused by the head-on collision with a drunk driver, heal. And eventually they had. Things went back to normal.

The horrifying moment when both he and his father had thought that they might not get Mary back, that life could have been so damn different – that *fear* – had passed and they'd both been so thankful for it, that they'd ignored the warning signs.

Like the way that his mom could veer between being a little down, a bit low, a bit tired, to suddenly ecstatically happy, as if everything and everyone was *just so wonderful.*

She'd said that a lot, back then.

Even now, Jacob shivered in a kind of Pavlovian response to the phrase.

But she was there. She was alive. She'd gone back to work and normality had resumed. Perhaps that was why he and his father had ignored the warning signs that pointed to a prescription-drug addiction.

And when the insurance maxed out from medical bills and physio, they'd found other ways to pay for whatever kept Mary's agonising pain away. They'd exhausted their savings and Jacob's college fund. And how could they not have? How could they deny her pain relief when just one little white pill could make it all go away? But then it had been two pills. Four. Eight . . . Ten.

So he and his father had done whatever they'd had to, because Mary had suffered so much already and they were just so thankful to have her back. Weren't they?

'Dude?'

'What? Sorry,' Jacob apologised, realising that Hugo had been in the middle of saying something. He passed a hand over his face and shook his head out of his thoughts.

'You back in the room?'

'One hundred per cent.'

Hugo grinned at him, just as their phones beeped from a group message.

SKI 26:
NOAH
Lunch. Amendines. 30mins.
Last one there buys the round.

Jacob checked his watch. They were probably a lot nearer than Noah realised. It would only take them ten minutes to get down the hill and another five on the chair lift, back up to the midway station where Amendines sat, prime position between a couple of green slopes, a blue and a red.

'Chill, bro. We have time,' Hugo said, flicking his arm across Jacob's chest before falling back into the snow behind him.

Jacob gave in and followed suit, falling on to his back on the snow to stare up at the sky.

'How are you doing?' Jacob asked Hugo, wondering whether Hugo would take the chance to open up about things.

'It's tough, being back here. It's Christmas. Darian should be here,' Hugo said. 'Shit, there's a part of me that still feels like the Devereuxs should be here, right? And Avery and her parents. But after what happened on the island, Avery's college friend getting murdered, me being framed for it and all the truly nefarious stuff about Dennis Devereux coming out ... No freaking way, dude. When we're in Boston, that's fine, because they were never there. But being *here*?' Hugo broke off with a shake of his head.

'Have you heard from her?' Jacob asked, knowing that he'd managed to mend fences with his ex-girlfriend.

'Yeah,' Hugo's face changed, and Jacob saw a little bit of surprise and a little bit of happiness. 'They're actually in Spain right now. Leo's spending his vacations catching up with wherever Avery's managed to get to on her travels. And, dude, she got into animal school,' he said with no small amount of pride.

'I don't think it's called that,' Jacob replied, laughing.

'Of course not, but it winds her up and that's half the fun. But it's good. She's always wanted to be a vet.'

Jacob nodded absently. He'd not known Hugo when he'd been dating Avery. He'd heard enough smack talk from the lacrosse team players who had though. They were still fairly wary of Hugo; his anger had been the reason he'd been kicked off the team. And the rumours and scandal from the island hadn't helped. But to Jacob, Hugo had been nothing but a true friend.

'Is your mom doing OK?' Hugo asked, as if he'd sensed the change in his thoughts.

'No,' Jacob answered honestly.

'Are you?'

Jacob gave it some thought. 'Maybe.'

'That's good enough for now,' Hugo said, slapping him on the back, launching off the snow-bank, into his skis and hurling himself down the hill.

Shit.

The race was on!

Half an hour later, sweat streaming down his back, his cheeks freezing from wind and sunburn, with salt, sunscreen and snow in his nostrils, Jacob followed Hugo towards Amendines.

Hugo pulled to a stop at the chair lift and looked down the mountain.

'Hey, isn't that Anike down there with Gustav?' Hugo asked, pointing to a miniature slope below to the left of them, where a small button lift dragged little kids up on their skis while their parents walked beside them.

Jacob frowned and looked to where he was pointing. He could see Gustav dressed in some pretty high-spec gear, and Anike doing a great impression of a newborn giraffe before she managed to get her legs tangled and she fell. On a baby slope.

'I hope not,' Jacob said accidentally out loud, earning him a shoulder shove from Hugo. He laughed and looked back up to where Hugo was still looking at the pair. 'Dude, you've got it baaaad.'

'No I don't,' he denied. Jacob didn't believe it for a second, especially when a grin split Hugo's features.

'I saw the way you were looking at her last night,' Jacob teased.

'No idea what you're talking about, Arcilla. No idea.'

'Yeah, yeah, you keep telling yourself that.'

Jacob looked around at the beautiful slopes. Further up the mountain on the harder slopes, he caught sight of a figure dressed head to toe in black. Barely a smudge in the distance at this point, they cut down the mountain like a hot knife through butter.

Their speed was incredible – verging on reckless – but there was nothing out of control about the easy graceful movements of the skier. The sun made the brilliant white slope glow to the point where Jacob's eyes nearly watered trying to keep the figure in sight. He watched them tackle slopes that he and Hugo had been on not so long ago. Sweeping though the same turns, twisting out of others, Jacob took in the similarities and differences of their approach and what he might have done if he had the slope to himself like this skier.

'Damn,' Hugo said, having also looked up.

'Yeah,' was all Jacob could say as the figure drew closer and closer, completely unaware of the two gazes that were firmly fixed on them. It only took another few minutes – Jacob and Hugo both glued to their progress – before the skier came to the slope just above the plateau.

'Shit,' Hugo said, impressed, just as Jacob noted the Vandenburg-branded snowsuit that the skier was wearing.

Jacob blinked as he saw the slash of a blonde ponytail and knew instinctively that it was the girl from the night before. The staff member. Her skiing was aggressive. Confident. Dangerous.

She slid past them at a speed that fluttered his hair, but hadn't displaced a single snowflake.

They continued to watch her as she slowed down enough to join the green run without disrupting any of the less-experienced skiers and swept all the way down to the baby slope.

When she pulled up beside Anike and removed her goggles, Anike cried out in joy, hurled herself on to the skier and promptly knocked them both into the snow. Jacob thought he could hear their laughter from here.

'Must be Reilly Clarke, the host for the girls' chalet,' Hugo hedged with a shrug, his tone a mixture of awe and curiosity.

Huh.

So now Jacob had a name for the face. Reilly Clarke.

CHAPTER FIVE

REILLY

Reilly reached for the glass of lager and tried not to down it in one go. For just a moment she allowed the feeling of utter contentment rise and fall in her chest. It had been two years since she'd been on the slopes, and although she had things to do, things that needed her undivided attention, she'd not been able to resist an afternoon out on the mountain.

Just to see if she still had it.

Of course you still have it, her best friend's voice whispered in her ear, laughing at Reilly's self-doubt. Asma had always been her biggest supporter. And when Reilly's parents could no longer afford to take her skiing, Asma and her family had, trying to keep her Olympic dreams alive. And for a while, it had still looked like a possibility.

But then everything had changed.

'Le Cheval Noir? Seriously? You couldn't think of somewhere with better nightlife?'

Gustav plonked himself down on the chair beside her and eyed both Reilly and her glass of beer with something like disdain.

'I was feeling nostalgic,' Reilly shrugged, trying to justify the reason she'd brought him here.

'So, you wanted to play tourist?' Gustav sniffed.

'Humour me,' Reilly said, in the same tone she would have used to say 'bite me', making Gustav grin. He turned to face her, snuck his arms through hers, pulled her into a tight, strong hug and then ruined the moment by rubbing the top of her head as if she were still a child.

Gustav gestured to the barman for two beers and turned back to her, ignoring the awestruck looks being thrown his way from the evening crowd either coming in after an early dinner or still here after a late finish on the slopes.

Gustav might be the most sarcastic Swiss person she knew, but he was also a celebrity on the slopes. And she would have been too, had she been able to keep skiing.

'So spill. What happened? One minute you and that girl who followed you around—'

'I think you'll find it was me who followed *her* around—'

Gustav waved her semantics aside. 'And then pouff! Nothing. Gone.' He looked at her, utterly bemused. 'I thought you were going to come with me to the Olympics.'

So had Reilly.

'It's good to see you,' she said instead.

'Don't give me that shit. Why are you playing at being a Vandenburg lackey?'

Reilly pulled a face. 'I'm not a lackey.'

He raised a brow.

'Hosting's just a way to ease myself back into it. That and it pays well.'

'*Oui*, I remember now. Your parents. How are they doing?'

Again, Reilly pulled a face, not wanting to answer. This time because it was the truth that was hard, not the lie. Her father was bitter and angry – he drank too much and argued with her mother, who had never got over the disappointment of losing, not only her house and her status, but her friends, as well.

'I like the blonde, though. It suits you,' Gustav said when she didn't answer, picking up a tendril of hair before tucking it behind her ear.

Reilly grinned. She was beginning to like it too. It would probably take too much money and time to keep it up after these twelve days, but the blonde streaks made her feel . . . *pretty*.

Before she could finish the thought, the memory of Jacob Arcilla, Hugo's friend, staring at her as if stunned hit her hard and fast and completely out of nowhere.

'Where *is* your sidekick?'

Reilly swallowed, at the sudden jerk of her heart from his question. 'She . . .' But the words wouldn't come. The tears did though, pressing against the backs of her eyes. She hastily tried to blink them away. All she could do was shake her head, and when she looked back at Gustav she saw his gaze morph from confusion to disbelief.

'*Non.*'

She said nothing, because nothing would ever make sense of it. From the very first moment she'd heard of Asma's disappearance to seven days later when the police and rescue had called off the search. It wasn't true. It *couldn't* have been.

And then Reilly had received the letter.

'She *died*?' Gustav asked, appalled.

Reilly bit her lip and nodded.

'*Merde*, Reilly. Sorry,' he said, genuinely, a hand on her back. Warm, safe, comforting. But she didn't want comfort. Or safety. Asma hadn't had any of those things. So until Reilly got what she needed, *did* what she needed, she shouldn't have them either.

'To Asma,' Gustav said, raising his glass.

He'd remembered her name. Remembered who she was. And it was that that made the single tear fall down her cheek.

All Reilly could do was nod and take a mouthful of beer.

A moment later, the barman came over and slipped a piece of paper to Gustav, his thumb jerking over his shoulder.

'Seriously? That's all it takes?' Reilly asked, laughing in spite of herself.

Gustav looked at the phone number written on the piece of paper and over to where the barman had pointed. A short, stocky guy with a trim dark beard was staring back at him.

'Huh,' was all Gustav said before putting the number in his back pocket.

'I thought you liked them blond,' Reilly said, remembering a few too many nights when she and Asma, only sixteen years old, had snuck away from their chalet and joined Gustav who had always, no matter how careless he appeared, kept a very close eye on them, ensuring that they managed to have fun without getting into trouble. He'd been like an older brother and Reilly suddenly realised how much she'd missed him, despite not having seen him for a couple of years.

'Not since Sven,' Gustav replied, with a shiver as if traumatised.

'Fair enough. Don't mind me,' Reilly said, nodding in the bearded guy's direction.

'I don't mind you. *Most* of the time. But I want to finish my beer,' Gustav replied, playing hard to get with a wink at Reilly.

'So, what have you been up to?' Reilly asked, genuinely curious.

'Oh, you know, I dabbled a little with the Olympics. Picked up a little bit of gold here and there and decided that what I *really* needed to do was make an obscene amount of money from these rich arseholes while I could, so that I can retire young and live a life of debauchery.'

'Living the dream,' Reilly said with a smile.

'Every day,' Gustav replied, taking another mouthful of his beer.

Just then the sound of a laugh cut across the bar, drawing Reilly's attention to the mezzanine floor.

There they all were. Minette and Noah pressed up against each other, his arm flung around her shoulder, laughing at something Hugo Vandenburg had said, while Anike and Jacob joined in.

Reilly had still been trying to avoid looking in their direction, but had kept a discreet eye on them from the moment she'd got there.

Just then, Minette looked at Noah, reached a hand to the back of his neck and pulled him in for a kiss that probably should have been left for behind closed doors. Minette shouldn't be allowed to be happy. She shouldn't be allowed to do what she'd done and get away with it as if nothing had happened and she hadn't ruined someone's life.

And then Reilly felt Jacob staring at her.

Her brain short-circuited. What was it about this guy that did that to her? She'd never experienced anything like it. She flushed from head to toe as if she didn't know whether to be angry or happy or sad.

'Oh, I see how it is,' Gustav said, with an eye over her shoulder on the table where Hugo and his friends were sitting.

'What do you mean?'

'*This* is why you wanted to come to this tourist trap?'

Concern skittered down Reilly's spine. How could he possibly—

'He's hot,' Gustav replied, turning back to his beer.

Reilly blinked.

'Oh, don't get cute with me,' Gustav said. 'I've got eyes. He's hot. And he's not stopped staring at you, since he noticed you sitting here.'

'*Who?*'

'Tall, dark and handsome over there.'

Reilly choked on her beer, while her cheeks flamed with embarrassment.

'Thought so. OK. Fine. I see where this is headed,' Gustav said, downing the rest of the beer in his glass and getting up from his seat. 'I'm going to get mine, Reilly Clarke. You do you, and call me when you're ready to hit the slopes with someone who knows what they're doing,' he said saucily, before planting a kiss on her cheek and walking over to the guy with the beard.

'Hey!' she called out to him, but all Gustav did was raise his middle finger without bothering to turn back to look at her.

She laughed, half in shock, and half in appreciation. That was Gustav, and she'd always liked him for it, but—

'Reilly!'

She turned in the direction of where her name had been yelled across the bar to find Anike leaning against the mezzanine's wooden balustrade.

'Want to join us?' Anike yelled, either unaware or choosing to ignore the looks that turned in her direction, which may or may not have had something to do with the thigh-high mini skirt and over-the-knee woollen socks she was wearing above her fur-lined leather ankle boots.

A ski-bunny fantasy that more than one guy had noticed. Though – from just one look at the hearts in Hugo Vandenburg's eyes – they didn't stand a chance.

'Are you sure?' Reilly called, scanning the faces of the others at the table. Noah looked slightly bored, Jacob looked . . . *hot* . . . but Minette?

'Absolutely, come on!'

JACOB

'You guys don't mind, do you?' Anike asked, sitting back down at the table.

'It'd be a bit late if we did,' Noah said out of the side of his mouth.

Jacob didn't stop the frown that crossed his brow in time.

'Sorry, mate. Don't mind me, I just . . .' He shrugged. 'We've had some bad experiences with people trying to get "inside scoops" and sell them to the press. It's made me a bit nervous, that's all. I'm sure she's fine.'

'Oh, she's great, she's—'

'Coming,' Minette said quickly, before sitting up on the wooden bench that she and Noah were sharing.

'Hi, guys,' Reilly said slightly awkwardly.

'I didn't realise you knew Gustav,' Anike said, moving up to make room for Reilly in between her and Hugo. Hugo suffered the move with grace, but shot a frustrated glare at Jacob for good measure.

Jacob swallowed a mouthful of beer to stop himself from laughing.

'Yeah. From way back,' Reilly said evasively, which she smoothed out with a smile. Her gaze flicked to Minette who was whispering something to Noah and laughing.

'He's really cool. And didn't make me feel like an idiot once!' Anike exclaimed.

Jacob leaned back in the seat, trying to work out what it was about Reilly that had caught his attention. She definitely wasn't older than him. Her blonde hair reached below her shoulders, but not much further. It framed a face that was both strong and fine.

But her eyes – they were the kind of crystal blue that made him think of the bottle of curaçao his dad had bought a decade ago to make some fancy cocktail his mother had decided she needed to have at their next dinner party. And in his mind the sound of his mother's laughter echoed over the moment Reilly Clarke looked across the table to lock eyes with him.

Unable to hold her gaze, Jacob looked down and picked a hangnail, berating himself for having silly thoughts. He hadn't had a girlfriend since Laura. They'd broken up shortly after his mother's accident and he couldn't blame her. She'd not signed up for a boyfriend who needed to be home on a Friday night to look after his mother, instead of hanging out with her. They'd only been together a few months and she'd been pretty torn up about the break-up. Probably more than him in hindsight.

And as for whatever it was that drew him to Reilly? It was unlikely to be anything more than how hot she was. She probably had a horrible personality and a terrible sense of humour.

Only, a few hours, and a lot more drinks, later it was clear that he was wrong. She was funny *and* nice.

'Oh my god, what did you do then?' Noah asked, as everyone around the table hung on Reilly's every word.

She shrugged. 'I chucked his skis over the ropes on one side, his poles over the ropes on the other and beat him to the bottom of the course by thirty seconds.'

They all laughed at the story, and even Minette seemed to have loosened up a little. Jacob had been mindful of Hugo – aware that as the boss's son there might be some awkwardness about drinking with the staff, but Hugo didn't seem to mind. In part, because he'd spent much of the last hour-and-a-half with his eyes glued to Anike's legs. Something that neither Jacob, nor Anike herself, had missed.

Hugo looked up to find Jacob catching him out *again*, bit his lip to stop himself from laughing and looked away.

'So, what time are we hitting the slopes tomorrow?' Hugo asked.

'As early as possible, dude,' Jacob replied.

'Count me in,' Anike said gleefully.

Hugo winced. 'I think you might need to spend just a little more time with Gustav,' he suggested kindly.

'I know that, silly! I just wanted to be able to say that I was hitting the slopes,' she replied, casting a look at Reilly, who nodded with a small smile, as if Anike had got something right. Anike also seemed to be utterly undeterred by any sense of rejection, which was strangely refreshing.

Hugo blinked as if he, like Jacob, was wondering if he'd ever met anyone as shiningly optimistic and sunny as Anike Dossongui.

'If you can rouse yourself from your bed before two in the afternoon,' Hugo said, jokingly nudging Noah's shoulder, 'you should join us.'

'Hey, today was a one-off. I'll be hunting down fresh powder before you'll have woken from your beauty sleep.'

'Yeah right,' Hugo dismissed.

'What about you, Reilly? Will you be out on the slopes again tomorrow?' Jacob asked.

'Again?' Minette asked.

'Yeah. We saw Reilly out on the slopes earlier,' Hugo explained.

'You did?' Reilly asked, as if surprised.

'Yeah, it was seriously impressive,' Jacob added.

She frowned. 'Because I'm a girl?'

'No, because it was seriously impressive,' he replied sincerely, hoping that she'd read the truth in his statement.

'You ski a lot?' Noah asked, with Minette watching their exchange. Jacob wondered if he imagined some tension coming from that end of the table.

'I used to. I'm getting back into it. What about you?'

'Oh, I gave up skis a few years back. I prefer boarding. It's waaaayyy cooler.'

'No, it's not,' Jacob, Hugo and Reilly all replied in unison and then laughed.

Minette joined in, but her smile didn't quite reach her eyes.

'So, you up for it?' Jacob pressed his luck again.

Reilly winced. 'I've got quite a lot to do at the chalet.'

'If you want to go . . .' Minette dangled.

'Yeah, we'll cover for you!' Anike exclaimed happily.

'You should. Then I can see how really *impressive* you are,' Noah said with a grin.

'I don't believe this,' Anike exclaimed, slamming her glass on the table.

'What is it?' Reilly asked, following the direction of Anike's gaze to the bar below.

'Just my stalker,' Anike complained.

'Your what?' Hugo demanded.

Minette slapped him on the arm. 'No, Hugo, it's just her bodyguard, Karel.'

'It's like being in jail,' Anike wailed. It probably wasn't, Jacob thought, but Hugo seemed sympathetic. 'Bloody Jacques,' Anike cursed.

It was impossible to have missed the gossip about Anike – it had been splashed across social media for the world to see. Minette winced, Noah nodded and Hugo could have cracked a walnut with his teeth.

Noah leaned across the table and rested a hand on Anike's arm.

'I think you handled it perfectly and with great creative flare,' he said in all seriousness, making Anike laugh.

'I always did have an artistic touch,' she acknowledged with a modest shrug and a satisfied smile.

'I just wish the press had bothered to find out the truth. I can't believe that he got to cheat on me and then tell everyone that *I* was the one who was being "childish".'

'That's the thing about the press, they'll do and say whatever they want – especially if you have money,' Noah said, looking at Minette as if they understood that in a way that Jacob would never get.

'It's probably not a bad thing, Ani. I'm sure he's only here for your safety,' Hugo suggested hopefully.

'And to spy on me for Father.'

'At least the press will leave you alone here. Val D'Amer Doux doesn't have much patience for journalists,' Hugo stated.

'They wouldn't dare risk the income they get through tourism,' Noah added.

The entire table turned to look at where Karel stood at the bar. He didn't look much like the kind of bodyguard Jacob had imagined Anike might have. He was less Jason Bourne and more an older Jason Sudeikis, but dressed in ski gear he could have been one of any number of tourists, and he supposed that was the idea – to blend in, not to stand out.

Noah leaned forward across the table. 'I have an idea,' he whispered. 'Let's give him the slip and head over to Exeter.'

'What's Exeter?'

'It's a nightclub in the next village. We can get a car to take us. I'll order it now,' Noah said, the phone already in his hand.

'You really think we could do that? Give a trained bodyguard the slip?' Jacob asked, sceptically.

'Of course. I've done it loads of times with the guys my parents employ. They just need a distraction.'

Anike's eyes danced with excitement, and even Minette seemed eager. 'Do you think we could get away with it? Really?'

'Absolutely!' Noah exclaimed. 'If Reilly can go down there and tell him something like, Ani messaged saying that she needed help—'

'Hey, I don't think we need to worry him,' Hugo said, nudging Noah with his shoulder.

'OK, not that, but like, maybe Reilly gets worried because she's heard that we're all planning to go down to O'Connors, which everyone knows gets a bit rowdy . . .'

'But he's literally right there, watching us.'

'And what about Reilly?' Jacob said. 'She'll be left with Karel while we all slip out the back.'

Noah shrugged.

'I'm sure there's another way,' Hugo offered.

'It's fine,' Reilly said. 'Honestly, I'm happy to help. I was going to head back to the chalet anyway.'

'That's great!' Noah and Minette said together.

'Are you sure?' Jacob asked, and not because he wanted to spend more time with her – even though he did. He just didn't like the idea of her being the sacrificial lamb for their own enjoyment.

'Seriously, you guys go on. Exeter is a really great club – you'll love it. And don't worry about Karel. I've got the *perfect* way to distract him,' she insisted, with a naughty look in her eye.

CHAPTER SIX

MINETTE

Minette twisted from side to side in the mirror of the ultra-exclusive boutique in the heart of Val D'Amer Doux. The top hugged the front of her chest and reached her collarbone, but dropped away at the sides leaving her back dramatically bare.

The midnight blue looked good against the slight tan of her skin, courtesy of the sunbed she'd used before travelling to Switzerland. She'd made sure that before she saw Noah, she was picture perfect, just the way he liked her.

The critical eye she assessed herself with now was tinted by thoughts of what her mother would say. Or Noah, she silently conceded.

Narrowing her gaze, she caught the eye of the sales assistant behind her practically frothing at the mouth at the possibility of the commission she was sure to make on the five-thousand-euro piece of designer clothing.

'*Non.*' Minette shook her head and called for the next item of clothing that had been put aside for her when she'd first made the appointment. Minette slipped out of the top in the changing room, and reached for the glass of champagne, eyeing the smooth planes of her body.

She'd always had a slender body. But Noah liked bigger boobs, she thought miserably, looking at her chest. She'd tried to make up for it with sexy lingerie, but sometimes he almost seemed bored of her.

Minette flicked her gaze back to her face and peered at the dark smudges under her eyes. They'd got back from the club late last night after Reilly had somehow distracted Karel for long enough to allow them to sneak out. Minette had been thankful that Reilly hadn't joined them. She still couldn't quite put her finger on *why*, but the chalet host made her feel a little uncomfortable.

'Mademoiselle?' called the sales assistant, as she passed a hanger with the next item of clothing for Minette to try.

She inspected the burgundy silk, layers of swaying fabric falling from the thick waistband, into which was tucked the two dramatic pieces that would just cover her chest.

She lowered the side-zip and stepped into the circle of the skirts, settling the dress around her before going back out to the raised dais, in front of three mirrors that could offer her the best reflection of the clothing.

The sales assistant gasped in delight, hands clutched to her mouth in excitement.

It was good. Very flattering, pressing tightly against her torso, and the way that the skirts moved when she walked revealed a slit that was nearly indecent – but not quite.

She *loved* it.

'Oh, *un moment, s'il vous plait*,' the sales assistant said, before rushing off.

Minette looked at herself and swished the skirts, loving the way that the material slid against her skin.

The sales assistant returned with a velvet box and presented it to Minette with the lid open.

Minette pressed her finger to her lips in surprise.

On the black velvet was a ruby pendant the size of a small egg. The colour of the precious gemstone was rich and dark, the same blood red colour of her dress.

'*I couldn't*,' Minette said, even though she very much wanted to try on the incredible necklace.

'*Mais oui!* You must,' insisted the assistant as she slipped the necklace from the box and opened the clasp.

Minette turned to allow the assistant to fasten it behind her neck and the moment the necklace pressed against her skin, she knew the assistant had been right.

She *had* to have it.

'How much is it?' Minette asked, without taking her eyes off the way that the pendant glimmered in the boutique's lights.

The sales assistant wrote down the number on a piece of paper, as if it were uncouth to mention the number out loud, and Minette nearly laughed.

She looked at the zeros and shrugged off the price. It was fine.

The dress was exquisite, but with the necklace it was exceptional. And she'd been looking for the perfect thing to wear to the Vandenburg Christmas Eve drinks and this was it.

She waved away the sales assistant, telling her that she'd need shoes and underwear to go with it. The sales assistant rushed to fulfill her request before Minette could change her mind.

She wouldn't. She looked incredible. She *needed* to.

Last night, Noah had been . . . fine. He'd been absolutely fine. *Of course* it was going to take a while to get used to each other after all that time apart. It was perfectly natural. It didn't mean anything that once they'd got to the club, he'd spent more time with the boys. Or that he'd been very kind to the few girls that had approached him, rebuffing them easily, with a rueful 'what can you do' glance her way. It had touched her that he'd even realised that she'd noticed. And besides, it had given her time to catch up with Anike, who had done everything possible to drive Hugo to distraction with her dancing and flirting.

Her phone vibrated from inside her purse on the small table beside the gold framed mirror.

SKI 26:
HUGO
Last one to the bottom buys the drinks.
JACOB
Guess it's on you then, bro.
NOAH
I'm down already!
ANI
Hey, don't I get a head start?

Minette's fingers hovered over the keyboard but she didn't know what to say. She felt as if she were being left out, all the while knowing perfectly well that it was her own choice. But it didn't really feel like her choice when the ski boots felt like torture devices against her shins and she'd been in agony the last few times she'd forced herself to ski.

No, she'd finish off here at the boutique, have lunch with her mother at the Rubicon – the Michelin-starred restaurant at the Vandenburg Hotel – where the chef would make something special and off-menu for her mother, and then Minette would head to the gym at the spa centre.

She looked over the selection of shoes and lingerie the sales assistant offered and chose two pairs of heels and two underwear sets, handed over her card and had the entire lot packed up and sent to the chalet.

Minette redressed in the layers of thermal silks and the black one-piece ski suit, before heading back out into the village.

The icy wind immediately bit at any exposed skin and Minette adjusted the rabbit fur headband that covered her ears and held her hair back, before slipping on a pair of Chopard sunglasses.

Despite the fact that most people were out on the slopes, like Noah, Hugo, Anike and Jacob, the village was still a hot spot for tourists and this street in particular was for the shoppers. Minette passed the LVMH storefront and eyed the mannequin in the window.

She was still a little angry at her father for, once again, not coming with them to Val D'Amer Doux this Christmas. He'd promised. She'd *made* him promise after last year, because her mother was always so much *worse* when he wasn't there. Charlotte Aillet didn't even bother to try and pretend that she liked her daughter. So before he'd left for Hong Kong her father had given Minette his credit card, and now she wondered how much damage she could do to it in this shop.

Minette She checked her watch and realised that she'd probably be late for lunch with her mother if she continued shopping. But that didn't mean she wouldn't be back.

She messaged the car service and had it take her to the Vandenburg Hotel. Standing out from other hotels in the area because of its height and opulence, even Minette was awed by it. Stepping into the foyer she was immediately enveloped in warmth. Her snow boots thudded dully on the rich moisture-wicking carpet that bordered the dark marble flooring. Thousands of long, thin strip lights, hung down from the ceiling like windchimes that didn't move, but looked impressive. To her left was a seating area with egg-shaped chairs with buttery leather on the inside and a sheaf of pink copper on the outside. After the bright white of the snow and the mountains, the foyer was a blessed relief on the eyes.

Minette had pulled her phone out to call her mother when she caught sight of James Scarisbrick, striding through the foyer determinedly. She went to raise her hand, but let it drop again when she realised he hadn't seen her at all. Frowning, she wondered where he was going.

Just then her phone rang, distracting her.

'Maman,' Minette answered.

'I won't be available for lunch,' her mother announced.

'Oh, is everything OK?'

'*Bien sûr.*'

Minette frowned. If all was OK, then why were they rearranging lunch?

'I'm sure your chalet girl can make you something, and if not, just go out. I'll see you at the Christmas Eve drinks tomorrow evening.'

Minette bit her lip and heard her mother sigh and immediately braced herself.

'Oh, Minette, don't be difficult. I'm busy. Besides, isn't that why you have your friend? Where is she?'

'She's at her lesson with Gustav.'

'You know, if you actually went out on the slopes, you wouldn't be in this position. I'm sure it's not normal for girls your age to want to have lunch with their mothers. I know I didn't.'

'*Maman*,' Minette pleaded, feeling the sting of heat on her cheeks.

'Part of being an adult, Minette, is managing to occupy yourself.'

Minette bit her lip again, the sharp sting of her mother's disappointment and rejection digging into old wounds and before she could say anything further, her mother ended the call. Her phone vibrated a second later with a message from SKI 26. It was a picture of a huge platter of burgers and fries in front of Hugo, Jacob and Noah, who had his arm slung around Ani's shoulders.

HUGO
Wish you were here, Mini!

Shoving aside a devastating spike of jealousy, Minette messaged the car service to take her back to the chalet.

REILLY

She had the chalet to herself. She knew Anike was with the boys at lunch because Gustav had messaged after dropping her off at the on-piste restaurant. And Minette was having lunch with her mother, so Reilly had given herself an hour.

Sixty minutes to do what she needed to do. Get in, look for proof and get out again.

Reilly took the three flights of stairs to the top floor of the chalet, ignoring the elevator that had been installed because apparently the rich were *that* lazy.

It had been a tough transition from the kind of money Reilly's family had before her father's business went bankrupt, to their financial situation after. The school she'd ended up in had been rough and it had been difficult for Reilly to straddle that world and the world she inhabited during her vacations with Asma and her family.

There'd even been times when Reilly had told her mother she didn't want to go. And whatever her mother's faults, she had at least known that the holidays would be good for Reilly. Her mother had convinced her to go, to enjoy it, to forget just for a while what she didn't have, and to be thankful and grateful that the Chaudhurys wanted to give her an amazing vacation. Reilly had sulked and stropped and pleaded and she'd never been so thankful that her mother had been right. Just five minutes in Asma's company and she'd forgotten all her fears.

Reilly stepped out on to the large landing beneath a huge skylight that let in the early afternoon sun, warming her wherever it touched her skin. To the left was the large suite Anike was using and to the right was Reilly's destination: Minette's room.

Reilly's hand stilled on the door-handle. If she got caught . . .

She wouldn't. She'd made sure of it. Both the girls were out.

Reilly pulled on the brass handle and pushed the door open. She'd been in here when she'd given the girls a tour of their rooms, but she'd not visited since.

The chalets all had a cleaning service, which had just left – the Vandenburgs clearly recognising that the chalet host's duties were to be on-hand for the clients and as such couldn't be distracted by such trivial things. Not that Reilly was complaining. It had taken an army of five just over two hours to clean the entire place top to bottom, to the exacting standards of Savannah Coates.

Stepping across the threshold, Reilly looked around the enormous room. She didn't know what she'd been expecting, and it was clear that any trace of mess that Minette might have left had been tidied away by the cleaners. But that wasn't really why Reilly was here.

The super king size bed jutted out from the wall, at right angles to the floor-to-ceiling windows. Fur throws in different colours were laid beautifully over the perfectly made bed. In the corner, a circular wooden-chair swing covered in plush cushions hung from the ceiling, perfect for looking out over the rows of mountains that stretched into the distance beyond the glass.

Reilly went over to the table on the opposite side of the room where a laptop and a set of chargers were neatly placed in rows.

Putting the bag she'd brought with her down on to the bed, Reilly slipped into the desk chair, and levered open the thin computer and hoped that Minette was too lazy to have made her password complicated. The girl had her phone glued to her palm most of the time, so there was almost no way that Reilly would be able to get access to that. But this?

She checked her watch and set the timer.

The laptop booted up and presented her with a pin request.

The cursor blinked at her mockingly.

Reilly pulled out the list she'd been working on for the last few days. One side had possible passwords and the other had possible pins. She knew that the chances of her being able to get in to it were slim. Especially given that this model of laptop only allowed her four tries until it locked her out.

Which meant she only had *three* tries, stopping *before* it locked so that Minette didn't notice a thing.

With sweaty hands, Reilly smoothed out the paper.

2019 — the year that they all started at the Institute.
2869 — the pin code to Minette's dorm room at the Institute.
2021 — the year Minette and Noah became official.

There were more. Lots more. But she still had time ahead of her. This was only the third day. If she had to, she'd come in here and try again every single day. Because there was no way that Reilly would be leaving here without the proof she needed. No way in hell.

With the thread of anger making her fingers shake, she chose the one she thought most likely: 2869.

It's just easier this way.

Asma's voice sounded in her mind and Reilly remembered it from when they'd been putting their stuff in a locker at the swimming pool in Courcheval three years ago. 'It's not a big deal Reilly.'

'Of course it is! All you did was change the dorm code.'

'And I won't do it again,' Asma had said.

'She locked you out of your room for a week!'

'And I won't do it again.' Asma had shrugged. 'It's just easier this way.'

It's just easier this way.

Three years later, and those words had taken on such a different meaning. Asma Chaudhury, her best friend – the brightest, funniest, kindest girl Reilly had ever known – was gone.

And it was all because of Minette.

Reilly typed the numbers into the box on the screen and held her breath as she hit enter.

PIN NUMBER INCORRECT

Shit.

She swallowed and looked at the next number.

Her pulse had begun to race and she needed to calm down. She'd known that it might not work straight away, but she'd hoped it would. She'd really hoped.

2019.

Her fingers punched against the keys on the laptop.

Enter.

PIN NUMBER INCORRECT

Double shit.

2021.

Enter.

PIN NUMBER INCORRECT

Reilly slammed her fist down on the table.

ONE MORE ATTEMPT BEFORE ACCOUNT LOCK

She glared at the message on the laptop and closed it down, frustrated.

She'd had to wait so long to get this opportunity . . . having to finish school, having to find the right time, the right *place*, to make her move. Oh, she'd used that time wisely, researching and organising. And when Lisolette had got a job at the Vandenburg Hotel - the same Vandenburgs that Minette spent Christmases with, it had felt as if everything was falling into place. As if it was meant to be. So, yeah. Reilly had waited this long. She could wait a little longer.

She checked her watch. She had probably another thirty minutes before she should get back downstairs. She needed to be focused and methodical. She was looking for anything that would tie Minette to Asma's death.

She went to the chest of draws, taking the bag with her. One by one she pulled them open and very carefully felt her way through the contents to see if Minette had chosen to hide anything there. Nothing in the drawers. Nothing in the wardrobe. Reilly pulled out the suitcases and carefully felt through the pockets in case she'd left anything in them. Nothing.

Fighting her irritation, Reilly went over to the bedside cabinet, throwing the bag on the bed again, before yanking open the drawer and knocking over the iPad she'd not realised was an iPad. She'd thought it was a photo frame, but now she looked at it, Reilly realised what it was as it cycled through photographs of Minette.

She picked it up and sat on the bed, swiping a finger over a picture to move the gallery along.

Posed photos of Minette and Noah from social functions. One of Minette's father. She studied his face, wondering about the people who had brought up Minette. Wondering if they were proud of their daughter. Wondering how much they knew about her and whether they would protect her if they learned the truth.

That Minette was a bully who had driven a fun, kind, beautiful girl to take her life.

'What are you doing in here?'

Reilly's heart jerked hard in her chest.

'Oh!' she exclaimed. 'You scared me,' she scolded Minette.

She watched suspicion turn to confusion on her features, Minette hardly expecting that as a response.

'I came to leave you a little gift from the Vandenburgs,' she said, holding up the bag she'd placed on the bed. 'Sorry, I was clumsy and knocked over your iPad and I got caught up in the pictures,' Reilly said ruefully. 'You and Noah look so good together.' Reilly pointed at the picture of their graduation from the Institute.

Something Asma never got to do.

'I thought the chalet had cleaners,' Minette said.

Reilly frowned. 'They do. As I said, I was just here to leave you this gift. I'm going out this evening and I didn't want you to miss it. It's something special from your hosts. Anike has one too,' Reilly said, pointing through the open door to where she'd put a similar bag on the bed of Anike's room earlier.

Minette looked behind her, saw the bag and nodded slowly.

'And also your things arrived from the boutique. They've been hung in your wardrobe.'

'Thank you, Reilly. Sorry, I just wasn't expecting you here.'

Neither was I, Reilly thought as she excused herself and made her way back down the stairs, heart thumping with so much adrenaline that pins and needles nipped at her fingertips.

She got to the bottom of the stairs and looked back up to find Minette staring down at her, her gaze unreadable.

CHAPTER SEVEN

JACOB

'Are you ready?' Hugo asked.

'Absolutely!'

Jacob had been hearing about the spa centre for the entire semester. He'd had *dreams* about the place and he'd never even been there.

'OK, kids,' Mark said, coming out of the living area as Nils cleared away the table after their dinner.

Hugo winced, but it was so comical Jacob couldn't help but laugh. It had been clear from Mark Vandenburg's tone that he'd meant it jokingly.

'Have you got water as well as the stupid amounts of alcohol you think you've so cleverly hidden in your bag?'

'Yes, Dad,' Hugo said in a tone that screamed 'eye roll'.

'And snacks for later to sober you up just enough so that no one is sick in the hot tub?'

'Yes Dad.'

'And protection so that no one—'

'Dad, Dad, Dad, Dad, Dad!' Hugo yelled, sticking his fingers in his ears.

'Have you?' Mark demanded without budging.

'Always and only for just-in-case purposes,' Hugo ground out from beneath clenched teeth and eyes squeezed shut.

Jacob hid his smile, pretending to rub his jaw, but the grin on Mark's face and the love in his eyes was worth any embarrassment he could throw at Hugo, and the way that Hugo hugged his dad showed exactly the same thing.

'OK. Get out. I don't want either of you back until the early hours,' Mark commanded. Before adding in a whisper, 'But if for any reason you want to come back sooner—'

'Dad—'

'This door is always open and you,' he said turning to Jacob, 'are also always welcome.'

Touched into speechlessness, Jacob only moved when Hugo threw an arm around his neck and dragged him out the back exit of the chalet and into the freezing cold, where they would make the less-than-five-minute walk to the spa centre. It was accessible to each of the chalets, but had been – for tonight – commandeered by the gang, so no adults were going to interrupt their fun.

'That was . . .' Jacob trailed off, not quite knowing how to put what he was feeling into words.

'I know. Sickeningly emotionally supportive, whilst being funny and really kind and still being a parent. The world doesn't deserve Mark Vandenburg,' Hugo said, his words white clouds on the cool air. 'He meant it, by the way.'

'Mm?' Jacob asked.

'Our door is always open,' Hugo said, his gaze straight ahead on the snowy path that glowed in the moonlight.

Their generosity touched Jacob deeply.

'But now we drink!' Hugo cried into the night.

Over the crunch of their boots in the snow, Jacob soon heard the dull thud of music echoing off the snow-covered trees and out and down the mountain. They rounded the corner and—

Oh shit.

Actually, Jacob might have said that out loud, he wasn't quite sure. But when Hugo had told him that there was a spa centre that had everything they'd need, he hadn't quite been expecting . . . *this.*

'Hugo,' was all he seemed capable of saying.

'Yeah, I know. It's a bit much. But no expense spared is my dad's – *Darian's* – motto. And it's here, so . . .'

The long bungalow was all soft buttery wood and gleaming glass. Up lit, with a wedge of snow on the roof, it looked like a gingerbread house and offered just as many treats inside. Jacob spied what looked like a fifty-metre pool as well as a fully kitted-out gym, a sauna *and* a steam room.

'We've been here three days and it's only *now* you show me this?'

'Didn't want to spoil you all at once.'

Jacob followed Hugo up on to the porch and around the corner, where he stopped in his tracks.

Not too far from the edge of the forest, which bordered one side of the building, a hot tub was bubbling away, steam rising and swirling in the night sky. Anike, Minette and Noah were already there, the music loud enough to feel, but clearly not enough to bother anyone. The nearest neighbours were their parents and the staff and they were far enough away.

Anike caught sight of them and let out a squeal of delight at the same time as thrusting an open bottle of champagne into the air.

'Come on, we've been waiting for you,' Noah grinned, before taking a long drag on a cigarette. 'Don't want you to miss all the fun,' he said, leaning down to press his mouth against Minette's in a kiss.

Ten minutes later, Jacob was in his swimming shorts, chest deep in bubbling hot water with a shot in one hand and a glass of champagne in the other. If this was how the other half lived, he wasn't complaining.

The sweet cherry scent from Anike's vape twirled into the steam from the hot water and drew his gaze upwards to the incredible array of stars overhead. Music was thrumming in his veins and he felt for the first time since they'd got here that he was truly relaxing. To his left, Hugo was flirting outrageously with Anike and Minette was now on Noah's lap, facing outwards. He didn't mind feeling like a third wheel. It had never bothered him before. But it did mean that it left him free to spend an inordinate amount of time thinking of a particular blonde.

For a few hours, they talked and laughed. Noah offered him a cigarette, Jacob happily refused and when Noah started to press, he simply said, 'Body is a temple and all that.'

Noah side-eyed him, but Hugo backed him up, saying, 'They take that shit seriously at Harvard.'

Jacob had absolutely no intention of opening up about his feelings on smoking. Yeah, he knew that the kids his age did it as easily as drinking. But they clearly had no experience of addiction. And as the son of an addict, there were two ways he could go. He could follow in his mother's footsteps, or he could take a different path. And he'd take the different path – because he'd never do that to the people he loved.

He knew it wasn't her fault. And he would never, *ever*, blame his mother. No, it was the prick doctor that had prescribed her unnecessary opioids and got her hooked.

Jacob looked away and got himself under control, before forcing himself back into the 'party mood'.

'Hey, are you hoping to go to Costa Rica this summer?' Anike asked Minette.

Minette shrugged. 'Maybe. Why?'

'I just thought it would be really cool if we could all meet up there in July.'

Jacob bit back the 'yeah right', clawing in the back of his throat. He wasn't going to get that lucky twice.

'You're usually at Mokani,' Noah said to Hugo. 'Are you going back there this year?'

Hugo rubbed the back of his neck, a sad look in his eyes. 'They're selling it.'

'Shit, really?' Noah asked, sitting up and dislodging Minette from his lap.

'Why? Daddy wanna buy it?' Hugo asked angrily.

'I mean, yeah. But that's not what I meant.'

'I know, sorry,' Hugo said, reining in his temper quickly. 'It's just still so fresh. But would he really be interested in buying it after what happened?' he asked.

Noah waved him off with a hand. 'That wouldn't bother him.'

And Jacob didn't know what he was more bemused by. The fact that kids his age were talking about buying and selling an entire island, or whether Noah's parents didn't care about a little thing like murder.

That's what made him feel out of place. This was a kind of living that he'd never have access to. No matter how much he earned or, if he was lucky enough, won on the lottery. *This* kind of money? It was generational. It was in their genes and made them different. Made them think differently. Feel differently.

Out of the corner of his eye, Jacob saw movement in the forest, and thought he heard the crunch of footsteps in between the beats of the music. He flicked a gaze at his watch. One forty-five. He peered into the distance and saw a familiar branded ski jacket and a flash of blonde.

And as quickly as he'd got into the hot tub, he was out, shoving himself, half wet, into his thermals and jacket, and heading towards the private forest track as quickly as he could.

'Where's the fire?' called Noah.

'Sorry! Didn't realise the time. My folks will lose their shit,' he called over his shoulder, knowing full well that if his mother wasn't asleep, she'd be bombed and out of it, and his father would either be staring at a blank wall or shouting at his wife.

He didn't want to go back there, but he hadn't really wanted to stay in the hot tub talking about Costa Rica and future events that were as far removed from him as the moon. He wanted something normal. A conversation. A laugh. He wanted *Reilly*.

REILLY

Reilly shrank into her ski jacket, the frigid temperature stark after the warmth of Lisolette's little apartment, down in the town. She could have used the car service to bring her back to the chalet, but Reilly had wanted to take the thirty-minute walk to clear her head. Or refocus at least.

Lisolette had aged in the two years since she'd last seen her. The grey hairs had shocked Reilly a little. In her mind, the loving, affectionate housekeeper, who had fussed over both girls as if they were her own and run the Chaudhurys' Courchevel chalet with a soft touch, had been preserved in amber, held still in time, just like Reilly's precious memories of Asma.

Reilly had never wanted to involve anyone in her plans, let alone Lisolette. But when it became clear that, as a trusted employee of the Vandenburgs, Lisolette could help position Reilly *exactly* where she needed to be to get the proof of what had *really* happened to Asma, Reilly'd had no option than to share what she knew had happened to the girl they had both loved like family.

The first time Reilly had noticed something different about Asma was the second summer after she'd left. In hindsight, they'd just been so happy to be with each other that first year, that their summer and winter together had passed in a blur. Maybe if she'd seen it then, or if she'd done or said something earlier, then things might have been different. Might never have escalated the way they did.

That second year, Asma had seemed a little distracted – not as *happy*. They'd celebrated her fifteenth birthday on New Year's Eve with cake and Reilly had even managed to sneak a bottle of Bacardi into their rooms without her parents noticing. They'd been so sick the next day and, although everyone knew why, Asma's parents went along with the twenty-four-hour bug story that they'd told them.

But it was the insecurities that Reilly had noticed then.

Only if you want to.

Are you sure? I don't want to bother you.

Do you really want to come?

The hesitancy that had seemed so alien coming from the bright, bubbly, happy girl who Reilly had once known. Reilly and Lisolette Keller had shared more than a few concerned looks. And if Reilly had tried to ask her about it? Asma had simply replied, 'Please don't. Let's just enjoy this.'

The summer just before sophomore year had been the worst. Asma's phone had pinged and pinged and pinged. She wouldn't explain or let Reilly see her phone. And one night, after Asma had fallen asleep, Reilly had snuck over to the phone, remembering the code that Asma seemed determined to use for everything – 2869 – and almost wished she hadn't looked.

The notifications had been from Instagram.

A post from a girl who Reilly had recognised from the Institute. The girl Asma had been forced to dorm with after Reilly had left: Minette Aillet.

As if someone had thought it would be a good idea to put the *least* popular girl in school with the *most* popular.

The post was a picture of Minette and Asma in their dorm room. It seemed innocuous at first glance, but it was the comments that gave it away.

> Portrait titled 'Me and my pet' 🙄
> When are you going to just get rid of her?!
> #bestfriends #yeahright 🙄
> Oh my god. How can you stand it @MinetteAillet??
> One day she'll just get the message and leave! ✌
> #takingoutthetrash

The messages went on and on. Mean, spiteful, hurtful. Hundreds of them, from people at the school, from strangers jumping on the bandwagon. Minette had tagged Asma so that she'd see every single one of them. Reilly's eyes had watered at the thought of Asma seeing these as they came in.

She looked up to find Asma staring at her in the dark.

'Why didn't you tell me?' Reilly had asked.

'What can *you* do about it? I just want to use the time we spend together to forget about it. Before I have to go back. Please, Reilly. Can you give me that?'

Reilly hadn't been able to refuse such a heartfelt request.

But, from then on, she'd checked Minette's social media accounts regularly.

Which was how she'd found a reference to the sex tape that someone had shared of Asma and her teacher. At first, she'd had to follow the rumours from comment to comment, not quite understanding what Asma's school peers were talking about.

She'd never seen or found the footage. Never wanted to. She'd known immediately it was fake. Asma would never do that.

Reilly had reached out to Asma, but her friend had already started withdrawing. Not answering messages for days.

I just need to make it to the end of term and then I'll be back home and everything will be fine.

Reilly thought the helpless fury she'd felt then had been agony. But it was nothing compared to what came next.

Because one night, after returning home to Kerala, Asma took her family's boat out on to the lake at dusk by herself, just before a devastating thunderstorm and she'd never made it back.

Her parents had called the authorities, but the conditions of the storm and the night meant that they could only do so much. By morning, pieces of the boat had been found washed up on the shoreline. Search and Rescue had looked for her for seven days – longer than they usually would have, because of her age and probably because of her parents' money.

Lisolette had been the one to call Reilly alerted by the Chaudhurys' house staff in Kerala, knowing that Asma's parents would have been too distracted to reach out to the girl who was like a sister to their daughter. The shock and pain in Lisolette's voice had been matched only by Reilly's own devastation.

Reilly had begged her father to let her go to India. And after two days, he'd relented. He'd flown to Kerala with her, ignoring his wife's protests about the money. He'd sat grim-faced and resolute with Mr and Mrs Chaudhury as Reilly had sat huddled next to Lisolette, all praying for a different outcome than the one that was looking most likely.

Lisolette had held Reilly's hand – quiet, dry-eyed, but with a ferocious intensity – as if she were holding them both together. Until the police delivered the awful news no one wanted to hear. That day grief became a living, breathing monster that had nearly consumed Reilly.

That had been true agony.

That same day, Reilly's father announced that they needed to return home. She missed the funeral; missed her chance to say goodbye to her friend. And when she'd got home, the letter had been waiting for her.

I'm so sorry, Reilly. Please forgive me. It's just easier this way.

And it had been that letter that Reilly had been forced to share with Lisolette for her to understand and to know what Reilly was here to do. To understand, so that if things went wrong – if things went *right* – then Lisolette would be prepared for the fall out from having recommended Reilly for the position with the Vandenburgs.

'Reilly? Reilly! Wait up!'

The shout from behind her startled her from her thoughts and she hastily wiped at the dampness on her cheeks before Jacob could catch up.

'Hey, I saw you walking and . . . Are you OK?' Jacob asked, peering at her in the darkness as if he could tell that something was wrong.

'Yes, of course,' she replied with a smile as fake as could be.

He raised a hand as if to push back the hair from her face to see her better, but let it drop and it was only after he did that Reilly realised that the gesture should have felt overly familiar, but didn't. And for some reason, she wished he *had* brushed the hair back from her face. Wished she could have felt the warmth of his skin. Wished she could have turned to him for comfort.

They stood there, staring at each other in the moonlight.

'You don't have to lie to me,' he said, his eyes not leaving hers once. They were a dark brown, she realised, with a green circle near his pupils.

'That's kind of you,' she said politely.

'No, I . . .' He trailed off, looking frustrated as he glanced back in the direction of the spa centre. She'd heard them all laughing in the hot tub as she'd passed. 'I . . . I just wanted to have a normal conversation for a few minutes. One that wasn't about champagne and trips to the Maldives and about selling islands,' he admitted as he rubbed the back of his neck.

'It's a hard life these rich kids have,' Reilly offered.

'Like, sooooo hard, babe,' he said, rolling his eyes and affecting a Californian girly twang.

Despite herself and the direction of her thoughts, she surprised herself and laughed. Shocked, she put a hand over her mouth as if to hide it, but he snagged her wrist.

'Don't. That was the most beautiful thing I've seen for weeks,' he said, too quickly to be a line.

'Only weeks?' she teased.

He raised an eyebrow and she felt it; the spark that ignited her body.

'*Years*,' he said, biting his lip and giving her a head-to-toe look.

Now that *was* a line and it should have been ridiculous, but somehow it wasn't. Somehow she felt it – felt how much he appreciated her – jerking awake something in her that she hadn't felt for so long she could hardly put a name to it.

Desire.

'Can I walk you back?' he asked.

She narrowed her gaze. She should say no.

'I mean, even if you say no, I'll simply wait and follow a few metres behind, but only to make sure you get back to the chalet OK. Seriously,' he said, his tone matching his words and his hands raised in surrender. 'No strings, no funny business. Just want to make sure you're safe.'

The laughter died in her chest, his concern touching her deeply as she wondered when the last time someone had looked out for her had been.

Asma. It had been Asma.

'OK,' she said, giving in and turning back towards the chalet. Jacob fell into step with her easily. They made small talk all the way back to the chalet, which she found oddly soothing.

'Good night, Reilly,' Jacob said with a small smile watching as she let herself into the chalet from the back door.

She looked up before she shut the door, knowing that he heard her softly spoken, 'Good night, Jacob.'

And she went back to her room, feeling unusually warmed by their strangely intimate exchange.

CHAPTER EIGHT

MINETTE

With Anike on one arm and Noah on the other, Minette stepped into the winter wonderland that was the Vandenburg Christmas Eve party. Karel had driven them further up the mountain, beyond the Vandenburg chalet, to a look-out point that had been constructed just for that evening.

A large white marquee nestled into the mountainside and against the edge of the woodland. Lights woven into branches made it look as if it were a forest of Christmas trees. On the far side of the marquee, a wooden deck stretched out beyond the slope to hang over the sharp drop to form a viewing platform.

Anike squealed in delight at the sight. 'It's incredible!' she exclaimed, jumping up and down in her impossibly high heels, her long locs bouncing over her shoulders and her dress clinking softly as the thousands of glittering diamonds moved against each other. Undeniably, Anike looked amazing.

Last night, she had come running into her room after Reilly had left, carrying the same red velvet bag that Minette had been holding in her hands.

'*OhmygodOhmygodOhmygod.*' The diamond tennis bracelet and matching earrings had almost slipped through her fingers in her excitement. 'These are GORGEOUS!' she had gushed over the gift that the Vandenburgs had given them. They perfectly matched the 'ice' part of the Fire and Ice theme for the evening and they were clearly meant to be worn to the party, but Minette had chosen to wear the ruby pendant she'd bought the day before.

That she stood out – like a drop of blood on the snow – didn't bother Minette at all. Because it had been worth it to see the way that Noah's eyes lit up when he saw her.

It always mattered to her that he liked how she looked. She could face her mother's disinterest if Noah was happy. She reached out a hand to stroke his arm, only partially aware of how tactile she was with him.

'Touch starved,' he'd once teased.

And she'd not been able to work out if he had been complaining or not. Sometimes she couldn't tell with him until it was too late.

Minette scanned the faces of the Vandenburg guests. Her gaze skated over Karel who was already melting into the background. Everyone who was anyone within a fifty-mile radius was here. There were a couple of A-list actors, local politicians, models, one Hollywood director, a foreign dignitary and a minor English royal and his girlfriend. Minette had crossed paths with him enough times for it to feel intentional. She knew her mother's hand when she felt it.

She'd never understood how her mother – a truly powerful, professional woman whose identity lived and died with her work – expected her daughter to grow up to only be a piece of glitter on the end of someone's arm.

Minette had always harboured dreams of living up to – or at least being equal to – her mother's fierce reputation.

It's sweet that you want to try, Mini, but you'll find it too difficult.

You don't have what it takes. Noah does. You've done well to attach yourself to him.

As if *that's* why she'd got together with Noah. As some calculated move to secure a future her mother didn't think she could get for herself.

Minette let her hand drop from Noah's arm which he didn't seem to notice. Or he had and he'd just ignored it.

Tension pulling her shoulders tight, she turned to find Hugo making his way towards them carrying a tray with five shot-glasses of Gran Patrón Platinum. She forced a smile to her lips and reached out to kiss his cheek when he arrived.

'*Willkommen, bienvenue,* welcome. *Mesdames et messieurs* for your evening's entertainment, please allow me to whet your taste buds with this divine offering,' Hugo said grandly, before bowing with a flourish.

Anike squirmed, and Minette couldn't help but smile. Their flirtation was reaching fever pitch and she remembered what that had been like for her and Noah in those early days.

She'd noticed him on her very first day at the Institute. It had been impossible not to – his thick, chestnut hair just a little grown out and careless; tall and pale, in that British way – he just moved differently to the other boys in their year. She and her friends had all had crushes on him.

Minette had never found it difficult to make friends and, not only was she rooming with one of her best friends, Eloise, but she was close with the entire dorm wing for their year. Minette was the most popular girl and Noah was the most popular boy, so it was only natural that they'd got together in the end. Even though he'd made her wait for it.

There'd been a few times when Noah had snuck into their dorm room. Eloise had risked detention for them to have some time together, by sleeping in one of the other dorm rooms for the night – but it had been worth it. Things with Noah were perfect. Until Eloise's father had been transferred back to Australia and taken his daughter with him. That's when Minette had got a new roommate.

Asma Chaudhury.

The sound of glass smashing on the floor cut into Minette's thoughts and drew her attention to where Jacob's mother was staring at the broken glass on the floor, looking embarrassed.

'It's OK,' Minette heard Mark say. 'We'll have it cleared up in no time. Can I get you another drink? Or something else?'

Minette glanced at Jacob, who was staring at his mother, but she couldn't read the expression in his eyes.

'Tequila?' Hugo offered again, still holding the tray of shots.

'*Merci*,' Minette replied, taking her glass along with the others.

They all chinked their shots together before downing the Patrón, the burn satisfying on her throat.

'Standing out as always, I see, Mini,' Hugo observed her dress, happily enough.

Minette shrugged a bare shoulder, thankful and halfway impressed that even though the marquee was situated on the side of a mountain, it had warmed to a temperature that made such things possible.

'I think she looks amazing,' Anike replied, leaning her shoulder against Minette's. Minette blushed, delighted, but when she looked up at Noah his gaze was across the room.

'I'm sorry, I didn't realise that the theme was so strict this year,' she lied, the blush turning to embarrassment.

Hugo pulled a face. 'No one minds, Mins. Anike's right, you look gorgeous,' he said, easing some of her discomfort.

'How long do we have to stay here for?' Noah bent to whisper in her ear.

'It's the Christmas Eve party,' Minette whispered back, with a slight frown. 'We always come here.'

Noah looked at her, expressionless, before turning away again. She rolled her shoulders, smiling at Jacob when she caught him looking.

'Actually, I think we have to go and speak to our parents,' she announced, having felt the weight of her mother's impatience from across the marquee.

She and Noah excused themselves to do their 'parental duty', promising to be back the moment they could get away.

Together they moved between the guests and the wait staff, all dressed discreetly in black with the Vandenburg logo on their chests. Minette tried to ignore the way that Noah's gaze lingered on one of the staff she thought she recognised as Noah's chalet girl.

A light sheen of sweat broke out at her neck and suddenly the warmth of the marquee felt a little too much.

Champagne cocktails were being passed around by staff, and despite knowing that it would draw disapproval from her mother, she picked one off the tray of a passing waiter and carried on without missing a beat.

She was feeling oddly reckless tonight. She'd forgotten that with the incredible highs of dating Noah Scarisbrick, came the incredible lows. Ones that had been dampened from having spent the last three months apart.

Jealousy was a cruel twist in her chest, making it almost hard to breathe.

Don't be silly. Don't risk what you have over some childish insecurity.

She took a mouthful from the flute, ignoring the side-eye that Noah gave her as they joined the small circle created by her mother and Noah's parents.

'Ah, there you are. I was just letting Charlotte know about your *good news*.'

Minette frowned, not quite sure what James Scarisbrick was talking about.

'Yeah,' Noah said with a bashful smile. 'It's a really great opportunity. I'm thrilled. They announced it about a month ago, but it's taken time to filter through. Obviously, it will mean spending a year in the States, but getting an internship with Trows and Hamlet was a . . .' Noah shrugged, 'a one in a million shot.'

Stomach taut and pulse racing, Minette felt the sting of exclusion – of his rejection – as if it had been a slap in the face. She had absolutely *no* idea what he was talking about. A year in America would take him even further away from her.

'Obviously, it means it will be harder for us to see each other,' he said, finally deigning to look at her as if he knew exactly what she was thinking about. 'But we'll make it work, won't we, Mins?' Noah slipped an arm around her waist and pulled her into his side, with such a look of affection, she nearly believed it.

JACOB

Jacob eased himself under the heater that was blasting at such a powerful force that no one needed to wear any of the layers that were usually a life-or-death requirement out on the mountainside at this time of night.

He was standing on the wooden deck that had appeared overnight, on the perch just above the Vandenburg chalet. It sprouted from the enormous marquee behind him where the Vandenburg Christmas Eve party was currently in full swing.

Jacob had just needed a moment to catch his breath. He took a mouthful of beer, having developed a disliking for the taste of champagne. A statement that, should he have the temerity to utter, he was sure would fill Noah Scarisbrick and Minette Aillet with abject horror.

He swallowed and felt guilty for his thoughts. They weren't bad people. He just ... needed to get his head out of his arse and enjoy it. Especially when 'it' was so incredible. The marquee had been draped in silks and satins and filled with chairs covered in furs and cushions, and circular seats that hung on chains from the tent's ceilings. Four wood-burners, sitting on expensive-looking silk rugs, warmed the space. Jacob half expected Mr Tumnus to emerge, to warn him away from rose-flavoured Turkish delight.

'Fancy meeting you here,' Gustav said, sidling up beside him and looking appreciatively out over the white slopes of the mountains.

'*Such* a surprise,' Jacob joked.

'Had any good slope action?'

'Yeah, quite a bit actually,' Jacob said, thinking about the time they'd spent out there today. He and Hugo had caught some fresh snow early that morning, taking several chairlifts up and over to another part of the mountain and slowly made their way back in time to meet up with Noah and the girls for lunch. Minette had caught the lift up and back down the mountainside again after.

'What about you?' Jacob asked.

'I've been earning my keep, I'm afraid,' Gustav replied sadly. 'But I'll get out there tomorrow before the hordes descend for Christmas Day skiing. I'm heading off-piste if you want to come?'

Jacob smiled. 'I'd love to . . .' He really would have.

'But?'

Jacob nodded over to where his parents were huddled, looking as if they were on the brink of an argument. Probably because his mother was on the verge of causing a scene. He'd been hoping that, away from home, away from the States, she might have been able to leave the pills behind. But no. He could see the warning signs. Her laugh, just a bit higher and harder than it usually was. Her gestures a little bit wilder. Her steps a little more unsteady. He hoped that most people here would pass it off as a little too much to drink. *Please, god, let them think that*, he thought, discomfort swirled in his gut.

Gustav turned an assessing eye on him. 'Pills?'

Jacob inhaled, buying himself some time before answering. He'd never really spoken to anyone about it. Never really admitted it out loud – not even with his father.

Screw it. He hated secrets. He hated his mother's addiction. Hated how heavy it all felt sometimes. But no one had ever seen it before.

Jacob nodded once.

'I'm sorry. That's tough. How long?'

'Three years.' Jacob confessed.

'How bad?' Gustav asked, his tone matter of fact, which Jacob appreciated.

'Bad enough to burn through their savings and some.'

Gustav looked at the ground. 'I know a few skiers who got caught up in that shit after a bad fall. Or one too many bad falls. It's a horrible disease.'

Disease. That's what it was. That's what Jacob had to start thinking about it as.

'Listen. I know some good centres. Really good centres. They're in Europe, but they do excellent work. If you want the names . . .'

'Yes,' Jacob replied, without a second thought.

Gustav held his hand out for Jacob's phone, and Jacob unlocked it before passing it over to him.

'I've sent a message from you to me, and I'll reply to it in the next couple of days,' Gustav said after a few taps on the phone screen before returning it to Jacob. Gustav raised his glass, about to take his leave.

'Have you seen Reilly today?' Jacob asked, before he could stop himself. It came out urgent, and probably desperate.

'And why would I have seen Reilly Clarke?' Gustav grinned.

'You two seemed to know each other,' Jacob hedged.

'You like her?' Gustav asked with narrowed eyes.

'Yes,' he replied, instantly and confidently.

'Mmm. We'll see then,' Gustav said.

'See about what?' Jacob said, but he was speaking to nothing but space as Gustav had already headed across the marquee to talk to a group of people standing by the bar.

Jacob caught sight of Noah and Minette talking to Noah's parents and then cringed when he saw his mother chatting to a local politician, her hand brushing up against his shoulder in a suggestive way.

His father, now talking to Mark Vandenburg and a male model Jacob was sure he'd seen on the cover of *GQ* magazine, kept shooting looks his mother's way. The marquee was busy, but exclusive. Everyone dressed in finery utterly at odds with the freezing temperatures outside, which were kept firmly at bay by the power of electricity, gas and wood. Jacob wondered if almost every possible combustible was being used to generate the kind of heat that allowed the men to walk around in shirts and the women to walk around in sleeveless dresses.

From the soft glow of the lanterns that lit the stunning space, he caught Hugo's eye. Nodding at Jacob, Hugo whispered something to Anike before they made their way out of the tent to reach him.

'You hiding?' Hugo ribbed.

'Na, just trying to decide which slope to do next time we're out.'

Anike squinted into the distance and raised her hand and pointed. 'That one!'

Hugo pressed his lips together and made reassuring noises. 'Mm hm.'

'You don't think I could do it?' she asked.

'I think you could do whatever you set your mind to,' Hugo replied diplomatically, before sending Jacob a wink, which Anike saw and promptly slapped his arm for.

'Hugo!'

'I meant everything I said. I just didn't say how long you'd have to practise before you get there.'

Anike pouted and then laughed, before turning her attention to Jacob. 'Are you having a good time?'

'Yes,' Jacob said, only half truthfully.

'It's just that you were out here alone . . .'

'No, I was speaking to Gustav,' he said.

'Ahh, that's OK then,' she replied, as if being on your own was a truly awful thing.

Jacob flinched when his phone vibrated in his pocket and then heard an echoing sound from Anike and Hugo's phones. He checked the screen and frowned.

SKI 26
UNKNOWN NUMBER
Are you having fun yet?

'Who sent that to the group?' Jacob asked.

'I don't know,' Hugo said, keying in his pin and pulling up the full conversation.

Jacob looked back into the marquee to see Minette and Noah staring at their phones in confusion before they sent a querying gaze his way. When he shrugged, they excused themselves and came to join them.

'Who sent it?' Noah asked when he arrived.

'I just asked the same thing,' Jacob said.

> **SKI 26**
> **UNKNOWN NUMBER**
> Enjoying drinks with your new bffs?
> How well do you *really* know each other though?

'Could it be a mistake?' Jacob asked.

'No,' Hugo said. 'It's within the group chat. Someone would have had to add the number to the group, but I didn't do that.'

'Who is it even addressed to?' Anike asked.

> **SKI26**
> **UNKNOWN NUMBER**
> Someone's been naughty.
> They've been keeping secrets.

'Look, can you just delete whoever it is? Or block their number or something?' Noah asked.

'That's what I'm trying to do,' Hugo replied, irritated as his thumbs tapped and swiped over his phone screen.

Jacob scanned the messages in the group chat.

What the hell was this about?

'Done,' Hugo announced, smugly, and took a mouthful of his beer.

Unknown number blocked.

Their sighs of relief puffed out into the night air.
'What was that?' Anike asked.
'No idea,' Minette replied, looking at Noah and running her hands along his lapel.
'It happens,' Noah dismissed. 'Someone trying it on. A scam – probably just looking for money. It's a little more sophisticated than usual, but still the same. It's always about money.'

Jacob wouldn't really know about that, so he'd have to take Noah's word for it.

SKI 26
UNKNOWN NUMBER
Look what I saw the other day . . .

Jacob frowned. Whoever was sending the messages had picked up directly from where they'd left off. As if it hadn't even mattered that they'd been blocked. Either one of the group had malware on their phone, or whoever was sending the messages had beyond-stellar hacking abilities. Either way, the message couldn't easily be ignored. A sense of expectation, even eagerness, built as if it were a car crash he was slowing down to watch, unable to look away.

It didn't take long for the attachment to come through and when it did, the picture made everyone in their small circle gasp in shock.

'Shit,' Hugo said, glaring at Noah.

'This is bullshit. That's not me, I swear. I didn't …' He turned to look at Minette who hadn't taken her eyes from the screen of her phone that showed a picture of Noah with his tongue stuck down some other girl's throat, one hand on the girl's chest and one on her ass.

'Mins, I swear, it's fake. It's not real. I didn't do this,' Noah insisted. 'Please, you have to believe me.'

'Of course I do,' Minette replied, sounding more robotic than Alexa.

SKI 26

UNKNOWN NUMBER

Sorry, Mins. Your boyfriend's been naughty.

But don't worry. I'll be there for you. See you soon. 😉

CHAPTER NINE
MINETTE

Christmas music played through the hidden speaker in the living area of the Scarisbricks' chalet. The large Christmas tree was decorated tastefully in reds, golds and greens. The scent of pine in the air mixed with the smell of the roast turkey being brought to the table on a trolley pushed by their chalet host, now that the dishes from the prawn cocktail starter had been cleared.

The Scarisbricks made approving noises as dish after dish was placed on the table. Roast hassleback potatoes, sautéed Brussels sprouts with bacon lardons and slivered almonds, baked beetroot, rosemary and Camembert, three different types of stuffing, carrots with honey and thyme. So much food and Minette could hardly stomach any of it.

She was so frustrated she could scream. She wanted to throw her plate against the window and sweep all the food from the table.

They had been eating in painful silence for the duration of the meal so far. The room was filled with so much tension it was inconceivable that anyone could actually eat.

The only sound being hidden by the background music was the scraping of knives against plates.

Sorry, Mins. Your boyfriend's been naughty.

Hugo had deleted the entire group chat after that last message had come through. Noah hadn't even had to ask. And they'd not talked about creating a new one.

Questions like how the person had managed to access the group chat and so quickly, and *repeatedly*, after being blocked, had been buried beneath the more salient question as to *why*.

The way that everyone had looked to her as if she would know, as if she could make sense of any of the messages that had been sent last night . . .

All Minette had been able to do was smile and tell everyone it was clearly just a prank. Maybe someone Hugo knew, or someone technologically savvy enough to have accessed their phones somehow – but it didn't really matter, because it was fake.

I didn't do it! I wouldn't do that. You have to believe me.

Only, for some strange reason, instead of hearing those words in Noah's voice, in Minette's mind it was Asma's after the fake video of her and one of the teachers had been sent around the messaging app that was used by ninety-nine per cent of the school.

But even if anyone *had* believed Asma, they'd never said. Because it had been far too fun, far too scandalous, far too *entertaining*, to believe that she and Mr Carter had got it on in the chemistry lab.

Only this? Noah and the girl? This wasn't fun at all.

Noah risked a glance at her, but Minette kept her gaze on the empty place on the table where her plate would go.

This wasn't how it was supposed to be. She wasn't supposed to be fielding questions about Noah's fidelity, or wondering why he hadn't told her about his internship. She was supposed to be having the best time ever with her new best friend and her boyfriend, living life to the fullest in one of the most exclusive resorts in Europe, at one of the most perfect times of the year.

Tina put a plate down in front of Minette and one in front of Noah. No one dared touch their plate until Noah's father did. And James Scarisbrick waited until Tina had left. Which was why the food was practically cold by the time anyone tried to eat it.

Had he done it? Had Noah kissed that girl? The picture was so dark, she hadn't been able to see the details, who the girl was or where it had been taken.

It's AI, Minette, anyone can see that.

Only when she'd looked at Hugo and Jacob, they couldn't meet her gaze. And the fact that no one had supported him had only infuriated Noah.

'I won't say it again. I'm not in the habit of having to repeat myself, certainly not to you,' he'd whispered in her ear so that the others couldn't hear.

'I know it's not real, Noah. Please, give me more credit than that,' she'd said in front of their friends.

He'd held her gaze, eyes narrowed, until he'd taken her words at face value.

But the conversation echoed in her mind as she pushed the food around her plate.

She risked a glance at the head of the table, from where James Scarisbrick dominated *everything* and suddenly missed her father. Missed the way that he made her feel wanted, the way that he would have tried to make conversation, to include her and everyone else around the table for that matter. Here? With Noah's father? It was the complete opposite. As if everyone were subject to his whim.

As if she'd made it happen, James threw his napkin on to the plate he'd barely touched and stalked from the table and the room, disappearing down the hallway towards the study. Minette struggled to swallow a mouthful of food and nervously took another sip of her wine, catching a glare of disapproval from Janet Scarisbrick, who never drank a drop of alcohol before 7.30 p.m.

Noah's fork screeched against his plate, causing Minette to jump and her mother to hiss under her breath, 'Minette! Don't be so dramatic.'

It was the first thing anyone had said in nearly fifty minutes. As if that were normal. *None* of this was normal, Minette wanted to cry. And why did she feel as if she were the one to blame? Why had the message involved her at all?

For five more painful minutes they carried on in complete silence, until Noah put down his napkin and left the table to follow his father.

Something was wrong between James and Noah, but Minette couldn't tell what. All she knew was that she had to find out.

She waited before excusing herself, hoping that her mother would think she needed to use the toilet, but not notice that she was going in the opposite direction to the bathroom.

Breath locked in her lungs, heart pounding in her chest, Minette tiptoed down the hallway, determined to know what Noah and his father were talking about.

If she was caught . . .

Well, she didn't *know* what would happen if they found her listening in on their conversation. It would be bad. She knew that much.

Her heels dug into the soft pile of the carpet lining the hallway and she was thankful that it masked the sound of her footsteps. Off the corridor was the room James used as a study while he was here, and further down was Noah's room.

She stopped just outside the study, where she could see into the room through a small gap in the door that hadn't been shut completely.

She could just about make out Noah standing in the centre of the room with his hands clasped behind his back. Frowning, she tried to press her ear closer to hear what was going on.

'. . . what are you playing at?'

'I'm not playing at anything, sir,' Noah replied.

'That internship you convinced me you wanted is public. Very public. And I warned you about what would happen if you brought any undue attention to yourself throughout its entirety. So, I'll ask you again, what are you playing at?'

'Nothing, sir,' Noah repeated.

A muffled noise followed James's statement and, creeping as close as she dared, Minette peered through the door.

A shadow passed in front of the crack and she realised it was James, coming out from behind the desk to face his son. Her heart thudded painfully in her chest just moments before James raised his arm and struck his son across the cheek with the back of his hand. A resounding crack rang out.

Stifling her gasp of shock with a hand across her mouth, Minette reeled from the sudden violence but was unable to tear her gaze away.

'No?'

And once again, James struck his son across his face.

A wedge of Noah's dark hair fell over his forehead, a red mark already blooming across his cheek. But he'd done nothing to stop his father. Not tried to plea, or beg, or ask why, or even stop James from hitting him.

As Noah straightened, his gaze turned towards the door and Minette thought his eyes narrowed, catching sight of her. Scared, she pulled back from the gap and pressed against the wall.

'What did I tell you?' she heard James shout.

'Don't get caught,' Noah said quietly.

'I didn't hear you.'

'Don't get caught, sir,' Noah said, projecting his voice loudly enough to easily reach where Minette hid in the shadows of the hallway.

Her stomach plummeted. Were they talking about the picture? Or something else. If it was something else, what had Noah been doing?

From behind her, Minette heard the snap of her mother's fingers.

At the far end of the hallway her mother pointed to her side, the command clear. She'd been discovered, listening outside the office, but her mother was clearly avoiding making a scene – for which Minette should be thankful.

'What do you think you are doing?' Charlotte demanded as soon as Minette was close enough.

'I was just leaving a Christmas present for Noah in his room,' Minette explained, having prepared an answer just in case she was caught. What she would have actually done if Noah had revealed that they'd already exchanged presents, she wasn't sure. But at least she didn't have to worry about that now.

Whether or not her mother believed her, Minette couldn't tell, but she led her back to the dining room in silence.

It was only when she was sitting back at the table in front of her now stone-cold plate of food, that Minette realised she'd said almost word for word what Reilly had told her, when she'd found the chalet girl in her room.

JACOB

'Thank you, Marcus,' Jacob's dad said, as Marco took away the plates of the first of what promised to be an interminable three-, if not four-, course Christmas meal.

The smoked trout on slivers of toasted sourdough and a gravlax sauce had seemed pretty posh to Jacob, but it was damn tasty. Not that he would have said no to a shrimp cocktail. He'd looked across the table at his dad just as they were tucking in, half convinced that he was thinking the exact same thing, especially when they shared a secret smile.

Jacob tried to ignore the way that his mother picked at the roast turkey and the smile that his father had worn dropped away at the edges.

'Would you like some green beans, Mom?' Jacob asked.

She nodded, but her gaze went right through him and he honestly couldn't tell whether she was buzzed again, or suffering from withdrawal. And then Jacob realised, that it didn't really matter. The result was almost the same. A zombie sat opposite him, in place of the beautiful, fun-loving, kind mother she had been before the accident.

'So, what do you think of the other guests?' Jacob asked, trying to make conversation as he reached for the wine that his dad let him drink when he was at home, preferring him to do so out in the open rather than getting reckless in secret.

'Mark's great,' his father said. 'Actually, he might be interested in making a donation to the pro bono work I'm doing.'

'That's cool,' Jacob said sincerely. His father lived and breathed his law firm. But pro bono work had always been his passion and his reason for pushing so hard. But recently his father had been forced to take on more fee-paying clients in order to pay for the drugs his mother was using more and more frequently.

Neither he, his father, nor his mother were under any illusions. The only thing that had stopped his mother from doing something either stupid or desperate was the fact that they were buying her drugs with money from their savings. But it couldn't continue that way for much longer.

'Well, if I were a cynic—'

'Which you're *not*,' Jacob interrupted.

'Which I'm not,' his dad agreed jokingly, since Sandro Arcilla was in fact a fully-fledged, card-carrying cynic of the highest order, 'then I'd say he's probably got an image problem after what happened on that island. But –' he held his glass out to Jacob in acknowledgement '– the guy loves the crap out of his son, which makes him one of the good guys in my book. Not to mention, offering us this place completely free of charge.'

Jacob smiled and raised his glass in return.

It eased something in him to know that his dad liked Mark Vandenburg. In part because he really liked Hugo. Jacob knew he'd got a bad rep after his behaviour last year, before Jacob had got to Harvard, but it was clear how much work Hugo was putting in to mend his ways, how much effort he put into the team with no guarantee that he'd get back on it himself. Even the coach had been impressed and they were both secretly hoping that Hugo would make it back on the team before the end of the academic year.

'As for the others . . .'

'Yeah,' Jacob said, not needing his father to put into words how unimpressed he'd been with the Scarisbricks.

'What are the kids like?'

'Well, *not* kids for starters.' Jacob replied.

His father waved aside his complaint, and Jacob smiled. 'They're OK. I think,' he said, remembering the strange message that had found its way on to the group chat last night.

'Something wrong?' his father asked.

'I don't think so,' Jacob hedged.

His dad raised a brow. 'If there's any trouble . . .'

'There won't be,' Jacob assured him.

'Yeah, but if there is . . . Remember. These people have *money*,' he said, lowering his voice.

'Why are we whispering?' Jacob whispered with a grin.

'Argh, you know what I mean,' his father said at a normal level.

'Make sure your ass is covered, and you know where the exit points are,' they said together in unison.

Three years ago, his mother would have joined in, but now she was just staring out of the chalet window at the snow that had begun to fall.

'Mary, you should try and eat something,' his father cajoled, as if she were still the patient recovering after the accident.

No one talked about the painful irony of a drunk driver causing the accident and making his mother an addict. It wasn't funny and it sure as shit wasn't fair.

And pretending everything was fine was just a lie. Trying to handle it themselves wasn't working, and none of them trusted Mary's health with the same doctors who had strung her up on this stuff in the first place.

'I was talking to someone about rehab centres—'

'I don't need to go to a centre, Jacob,' his mother said, her voice almost cruelly detached. 'I don't,' she said shrugging, despite the hollow-eyed look that stared back at him. 'Honestly, I'm good. Last night . . . was just . . . last night. An aberration. Besides, that was it. The last of it. I haven't got anything left. I'm done. Easy.'

Only it wasn't easy. Because they'd heard this before. Over and over again. The denials and the promises, and the begging and the pleading. *Just a little more. One last time. Just to get through this week. Then I'll be fine.*

Jacob looked up at his father, his pulse pounding angrily in his veins.

'If you're going to use my college fund, I'd rather you use it on a rehab centre than more drugs for her.'

Mary slammed her palm down on the table.

'You will not talk about me like I'm not here,' she commanded, her sudden animation startling.

'But you're not, Mom. You're not here,' Jacob accused with all the hurt that his words cost him to say. 'And we can't keep pretending that you are. Did you see her last night?' he asked, turning to his father.

'I was fine last night!' his mother insisted.

'No, you weren't, Mom. You hit on a French politician, you dropped your glass in front of everyone, you spent twenty minutes in the toilets and Dad had to walk you out the back, so no one could see that you were wasted.'

Which was precisely why he couldn't have cared less about the messages on the group chat and whether Noah had cheated on his girlfriend. It sucked for Minette, but honestly? He had bigger things to worry about.

His father stared at him. They'd never talked about it. Never acknowledged it for fear of setting his mother off. But Jacob couldn't take it any more. Sandro stared at him as if wondering how his son had turned into an adult overnight. But it hadn't been overnight. It had been every night since his mother's accident. Every night wondering whether this would be the night that pushed his mother too far, if she'd do something stupid like cause an accident or OD.

'I'm going to my room,' Jacob said, putting his cutlery down and leaving the table.

'Jacob?' his dad called after him, but Jacob just didn't have the energy to fight it any more.

He ran up the stairs to his room on the top floor of the chalet and shoved open the door.

The room was amazing. Nothing like Hugo's, but still amazing – which made it even more ridiculous that Jacob didn't take notice of any of it. He threw himself down on a sofa, his head falling back off the arm and hung upside down looking out at the mountain through the large screen windows.

What would the conversation have been like if his mother hadn't been addicted to pain pills? If they were like they used to be? Would they have asked Jacob about how he was getting on with Hugo? Would they have asked whether he fancied either of the girls who were there?

And if he'd been able to answer, what would he have told them? The girls are nice, but I like Reilly? The one with prickles on the outside, who looked at him with barely concealed tolerance, but then blasted him with a smile that hit him square in the chest. Would he have been able to confess that he'd never had such a strong reaction to a girl before?

And that he didn't know what he would do even if she *did* decide to give him the time of day, because the last time he'd been anywhere near a girl, he'd been fifteen and sweaty-palmed and nervous as hell. He hadn't been with a girl since, because between his mom, school and training there'd been no time left.

And now that he had found someone he liked, he didn't have the first clue how to ask her out and that made him feel like a little kid ... but it also made him feel like laughing because it was so *normal*. So mundane. And, Christ, he wanted to clutch at that with both hands.

He pulled his cell from his pocket and fired off a message to Hugo.

> Don't suppose you're about?

It didn't take long for three dots to appear.

> Dude, I wish. Mark has me locked into a twelve-course wine tasting meal. Just the two of us.

Jacob laughed, despite himself. He sent a couple of emojis Hugo's way and thought about the hot tub.

> Is it bad?

Jacob stared at Hugo's question. *Is it bad?* He was about to assure him it was fine when he heard his father's raised voice.

'You couldn't let him have one day? One day, Mary?'

Jacob typed on his screen.

> Is the spa centre open?

Hugo's reply was instantaneous.

Always. The code is 3674.

Jacob nodded to himself.
 Yeah. He was going to take a couple of beers and soak in the bubbles until his fingers turned into prunes and pretend that today hadn't even happened.

CHAPTER TEN

REILLY

GUSTAV
Left you a Xmas present at the hot tub.
P.S. Take your bikini!

Reilly inhaled the cold air deep into her lungs and straightened the strap of her bikini top beneath the thick layers of her winter jacket. Reilly shouldn't really be using the spa centre, but she figured every one was occupied with their Christmas celebrations and it would be fine. Gustav certainly wouldn't have sent her that message if he'd thought she would get into trouble with the bosses. She'd made sure that Anike had everything she needed for the evening before leaving. Minette had been at the Scarisbricks so while Anike was showering, Reilly had crept into Minette's room and opened up the laptop. Reilly had used up all three password attempts in less than five minutes and no matter how hard she looked, there was literally nothing in the room that linked Minette to the Institute, let alone Asma. Apart from the photos on the iPad, which had mysteriously disappeared.

Reilly had one week left. Seven days. She had to do better. She had to find a way of getting Minette to like her.

The last thing Reilly should be doing was wearing a bikini and heading to a hot tub. Knowing Gustav the mysterious Christmas present could be anything from a bottle of cognac, to new ski poles, to a signed photo of himself.

The last possibility made her laugh. She'd actually really like that.

She tipped her head back and blew out a stream of breath towards the night sky. She and Asma had tried smoking. Once. Some crazy moment of rebellion slash desperate need to be accepted by their peers.

But Reilly had never fit in. Not at the Institute – where she and Asma had both been labelled as dorky and 'sad' – or later, at her local high school. Everything that she'd not had enough of at boarding school – money, wealth, access – the students now thought she had too much of. Even though she didn't.

Poor little rich girl.

Reilly looked out at the snow-covered slopes, glowing in the light of the moon. They'd been packed earlier that afternoon, full of families making the most of their vacations. She had taken Anike out, because Anike wanted to practise more so that she could be good enough to go out on the slopes with Hugo. Reilly couldn't stop herself from smiling. Anike's enthusiasm had been infectious and it was impossible not to like her. She was far too good to be around someone like Minette.

Reilly's boots crunched into the thick layer of snow as she cut across the back of the chalets towards the spa centre.

Minette, who had engineered Asma's bullying like it was an art form. Who had, over a period of *years*, made her life so unbearable. It wasn't hard for Reilly to imagine. She'd attended that school. She knew what it was like. The whispers, the gossip, the canteen, the isolation and the humiliation. The power someone like Minette wielded to harness everyone around her to do her bidding. And how the bullying was like a wave that grew and grew and grew until Asma drowned beneath it.

When the Institute had held a memorial service for Asma, Reilly had begged and pleaded with her dad to let her go. He hadn't wanted her to, but she'd been adamant and eventually he'd given in. The old main hall had been packed with current students, former students, parents, teachers and staff. A large photo of Asma was displayed on the stage, with her parents sitting up there next to the headmaster and Asma's form teacher.

And Minette.

Who had been crying prettily into her tissue. The death of her 'close friend', her roommate – Minette was apparently devastated. She'd soaked up all the condolences and all the support, all the 'you must be so shocked' and the 'I'm sorry for your loss' wishes.

That had been the hardest part. The hypocrisy of it had rendered Reilly utterly incandescent with rage.

Reilly followed the ski track down the hill a little, passing the chalet the Arcillas were staying in. She paused, looking up at the single illuminated room. Jacob's father passed in front of the window. He was tall, like his son. Handsome, the blueprint for how Jacob would age. She flicked her gaze over the rest of the chalet. All the lights were off, everyone tucked up in their beds, strangely early for Christmas night.

Her feet took her further down the mountain, skirting the back of the spa centre, not as surprised as she perhaps should have been to see spirals of steam winding into the night sky. At least Gustav had turned it on for her. Already she imagined how utterly divine it would be to sink into the hot bubbling—

'Reilly?'

Oh shit.

'Jacob?'

She blinked, and then spun round, trying to avoid the sight of broad shoulders, clearly defined *large* muscles and . . . *Urgh.* She had to get out of there.

The easy gentle laugh that came from Jacob sent a shiver down her spine.

'It's OK. I'm not naked.'

Thank god, thank god . . . But also, why not? Reilly quickly shook her head. *Oh, shut up!*

GUSTAV! I'm going to kill you!

'Are you OK?' Jacob asked, the smile in his voice reaching her.

'Yup,' Reilly replied, looking anywhere but at him.

For a moment there was nothing between them but the sound of the water bubbling and the cry of a bird in the night sky.

'Did you want me to go?' Jacob asked.

'No, of course not,' Reilly said. He was the guest, after all. What had Gustav been thinking! 'Look, I'm just gonna—'

'Don't! I mean . . .' Jacob trailed off into a loud exhale. 'I mean, actually if you don't want to leave, I could use the company.'

Reilly bit her lip, turning at the sound of *something* in his voice and getting another blast of that very sculpted torso. She raised her gaze to his face and the slightly satisfied smirk that had touched his lips was now a full-blown smile.

She should *not* be doing this.

But oh, she *really* wanted to. To be silly and flirt with a boy and pretend that revenge wasn't a word she knew, and the reasons for it hadn't tainted her life. Just for a bit.

'I promise,' he said, hands pressed together in a prayer. 'No funny business. Just two people sharing a, frankly a-mazing, hot tub overlooking a stunning mountainous nightscape ... with a couple of beers?'

It was so tempting. And he knew it too from the look in his eye.

'Please?'

Urgh.

'Fine,' Reilly surrendered, unable to stop herself from laughing when Jacob fist-pumped the air and whisper-yelled, 'Yes!'

She went into the spa centre and used the cubical to change, promising not to stay for long. One beer. Just one.

As she removed the layers of clothes over her bikini, she told herself she was making a mistake. That she shouldn't be doing this. But why, then, did it feel so ... *exciting*? Like a guilty pleasure.

There was something about the rush she got from Jacob that pushed out all other thoughts, that filled her up so completely that nothing else existed. No anger. No fear. No plans could be made. No thoughts could be finished. He was like the eye of a storm and she wanted so badly to stand there with him and just *breathe*.

She unfolded a Vandenburg spa gown and wrapped it around herself as she walked past the thick green potted foliage around the edges of the pool that probably cost a fortune to maintain in this climate.

Cool. Just be cool, she told herself as she opened the door and promptly squealed in shock from the blast of icy air that slapped her hard.

'Get in, get in!' Jacob urged.

Shivering, she ran over to the hot tub. 'Close your eyes!' she told him in a moment of sudden shyness, trying and failing not to laugh and, barely checking to make sure he *had* closed his eyes, she sank into the hot bubbling water that enveloped her. The moan she made took her by surprise and she blushed when she realised that he'd heard it.

'I did that too, don't worry,' Jacob said, with a laugh.

And she smiled. Genuinely. Warmly. Widely. The kind of smile that felt strange and unfamiliar.

'*Ohmygod*,' the words rushed out of her in one go, and she let the roll of laughter bubble up over her like the luxurious water in the tub.

'No judgement whatsoever,' Jacob said, grinning but looking straight ahead and not at her. Which . . . only made her more conscious of the fact that she actually *wanted* him to look at her. Wanted him to see her as pretty, as desirable, as someone he could *want*.

JACOB

Jacob was trying his hardest not to stare. In comparison to Minette and Anike who had brightly coloured, barely-there bikini designs, Reilly's almost functional blue two-piece should have seemed uninteresting.

If you completely ignored the woman wearing it.

Christ, get a hold of yourself, dude.

Then he caught her looking at him and once again he was reminded of blue curaçao. Her eyes bright – almost unnaturally so. Reaching around behind him, he grabbed a beer from the small case he'd brought with him. He'd intended to drown his sorrows in silence, but sharing a drink with Reilly was by far a better way to spend the night.

As she leaned forward to accept the beer, a few tendrils of her hair brushed the top of the broiling water and curled.

There was silence between them, but it wasn't awkward. Tense? Maybe a little. But not awkward. Jacob leaned his head back, enjoying the ease of it. He was so tired of the effort things required these days: his parents, university … Noah and Minette. The others were OK, but there was something about that couple that put him on guard.

He glanced across the hot tub, Reilly was looking up at the stars, and he looked away again, but the imprint of her face remained on the backs of his eyes.

Beautiful. In a striking way.

Jacob was almost one hundred per cent sure that she felt it; the attraction between them. The chemistry. Because it did feel chemical. It hissed and sparked and jump-started his pulse.

'So, do you come here often?' Jacob asked, leaning into the cheesy line so hard, Reilly *had* to know that it was a joke.

Thankfully she laughed. 'Really?'

'Sorry,' he said, his mouth a wry grimace. 'So, tell me about Reilly Clarke,' he tried again, but then her eyes shuttered and he knew he'd said the wrong thing. 'OK, scratch that too.'

Reilly smiled regretfully and for a moment he thought she'd try to leave. Before she could, he had to do something to keep her here.

'How about this – and absolutely no pressure. If you don't want to, we don't have to, and even if we do, it doesn't have to mean anything,' he offered.

She looked at him sceptically from across the hot tub.

'No,' he said, laughing. 'Nothing like that. My suggestion is this. I put one hour on the timer on my phone. Just one. And for that hour, we pretend to be completely different people. I'm not Jacob Arcilla and you're not Reilly Clarke. We're just . . .' He trailed off.

'Two people that happened to meet in a hot tub?' Reilly finished for him.

'Exactly! Exactly,' he repeated, thrilled that, not only had she understood, but hadn't actually told him to piss off.

Reilly looked tempted. *Really* tempted.

Please say yes, please say yes.

And Jacob found that it wasn't just because he wanted that line between them to disappear, but also because he genuinely, for one blessed hour, wanted to forget it all. His mother, his father, the fact he might not have enough money to go to school next year and be forced to transfer out of Harvard . . . All of it.

But perhaps it was foolish to want such a thing.

'OK.'

He saw what he'd felt reflected back at him in her eyes. Longing. Not for each other, but for something different. And *that* hit him hard.

He swallowed and grinned.

'OK?' he asked.

'Yes,' she said, a small smile on her lips, her hair falling forward a little as she nodded.

He wiped his hand on a towel before setting the timer on his phone. The countdown had begun.

And just like that, he suddenly didn't know what to say. Reilly's wide nervous eyes told him that she felt exactly the same way and it wasn't long before they both started giggling like school kids.

And then the laughter died away and that thing was there between them again. He felt the way he looked at her change, in response to the way she looked at him. Her eyes flickered over his face, as if she were studying him, taking in every little detail, asking and answering questions about him in her thoughts.

'What are you looking at?' he asked, curious.

She chewed her lip.

'You're handsome.'

He tried very hard not to blush. She thought he was handsome. The ego stroke filled him up to bursting point.

'Really?'

'Yes, though I think . . .' She hesitated as if wondering how far to push things. 'I think I'd have to get closer just to see—'

'Do it,' he said, the words rushing out of his mouth before he could stop them, desperate for her to close the distance between them.

She half smiled.

Jacob held his breath, wondering if she would. And then, slowly, she made her way towards him, the water and the bubbles getting in her way and holding her back a little.

She was within touching distance when she toppled and he thrust out a hand, clasping her elbow so that she didn't fall. Electricity zipped through them, both managing not to flinch from the contact. Her skin was smooth beneath the water, and it took Jacob more than he thought he had, not to haul her into his lap.

She took the last step to sit beside him and he felt the brush of her leg against his and had to clench his jaw to stop him from sighing like some silly schoolboy. She looked up at him, illuminated by the underwater lights that glowed in the night, and reached up to brush some hair that had fallen over his eyes away from his forehead. Her touch was delicate but, despite that, he felt the tremble in her fingers.

'You have your mother's eyes,' she said.

He felt a part of him shut down at her words.

'And you don't want to talk about her,' Reilly said softly.

Her hand lingered against his cheek, her finger following the line of his jaw, which he raised and she followed it down his neck to his collarbone, seeming to find the bumps and dips endlessly fascinating.

From here, he could see the curve of her shoulder, the rise and fall of her chest as she breathed. He wanted to touch her, but was half frightened that if he did, she'd bolt like a racehorse.

Her hand paused over his chest, her touch sending a scattering of goosebumps across his flesh, and when she looked up, her lips were barely centimetres from his, their breathing quick but inaudible over the sound of the bubbling hot tub. He felt the countdown on his phone ticking away the brief respite they'd given each other from being tied to themselves. Tied to the resort.

Slowly, so damn slowly, Jacob closed the distance between them, giving her plenty of time to move, to back away. To stop him.

God, please don't stop me.

But in the end, it was Reilly who closed the last bit of space between them.

The moment her lips pressed against his, Jacob was lost. Lost to her, lost to the kiss, just utterly lost to the swirling emotions that swept over him like a tide. Eventually they pulled apart, staring at each other, shocked, disbelieving not only that they'd kissed, but how amazing it had been.

'Well that was . . .' Reilly trailed off.

'Terrible. Let's never to do that again,' Jacob said, biting his lip, before pulling her back to him.

This time the kiss was more urgent. As if they were done exploring for now and just wanted more. Needed—

Beep, beep, beep, beep.

Jacob reluctantly broke the kiss, resting his forehead against Reilly's. Regret that it had ended all too soon practically drowning him.

They locked eyes. The buzz rushing through his veins having absolutely nothing to do with the one beer he'd had since coming to the hot tub.

'Time's up,' she whispered, her words puffs of air against his lips.

'It doesn't have to be,' he pressed gently, trying to keep the plea from his tone.

'We shouldn't be doing this,' Reilly said breaking eye contact. 'You're a guest, Jacob.'

Something twinged in his chest. Yes, he was a guest. But . . . he wasn't like the others. He knew it and she knew it too. And the fact that she might want this as much as he did, but couldn't act on it because of some stupid rich-person rule, was bizarre to Jacob.

'And if I wasn't?' he asked despite himself, despite the fact that he knew he shouldn't. Because, while it was a small line for him, he wasn't blind to the fact that there was much more on the line for her and he didn't want to push her or force her into anything.

'You *are* though,' she replied, holding his gaze until he nodded in understanding. Slowly, she got out of the hot tub.

Jacob closed his eyes and stayed put to give her the time and space to get changed, and all the while his insides were spinning out into a hundred different directions with a hundred different questions, feelings and possibilities.

You got it bad, dude.

Jacob swallowed.

Reilly came back out on to the deck, once again wrapped up in her outdoor clothes.

She turned to go, but he didn't want to leave it like that.

And before he could stop himself, he called out, 'Happy Christmas, Reilly.'

Her gaze looked almost sad, as she replied, 'Happy Christmas, Jacob,' before she disappeared into the night.

CHAPTER ELEVEN

JACOB

Jacob blew out an impressed breath. Ice skating wasn't entirely his thing and he hadn't exactly been overjoyed at the idea, but Hugo had told him that he wouldn't regret it and even if he did end up falling flat on his ass and making a complete fool of himself, he had to agree. This was ... *Impressive* – with a capital 'I'.

He looked around the rink on top of the Vandenburg Hotel. *On top of the damn hotel.*

Mirror-smooth ice stretched out to the size of a football field, with the most incredible views of the mountain range stretching across three countries. Around the rink was an elaborate and expensively safe clear polycarbonate fence. It was the ice staking equivalent of an infinity pool and it was stunning. If not quite unsettling.

They'd met in the lobby of the hotel, taken the lift to above the penthouse suite – Jacob didn't even know that there could be anything above a penthouse suite – and walked up a small set of stairs, straight on to the rink. There were canvas-topped benches and sofas, strewn with furs and throws and cushions and a waiter on hand to serve them steaming mulled wine or hot toddies, or whatever else took their fancy.

Hot toddies. Honestly, the longer he was here the further and further away from these people he felt.

The entire rink had been reserved for their use only so the only people up here were these guys, two uniformed staff members from the hotel and Karel – Anike's bodyguard – keeping a very watchful eye on them.

Shaking his head at the extravagance of the company he was suddenly keeping, Jacob strapped on his skates and leaned back against the cushions taking in the view. He wanted to send a picture of it to Reilly. And the thought was as stupid as it suddenly was urgent in his mind.

A part of him wanted to reach out and make sure that she was OK after last night. That she wasn't feeling uncomfortable or regretful over what happened. That was the last thing he wanted. But he didn't have her number.

He couldn't get the image of her disappearing into the night with a look of something like sadness in her gaze. It was strange. For some reason he didn't think that look was about him, or something he'd done.

He'd got back late that night, his mother had already gone to bed – or at least retreated to her room. He'd crept past his father who had been in the living room, staring out of the window and nursing a whisky that he didn't usually drink.

He'd paused. He could have joined his father; could have said something to smooth over the scene he'd caused at dinner.

But actually, Jacob hadn't wanted to take it back. He'd been right to call his father out on his silence and his mother on her addiction. The more they pretended it didn't exist, the worse it got. The more they facilitated her problem, the further away his mother became. Already he was beginning to feel that the only similarity that the woman in the chalet had with the woman who had been his mother was appearance. And that made it all the worse.

So Jacob had left his father alone, hoping that perhaps he might have heard what Jacob had been trying to say, and went to bed. His dreams that night had twisted and turned between Reilly and his mother which left him feeling deeply unsettled in the morning.

He'd woken wanting to message Reilly and thought about trying to reach out to her on social media, but he'd not been able to find her. It was possible that she had accounts under nicknames or something, but without knowing what they might be, it had been a bit of a dead end.

He picked up his phone and pulled up his messages, looking at Gustav's name.

Gustav would have Reilly's number, he was sure of it. Jacob was also half convinced that the Swiss guy would give her number to him if he asked.

Especially if he was just checking that she was OK.

Jacob could offer to delete her number the moment she told him she was fine. Surely that was just a nice thing to do.

It's a stalkerish thing to do, you idiot!

The sound of Hugo laughing at something Anike was saying cut into his thoughts.

Hugo had Anike, Noah had Minette. It was like the world was showing him that everyone was coupling off, as if it was purposefully reminding him of Reilly and that kiss.

Damn, he thought, rubbing his jaw. It really had been one hell of a kiss. He'd felt both like he'd won the lottery and as if something was slipping through his fingers at the same time. Some first kisses were awkward and had to be got out of the way.

That kiss last night had been . . . *perfect*.

He really hadn't liked leaving things the way they were – as if it felt unresolved. Hell, you didn't kiss someone like that and just walk away.

Before he could change his mind, he fired off a message to Gustav.

> Yo, happy Christmas! Say no if it's not a good idea, but do you think I could have Reilly's number?

Urgh. The moment he'd sent it Jacob regretted it. He should have asked Gustav to give her *his* number. *Idiot!* He closed his eyes. Whatever way he wanted to look at it, he *was* a guest and—

His phone vibrated, Jacob's eyes springing open to stare at the message he'd received from Gustav.

> This Reilly?

The message was followed up by a picture of her swigging from a water bottle, out on the slopes, with the same picture-perfect blue sky behind her that was above him. He smiled.

> Yeah. That one.

Gustav replied instantly.

> I'll give you her number on one condition.
> You don't mess it up!

Jacob replied, promising to do his absolute best not to mess it up and less than thirty seconds later received a contact card with Reilly's number on it. Jacob clicked back to the picture Gustav had sent.

Reilly's hair was loose, hanging over her shoulders. Her eyes were closed against the bright sun and the Vandenburg-branded ski suit hugged her, sleek and sophisticated. Not puffy and garish like on some of the other people he'd seen out on the slopes.

Aaaaaannnd, he was mooning over her like a lovesick teenager.

His mind was racing. Should he message her? He probably shouldn't. But he couldn't shake the feeling that she was someone special. If anything, messaging her might piss her off enough to tell him to back off and delete her number.

> Hey, it's Jacob. Hope you don't mind, I got your number from Gustav. (Don't blame him!) You can tell me to take a hike, but I just wanted to make sure you were OK. I shouldn't have let you go back to the chalet alone. That was a dick move. But yeah . . . I just wanted to make sure . . . Jacob deleted the last few words. I just wanted to know that you were OK.

He hit send and then shoved his phone in his pocket. Hugo peered over at him from halfway around the rink, and Jacob raised his hand in a wave.

Hugo threw him a glance that said, you OK?

Jacob nearly laughed. Everyone wanted to know if everyone was OK this morning.

Jacob nodded and shifted forward on the stupidly luxurious sofa he'd sat on to lace up his skates. Not that far away from him, on her own large sofa seat, Minette was tying up her skates. About eight sofas were arranged around the rink and he imagined that when it was full they would be much in demand.

He was about to join the others when his phone vibrated in his pocket. He grabbed for it immediately, fumbling and nearly dropping it on the ice.

UNKNOWN NUMBER
Hi.

For a moment, he'd wondered whether perhaps it was the texter from the other day, the one who had sent the picture of Noah. The thought sent an unpleasant jolt through him before he remembered that he hadn't added Reilly to his contacts, only used the number Gustav had given him. He filed that thought away for later and quickly added Reilly to his contacts before replying.

Hi.

So cool, so eloquent, he thought, rolling his eyes at himself hastily typing out another message to her.

> I didn't want to bug you, so if you want
> me to delete your number . . .

Three dots appeared in the chat box. Then stopped. He felt his heart drop. Then they appeared again.

> You're not bugging me.

Yes!

Jacob raised his phone and took a quick selfie before he could overthink it and sent it to Reilly with a message that read,

> Kind of wish you were here.

He got back a selfie of Reilly and Gustav both sticking their tongues out at the camera – at *him* – and he laughed.

> Not missing you at ALL.

Reilly teased, before quickly sending another message.

> OK. Maybe just a little.

And for some reason that felt like a bigger win than Jacob's last lacrosse game.

> Now go hang out with your friends, while
> I hang out with mine.

Yes ma'am.

Jacob slipped his phone into his pocket feeling so happy he was near giddy. He hadn't felt like this in years.

MINETTE

Minette laced up her skates, trying not to look over to where Noah was talking to Anike and Hugo. Jacob was on the next sofa over, but was typing on his phone. Minette *should* have been happy. This was the part of the holiday that she loved the most. Every Boxing Day they came out to the ice rink, but this year not even her favourite place could make her happy.

After overhearing the heated, shocking exchange between Noah and his father, Minette had returned to the dining table.

She'd not had a chance to speak to Noah alone before her mother dragged her out of there, put her in the car and sent her back to her chalet without another word. When she'd got back, Anike was already in bed and Reilly wasn't anywhere to be seen, which suited Minette just fine.

She'd slumped on to her bed wondering whether she should call Noah.

And say what?

That she'd seen what his father had done? Ask what his father had been talking about? Ask Noah about what he'd been *caught* doing? Ask him if he'd seen her spying on him – which she knew he would have *hated*.

Noah wasn't behaving as if he *had* seen her standing in the hallway. But then, would he? No. He wouldn't confront her about something like that. He'd keep that piece of information. Only using it when he needed to.

Minette stamped her feet into her skates and looked around. Space was a high commodity in Val D'Amer Doux, but the ice-skating rink situated on the top of the Vandenburg Hotel was like nothing she'd ever seen. It was so dramatically different to the rough and ready rinks found in other resorts where anything that took up possible skiing space was resented; this was a work of art.

The clear fencing was her favourite bit, making it feel as if you were skating on a cloud. Or an 'ice desert', she had once thought. Nothing for miles, but snow and ice. The first time she'd seen it, it had made her feel shockingly vulnerable, but once she'd skated on it, it had made her feel powerful. As if she'd overcome herself and connected with nature in a way she'd never done on the slopes.

'Hi,' Jacob said, making his way over to her on his skates. 'You left this downstairs.' He passed her the scarf she must have taken off in the foyer of the hotel while they were waiting for everyone to gather.

'*Merci*,' Minette replied, shooting a look at Noah, who didn't always like her talking to other guys. 'Are you much of a skater?' Minette asked, forcing herself to make conversation.

'Me?' Jacob asked. 'Noooo. I'm bad. Like, *really* bad.'

Minette smiled, mostly because she wasn't used to that kind of easy admission.

Just then, she heard Noah laugh again, the sound scratching against some sensitive thing inside her.

They hadn't really spoken more than a hello and a kiss on the cheek that morning, so she didn't really know what kind of mood he was in. She turned away to gaze at the mountainside hating how insecure she felt. Noah was probably absolutely fine, hadn't seen her standing there and didn't think that there was anything wrong between them at all.

'Hey, are you OK?' Jacob asked. The look of concern in his gaze felt . . . awkward. Over-familiar.

'Of course she is,' Noah said, coming to sit down on her other side, forcing her to move a little to create enough space for them all. Noah pretended not to notice, but Minette knew that he did. Noah noticed everything.

But he also hadn't even looked at Jacob, his focus on her as if he was waiting for her to confirm what he'd just said.

Tension coiled in Minette's gut.

'I'm wonderful, thank you for asking, Jacob,' Minette replied, forcing sunshine into her words.

'Shall we then?' Noah asked, offering his hand, which she took and let him lead her out on to the ice rink that had always been her domain.

The others had the slopes, but this was where she came alive.

You're so beautiful when you skate, ma chérie.

Her father's voice in her head was a comfort after the confusing subtext of whatever was going on with Noah. She felt *beautiful* on the ice. And maybe here, she could forget, she thought as she looked up to Noah's handsome face beside her. The familiar planes of his face, the wave of his hair, the slight ruddy flush that the cold air gave his cheeks.

Maybe she could forget whatever discomfort had dripped like acid in her stomach ever since she had seen the picture of Noah and that girl kissing. Trying to push that thought, she let the simple glide of one skate after another soothe her. Hugo and Anike soon joined them, keeping pace with Jacob who, as he'd confessed, really was quite terrible. For a while they all just got used to the ice, but it wasn't long before Anike encouraged Minette to show off some of her moves.

A slight blush of pride painted her cheeks as Minette broke away to do some loops and test her muscle memory on the ice. Frowning, she realised that she hadn't actually been on a rink since last year, which surprised her. All the chaos with finishing school and getting settled into the Sorbonne had taken over.

She picked up a bit of speed, pivoting so that she was skating backwards, watching where she was going over her shoulder as Anike and Hugo cheered her on. It felt nice to be the centre of their attention. To be appreciated for doing something impressive.

Minette practised a few small jumps to a spattering of applause and lost herself in the feeling. The excitement of speed; the ease, like breathing. She loved it.

Which is why she wasn't looking when Noah seemed to trip into her path.

Whether he did it on purpose or not, the toe pick of his skate had dug into the ice forcing a stop, but his momentum carried on into a huge, careening two-step lunge forward, straight into her side. It spun her around in a powerful punch to her shoulder and she fell down *hard*.

She landed on her back and side, and her head slammed against the ice.

Head ringing and world spinning, she tried to open and close her eyes a few times.

The ache in her shoulder throbbed, and tremors started to fissure out across her body.

'Mini! Mini, are you OK?'

'Don't try and get up, you hit your head pretty hard.'

Anike and Hugo were kneeling down beside her.

She tasted iron on her tongue and realised that she must have bitten it. Her hand shook when she went to feel the back of her head, almost surprised to not feel or see blood there. But there *was* a bump.

Minette's stomach knotted and she thought she might be sick, but she couldn't tell whether that was because of fear or the hit to her head.

She closed her eyes and saw the brief glimpse of Noah's hard, malicious gaze before he took her down. He had done it on purpose.

CHAPTER TWELVE

REILLY

Reilly was just putting the finishing touches on the small feast she had prepared for the girls' dinner that evening. Raclette had been one of Reilly's favourite things about ski trips, and as she stared at the half wheel of cheese that sat centre stage on the large dining-room table she was pleased with what she'd pulled together. Cornichons and pickled onions filled a large wooden chopping board, along with fanned slices of fresh fennel. A separate platter contained the little sausages that would be cooked on the individual grills that looked like mini hot plates.

There was also a cheese platter, in the highly unlikely event that the raclette wasn't enough. Camembert, gouda, Comté, gorgonzola, brie, goats cheese, a mature cheddar that was nearly eyewatering in strength; while crackers, grapes, olives, roasted salted almonds and fresh figs were also strewn across the picture-perfect table.

Reilly had put extra effort into creating what she hoped was an intimate and fun atmosphere for the girls. Tonight, Reilly would do everything she could to get Minette onside because time was slipping through her fingers. It filled Reilly with the kind of anxiety that made her want to scratch an itch that wasn't really there. She already felt bad for letting Gustav talk her into a day on the slopes and flirting stupidly with Jacob, even though it filled her with light, fluffy airy feelings that she just didn't know what to do with.

But she couldn't afford to waste any more time. Reilly would never be able to get this close to her ever again. She only had until the end of their vacation to find the evidence she needed to prove just how awful Minette had made Asma's life. And when she had that evidence, she'd share it with the world. No, it might not be enough to punish her legally. But the court of public opinion was what mattered to these people. And Reilly would make sure that they all saw Minette for who she truly was.

The slap of water against the edge of the large saucepan of new potatoes for that evening's dinner brought her back into the present and she turned down the stove before turning to open a bottle of red in case either Minette or Anike preferred that to the Riesling she had chilling in the wine fridge. Reilly had just picked up the bottle opener when the door to the chalet opened.

'No, she's doing OK. I'll let you know if that changes though,' she heard Anike say, presumably into her phone.

Reilly came to greet them with a smile, which promptly dropped the moment she saw Minette.

'Oh, Reilly, Minette had a really awful fall,' Anike explained.

'I've fallen a million times on the ice and this wasn't remotely *awful*,' Minette dismissed, but even to Reilly's eyes, she looked more than a little shaken.

'Do you want to go up to your room?' Reilly asked.

'What I want is for everyone to stop fussing,' Minette replied a little sharply, Reilly feeling the sting of it despite knowing how she could be.

'I'm sorry,' Minette quickly changed her tone, as if realising that she had been too harsh. 'I just ... I really am fine,' she insisted, despite walking gingerly over to the large sofa in front of the roaring fire Reilly had lit earlier.

Reilly exchanged a worried glance with Anike.

'I can make you a tea, or I can get you something stronger,' Reilly offered, a little unsure that alcohol was a good idea.

'Something stronger. Definitely.' Minette replied.

'The nurse at the medical centre said that you probably shouldn't—'

Minette shot Anike a glare that cut off her words.

'OK,' Reilly said, trying to diffuse the tension. 'I don't know how hungry you are, or what you might fancy. There's a Riesling to pair with the dinner, but we can forget *all* that if you fancy something else. It sounds like you've had a miserable day and I reckon we should turn that around.'

Minette looked back at her a little sceptically, eyes narrowed.

'Champagne?' Reilly offered with a smile. 'Lobster from Le Meurice? Venison from the Hotel L'Étoile? It can be arranged, all you have to do is ask.'

Anike's face turned from curious to eager, and even Minette looked a little tempted.

'Even if you wanted a cheeseburger from—'

'What's that smell?' Minette asked.

'The raclette? It's prepared and ready. If you don't want to do it yourselves, I can cook and plate it for you?'

Minette peered over her shoulder, her eyes growing wide at what must have been her first sight of the dining-room table. Anike followed suit and gasped. 'Oh my god, is that half an entire wheel of cheese?'

'Well, yes. But like I said—'

'Reilly, that looks incredible,' Minette said, in what Reilly thought was the first genuine moment of praise she'd received from her.

'I mean, if you want to get something else . . .' Anike asked Minette, all the while looking like she might be devastated by the thought of abandoning the raclette.

'No, I think it looks and smells divine. Thank you, Reilly,' Minette said.

'You're very welcome. Wine?' she asked, secretly pleased that she didn't have to make an emergency call to rouse the head chef at The Hotel L'Étoile on the twenty-sixth of December with such a request – which she of course would have done, and he would of course agreed . . . There wasn't a single person in the service industry who didn't know that when a Vandenburg staff member called, you answered.

Reilly watched Minette make her way over to the table gingerly. It must have been a pretty bad fall, she thought, briefly wondering why Noah wasn't here to look after his girlfriend. Reilly returned to the table and switched on the mini grills for the raclette.

'But, Reilly, where's yours?' Anike asked.

Reilly blinked. 'Oh, I didn't think that you'd want me to

stay,' she said as Minette chose what she wanted to load on to her raclette.

'Of course you must join us. This would be wasted on just the two of us,' Anike insisted.

'It certainly wouldn't be,' Reilly said, but she also wasn't going to miss the opportunity to get a little closer to Minette, no matter how against it the French girl seemed. 'But, OK, that would be lovely, thank you,' she added.

Reilly was back at the table with another raclette machine and pouring them all a glass of wine before anyone could take back the offer Anike had extended.

Don't screw this up.

Reilly knew it probably wasn't entirely ethical to take advantage of a girl with a minor head injury, but beggars couldn't be choosers. She had to find some way to get Minette to trust her.

'So, how did it happen?' Reilly asked.

'I didn't see – one moment Minette was about to do a gorgeous jump and the next she was on the floor, and Noah was standing over her,' Anike explained.

All Minette did was shrug and take a mouthful of her wine.

Reilly frowned, unsure about the sudden change in temperature. If she wanted Minette onside, she needed to pull it back.

'Well, I'm sorry. I'd actually wanted to ask you about skating as I'd heard you were really good at it.'

'Really?' Minette asked. 'Where from?'

Reilly blinked. 'Savannah. She said that you are incredible on the ice.'

Minette swallowed, and then nodded. 'It's my favourite place. My father used to take me when we'd come here all together.'

'Really? Does he prefer ice skating too?'

Whether it was the wine or the injured head, or a combination of the two, the talk began to flow a little more easily, all three girls chipping into the conversation that unspooled around family and vacations and friends.

Throughout it all, Reilly didn't relax once. She might have looked like she did, but she topped up Minette's and Anike's glasses significantly more than she did her own. And while she laughed as much as them, she was also clinging with desperate hands to the threads of conversation, ingratiating herself with Minette wherever she possibly could.

'I just think what you want to do with your life is amazing,' she insisted. 'Working at the UN. That's so aspirational.'

Minette smiled hazily and shrugged, before scrunching her nose. 'Maman doesn't think so,' she said, her eyes saying more than her words did.

'I think you'd be absolutely perfect for it,' Reilly insisted with all the fake warmth she could muster. 'If it's something you want, if it's something that will make you happy, that's all that matters.'

Anike swayed in her chair from side to side, before popping another sausage into her mouth.

'I'd kind of like to make Hugo happy,' she admitted. 'If you know what I mean.'

Minette laughed into her glass and Reilly couldn't help but smile. She could see those two working out. It would be quite sweet actually.

'And what about Noah. Is he *easy to make happy*?' Reilly asked, regretting it almost immediately when Minette withdrew.

That was strange, she thought. The power couple from the Institute having problems?

'Mmm,' Minette replied, trying to cover her luke-warm reaction.

Just then, Minette's phone started to vibrate.

'Ooohhh, speak of the devil,' Anike teased, as Reilly grimaced, because it took less than three seconds for Minette to snatch her phone, and excuse herself for the rest of the night, effectively ending Reilly's chance to get more friendly with Minette.

Damnit.

JACOB

Jacob took a mouthful of beer while watching Noah at the bar flash the waitress a grin. It was table service, but Noah had wanted to go up and ask about a particular type of brandy.

Brandy. What kind of nineteen-year-old orders brandy?

Hugo was sitting opposite him, typing on his phone and laughing to himself. Presumably he was chatting with Anike.

'Is Minette OK?' Jacob asked Hugo, knowing that had been the pretext for him getting in touch.

'Yeah, Ani says she's doing much better.'

It hadn't sat well with Jacob, how they'd just left Minette with the girls at the chalet and had come to the bar to drink instead. It was, in his opinion, weird that Noah had been fine with it. If it had been Reilly – or whoever his girlfriend might have been, Jacob mentally clarified – he wouldn't have left their side. He'd seen team mates go down easier and be pulled from the match over concussion warnings for less.

It had also surprised Jacob that he'd been the one to insist that they take Minette to the treatment centre to get checked out as a compromise to not calling an ambulance.

'It's not that big of a deal,' Noah had dismissed, and Minette had agreed. It was clear she didn't want to make a fuss, but Hugo had at least sided with Jacob, especially as his dad owned the place and said, unnecessarily in Jacob's mind, that he didn't want any more trouble to happen at his dad's resorts.

Jacob took another mouthful of his beer, trying to resist the temptation to message Reilly. In his mind, he ran over the brief exchange from earlier, feeling stupidly giddy about the whole thing.

> Not missing you at ALL.
> OK. Maybe a little.

But just thinking of it reminded him of the brief moment he'd thought her message had been from the person who sent that picture of Noah.

'Hey!' he called to Hugo, who finally looked up from his phone and slipped it into his pocket. 'Whatever happened with that unknown messenger?'

Hugo shrugged. 'I don't know. We closed down the group chat, so I guess they couldn't start up again.'

'What do you think it was about?' Jacob asked, wondering if Hugo had any ideas. He'd known these guys for longer, certainly. Jacob hadn't really bought Noah's suggestion that it had just been a scam. Even if the picture had been faked with AI or ChatGPT or whatever. Though, flicking his gaze back to where Noah was at the bar talking to the waitress, he wasn't entirely convinced that the picture had actually been fake.

Hugo followed his gaze.

'Hey, listen. I don't know, man, and I don't really want to get involved. What Noah and Minette have is like, something . . . *different*. Even when I was with Avery, and that shit wasn't entirely right – which was absolutely on me – it was a breeze in comparison to those two.' Hugo winced.

'I don't know what that means, Hugo,' Jacob admitted.

'It's just . . . it's just how things are with people who have this much money. There's a lot of unspoken pressure to be a certain way, be with a certain person. It's hard to explain.'

'. . . to someone who *doesn't* have that kind of money,' Jacob added for clarification.

'Kinda, yeah,' Hugo said as if he felt bad about it. 'But you're having a good time here, right? Like, I didn't bring you out here—'

'Oh, god no!' he rushed to reassure Hugo with a bit of a laugh. 'No. It's freaking amazing, Hugo, seriously. It's time away me and my folks desperately needed. And more than we could have ever imagined, let alone experienced. So yeah, I'm really, honest to god, having an amazing time.'

'That's good,' Hugo said, leaning back in the booth looking relieved. 'I'd feel like a complete ass if you weren't.'

'So now that we've established that I'm having a good time, what about you?' Jacob asked, curious.

'Me?'

'Yeah, *you*,' Jacob pressed, grinning.

'It's all good. Getting to spend time with my dad...' Hugo shrugged.

'And also spending time with someone else?' Jacob hinted.

'Ahh, bro, of course I love spending time with you,' Hugo said, batting his eyelids at Jacob. 'You never have to fish for compliments from me,' he teased.

'Not *me*,' Jacob said, waving him off. 'I was thinking of a gorgeous pair of dark brown eyes—' Jacob's words were cut off as a beer mat hit him squarely between the eyes. 'Ouch,' he said, rubbing at the non-existent sore spot, laughing. 'Dude, you're such a goof,' Jacob teased.

'Can't help it man, Ani is *hot*,' Hugo said, rubbing the back of his neck and looking bashful. 'And funny, and silly and she makes me... forget all the crap, which is nice, you know? But every now and then, she'll hit me with this stare that makes me feel like she cuts through all the bullshit and sees everything in me. I mean, she's a terrible skier,' he pressed on and Jacob couldn't help but laugh, because Anike was about as terrible at skiing as he was at ice skating. 'But I *like* her, man. Like, really like her.'

'So? What's wrong with that?' Jacob asked. 'I reckon she likes you too.'

'Really?'

'I mean, I've got *eyes*,' Jacob replied, thinking how obvious Anike's flirting had been and how surprisingly slowly Hugo was moving.

Hugo grinned and then his smile flattened just a little. 'It's just . . .' Hugo blew out a breath. 'I just . . .'

Jacob frowned, realising that his friend was serious. 'It's OK. No rush, also, no explanation needed,' Jacob insisted.

Hugo pulled a face. 'I don't want to mess it up, man. Like, I did *all* the wrong things with Avery, for all the wrong reasons. And I don't want to do that this time.'

'Well, I suppose the difference is that you *know*. You know what you did wrong before, so you won't make the same mistake again?' Jacob hedged, understanding more than he could say. Only in his case, all Jacob could see were pitfalls. All he could see was where it could go wrong. In part, because he could also see how right it could be. As if, instinctively, he knew what he and Reilly *could* have was something special.

'I guess so,' Hugo replied hesitantly.

'Well, *I know* so. You're a really great guy, Hugo, and you deserve to be happy.'

'OK, now piss off before you make me cry. Because I'm not having that. It'll ruin the family reputation.'

'I hate to break it to you but the family reputation is already ruined,' Noah teased, returning to the table finally.

'Bro!' Hugo said as if he'd been surprised by the snarky comment. Perhaps he was. But Jacob wasn't. There was something about Noah that made Jacob uncomfortable.

It was a little like how his mother was when she thought no one was paying attention. He noticed a difference. In how she carried herself or behaved. And Noah too. Like when he was talking to the girl at the bar, and the way, earlier on the rink, Jacob had the distinct impression that he hadn't liked Minette talking to him. And how Jacob wasn't entirely sure that Noah hadn't moved purposefully into Minette's path.

'Problem?' Noah asked, looking at where Jacob stared back, having accidently zoned out on his thoughts.

'None at all,' Jacob replied, his hands in the air in surrender. 'On another planet this afternoon. I've not been sleeping that much.'

'I've got something that could help if you like?' Noah offered.

Jacob new exactly what kind of 'something' Noah was talking about, and none of it would be legal. Jacob could see how that would play out.

US lawyer's son, caught with illegal drugs on the Vandenburg Resort.

'No thanks, but appreciated,' Jacob said easily.

Noah shrugged as if it were no big thing, but Jacob couldn't quite shake the feeling that he'd just earned a mark against his name, in the Englishman's eyes.

'How's Minette? Are you going to check on her?' Hugo asked.

'Yeah, *Dad*, don't worry. I called her earlier,' Noah replied.

'When?' Jacob asked before he could catch himself.

'When I was at the bar, Sherlock.'

'Sure, sorry, didn't mean anything by it.'

Noah turned away, and then smiled when he saw the waitress approaching the table.

'I hope you don't mind, gents, but I took the liberty of ordering us some proper drinks.'

Hugo met Jacob's gaze over the table, and Jacob got the subtle hint to leave it for now. But it was enough for Jacob to know that Noah's strange behaviour had been noted and not just by him.

CHAPTER THIRTEEN

MINETTE

When Anike had mentioned the idea of going to a club, Minette jumped on it. Especially as she was feeling better. She'd finally spoken to Noah yesterday, who had told her that of course he hadn't stepped into her path on purpose and apologised profusely for it, insisting that he'd never do that to her, that he wasn't like that.

And she'd wanted to believe him. She'd *really* wanted to believe him. Because, surely, he wouldn't have done that to her. So, they'd made up and things had been so much better since yesterday . . . since Christmas Day and, actually, since before that when those stupid text messages had appeared.

Minette shifted from foot to foot on sky high heels that were more comfortable than her train of thought. She was supposed to be using tonight to get things back on track with Noah. She needed them back on track. Because that's who they were. They were *that* couple. Most likely to marry. Most likely to succeed. To win.

And she wanted that. She wanted to have that. She wanted to prove to her mother that she could have Noah *and* succeed, no matter what Charlotte Aillet said. Minette was just as intelligent and just as determined, even if her mother didn't see it.

Minette's gaze scanned the club. It was new, having opened just two weeks ago. The cool, sleek black lines and ice-blue neon lights were different to a lot of places in Val D'Amer Doux that capitalised on the Swiss chalet vibe. It was good. It felt *exclusif*. The staff were all dressed in jeans and vest tops that glowed brightly beneath the UV lights.

The music was a combination of electronica and indie dance; it thumped in the air and the baseline vibrated through her body. The club was underground, and the crowd here were by invitation only. Not open to just any tourist, nightclub needed a platinum credit card at least. And from the icy gleam of diamonds and gold, these people had much more than that.

She caught Noah's eye as he approached from the bar and smiled, relieved that they'd made up. With the music throbbing in her bloodstream, not to mention the half a bottle of champagne she and Anike had shared getting ready, Minette was already pleasantly buzzed and she felt Noah's gaze all over her.

He wound through the crowd not taking his eyes from her and she loved it. She felt deliciously *hunted*. He stopped in front of her and dropped his gaze to her feet, slowly raising it over her bare legs, to the hemline of the delicate silver beaded dress that barely covered her backside.

She flushed at his appreciation of her, his desire for her soothing that insecure part of her that still felt vulnerable after the other day. He wanted her. He *still* wanted her.

Noah's gaze continued to skirt up over her body to the dress's low neckline and, as twin slashes of red appeared on his cheekbones, he closed the distance between them, pressing her back against the small table.

His fingers traced delicate circles beneath the hem of her dress on her thighs. Minette's eyes drifted closed as he dropped his head to place a kiss on her neck. Her head fell back, the soft ends of her hair splaying across her bare shoulders.

It was everything she wanted, but not here, where there were so many people. It felt . . .

'Noah,' she said, his name a gentle warning.

'Shhhh, it's dark. No one can see,' he said.

He kissed her lips more passionately.

'Noah,' she said again and this time she didn't know whether it was a plea or a protest.

'Incoming!'

Hugo's loud warning shout registered just moments before Noah suddenly pulled away, leaving Minette reeling a little.

Jacob and Anike's wide eyes and huge grins told Minette all she needed to know. They'd seen, if not everything, then at least enough. A painful blush rose to her cheeks, but Hugo laughed good-naturedly.

'So you two have kissed and made up?' he asked, making Minette frown.

'Nothing to make up, Vandenburg,' Noah said from across the table.

Hugo bobbed his head and, just over his shoulder, Minette saw Reilly.

'How did you get in here?' The question was out of Minette's mouth before she could call it back, and she was painfully aware of how that had sounded.

'Nice one, Mins,' Noah said under his breath.

Minette turned to glare at him. 'You know I didn't mean it like that.'

'Well, that didn't take long,' Hugo teased and Minette wanted to stamp her feet like a child. Why was everyone purposely misunderstanding her?

Reilly looked out over the dance floor and the flush on Minette's cheeks turned from one of embarrassment to shame. *Oui*, dinner last night had been fun, and it hadn't felt so weird, but that didn't mean she wanted to hang out with the chalet girl *all* the time.

'She's with me!' Gustav appeared from nowhere, slinging his arm around Reilly's shoulders affably. 'My VIP guest,' he explained.

Reilly was wearing a black, off-the-shoulder, thigh-length dress that clung to her body. It perfectly matched the black patent leather Louboutins and the slash of crimson red lipstick that she wore.

Anike squealed in delight. 'Oh my god, Reilly, you're *hot*! You look amazing. Soooo vintage!'

'Looking good, chalet girl,' Noah commented, Minette not entirely enjoying the way that he was eying Reilly up. For her part, Reilly didn't seem to know what to do with the compliment either. Her gaze flicked between Minette and Noah, before smiling and saying thanks.

A waitress appeared at the table with a bottle of Yamazaki and glasses, along with a small crystal ice bucket.

'Just a little sign of my gratitude for allowing me to teach such a delightful student,' Gustav explained, angling his head towards Anike for a kiss, which she obligingly put on the Swiss ski instructor's cheek.

'Nice!' Noah exclaimed, snatching up the Japanese whisky that was one of his favourites. Despite the fact that it made him mean and drunk in ways that Minette didn't like.

'I should be the one thanking *you*,' Anike insisted.

'Not at all!' Gustav dismissed. 'Anyway, *we* shall take our leave,' he said threading an arm through Reilly's without sparing Minette a glance. *Merde*. She hadn't meant anything by it, she'd just been surprised to see Reilly here, that was all.

'No, don't go!' Hugo cried.

'Please stay,' Anike begged.

This time, Gustav *did* look at Minette.

'Please,' she asked politely.

'Since you all asked so nicely,' Gustav announced with unnecessary dramatic flair. 'I've heard that this is where all the fun is at! Unless that was an exaggeration?'

'Absolutely *not*!' Noah exclaimed, removing the glass top of the bottle of whisky with a pop. Minette watched him inhale the scent.

She closed the distance between them, pressing into his side and placing a hand on his chest, wanting to regain that feeling of closeness, but he looked down as if he was slightly irritated by her and she let her hand fall away. Just then

Anike threw her head back and laughed at something that Hugo said.

Minette tried to remember if Noah had ever made her laugh like that, back when things had been good. Before they'd left the Institute. Before that stuff with her roommate. Back when she hadn't had to fight for his attention, or worry about it, because she was the prettiest girl in school. But they weren't in school any more.

Minette watched as Noah reached across the table to pour Gustav a drink. But when Noah turned that smile on Reilly, something vicious unwound in Minette's chest. Emerald bright and princess-cut sharp, it scratched against her insides. Jealousy, a hot acidic burn in her soul.

That damn picture rose in her mind's eye – the one of Noah with that girl.

It's not real, Minette. It's just someone trying to get to us. Don't let it work.

But *who*? Who was trying to get to them?

And why had they chosen that picture to do it?

JACOB

Jacob could hardly take his eyes off Reilly. Every time she moved, he discovered a new fascinating curve he wanted to trace with his hands.

He cursed and turned away before he embarrassed himself.

Gustav, Reilly and Noah were talking about the whisky, and Hugo was laughing with Anike. Jacob turned to Minette and smiled.

'How are you feeling after the fall yesterday?' he asked over the sound of music and conversations filling the small underground bar.

'Fine,' Minette replied tightly.

He couldn't work out whether she was just feeling a little off tonight, or whether something had upset her, but the one-word answer didn't give him much to work with.

'Hugo said you've been skating for years. I'm sorry we didn't get to see you properly in action,' he tried again.

Minette nodded, but her gaze left him and roamed over his shoulder to where Noah was now pouring glasses of whisky and explaining the different ways to drink it. With ice, with water, neat . . . as if no one else around the table already knew that.

Jacob frowned at the bitterness of his own thoughts and when he looked up, he saw Minette walking off towards the toilet.

He wondered if he'd been right yesterday about thinking there was trouble in paradise, despite the PDA that they'd interrupted just moments ago when they joined the table.

'Ice?' Noah asked, snagging his attention with a click of his fingers that should have been harmless but felt rude.

Jacob rubbed the back of his neck, eyeing the chunk of ice that had somehow been sculpted to look like a goose-egg-sized diamond. 'Na, I think I'm gonna pass.'

Noah looked at him like he was crazy.

'Suit yourself, mate,' Noah replied. 'More for us!'

Yeah. With once last glance at Reilly, Jacob headed to the bar, in search of something less . . . expensive. He passed Karel, trying to blend in with the club's crowd and failing miserably.

Jacob nodded to him as he passed, slightly surprised that he got a nod back in return.

As he pushed through the throng of people, Reilly's words echoed in his mind.

You're a guest.

But he was *nothing* like them. Minette might have tried to cover it, but she'd clearly been offended by Reilly's presence and equally uninterested in his own. While he waited at the bar, he turned to look at the table again.

He could see what Hugo saw in Anike. She was welcoming and easy-going. But Noah and Minette? They were something else.

His gaze crossed to Reilly, who looked up at that exact moment and he didn't, couldn't, look away this time. She broke eye contact, briefly, only to return it moments later, which made him smile. At least she was finding this as hard as he was.

A barman in a bright white T-shirt that glowed violet in the UV light approached and Jacob asked for a bottle of beer.

His phone vibrated in his pocket, and he pulled it out to see a message from Reilly. He looked back to the table while he unlocked his screen, but she was talking to Gustav. He read the message and smiled.

You need to stop.

Quickly, he fired off his reply.

Stop what?
Looking at me like that!
People are going to know.

He paid the barman an eyewatering amount of euros for his beer and took a mouthful, the hoppy bubbles sliding down his throat far too easily as he considered how to reply. He leaned back against the bar, not wanting to return to the table just yet.

He caught eyes with Reilly again and he knew exactly what to say, typing before he could change his mind.

> I don't like secrets.
> And I don't care if people know that
> I find you so damn
> hot it's impossible to keep
> my hands off you.

She blushed as she read his text from across the bar. And just like that, he knew he didn't want to be here. He didn't want to be surrounded by all these strangers with too much money and too many issues to count. He wanted to be anywhere else, just with her. He wanted to know why she liked skiing. He wanted to know how long she'd been friends with Gustav. He wanted to know what her favourite place to ski was, and what she was studying. He wanted to know what made her laugh and what made her cry, and who had been her first kiss and whether she would mind being his last ever kiss?

He was vaguely aware of Gustav clocking the looks they were giving each other, but he'd meant what he said. He really didn't care.

> Can I walk you home?

He watched her type back.

What, now?

> If you're happy to leave now, hell yes.
> But if not, I'll wait. As long as you want.
> All I want to do is walk you home.
> I should have done it Christmas day night.
> I want to correct that mistake.

Jacob watched Reilly bite her lip as she read his message, and gripped his bottle harder. She seemed to type something and then delete it. He took another pull of his beer as he watched as she put her phone away and he cursed. He'd pushed her too far. He shouldn't have said that.

She was staff. No, he might not have been one of them, but he wasn't like her either. She had income on the line, possibly even future work with the Vandenburgs and surely getting an in with them could be life changing.

Suddenly he felt like an ass and all he wanted to do was apologise.

By the time he looked up, Reilly had gone and Gustav was making his way over to where he was at the bar, with a knowing look in his eyes.

Jacob was about to apologise, when Gustav told him to get going.

'What?' Jacob asked, shouting a little, over the music.

'She's waiting for you. Out back,' Gustav explained. 'But she won't wait forever, so get going.'

Jacob didn't even wait for Gustav to finish speaking.

He'd started moving the moment he'd heard, 'She's waiting for you.'

Firing off a message to Hugo, and feeling guilty for the lie he told about having to get back to his folks, Jacob rushed to the cloakroom, shoved his arms into his winter coat and left the club.

He ran out on to the snow-covered side street and looked up and down for any sight of her. Nothing. He checked his phone, but there weren't any messages.

Shit. Had he missed her?

He started walking when he heard his name called from behind him.

He turned.

Reilly was standing there with a wonky smile, one booted foot tucked behind the other, swamped by her a ski jacket, and still she was more beautiful than any of the girls back in that bar.

He shook his head and made his way over to her.

'You wanted to walk me home?' she asked, her blue eyes sparkling like sapphires. He saw happiness, but he also saw vulnerability.

'Very, very much,' he said, biting his lip to stop himself from doing something stupid, like kiss her.

Excitement fizzed in his veins and, in that moment, he realised that this was the best Christmas present he could have had. Time with her. Just being in her company made him feel . . . alive.

She turned on her heel, her purse dangling from the end of her wrist, and slowly started walking back towards the chalet. She waited for him to catch up before picking up the pace.

'I don't like secrets,' he said, repeating the words he'd said earlier in his text message. He wasn't quite prepared to fully tell her why, and not just because admitting to having a junkie mom was a bit of a mood killer.

She looked up at him, but he kept his gaze firmly on the snow-covered path before them.

'OK,' she said, accepting his statement.

He nodded, still refusing to look at her until he got what he needed off his chest.

'But I'm guessing that you'd be in trouble if anyone found out that this . . .' he said passing his hand between them back and forth, 'could be a thing.'

Reilly swallowed and nodded.

'Is it *just* that?' Jacob asked, finally turning to look at her. 'Is it just because of work? It's not because there's a guy . . . or girl . . . or whatever,' he said, blushing from the awkwardness that he was suddenly drowning in.

Reilly bit her lip and smiled. 'There's no guy, or girl . . . or whatever,' she confessed, her cheeks a delicious pink, rather unlike the roaring red flame that he felt on his face.

'So, there's no one who would be hurt by us being together?'

'No,' Reilly insisted.

'If you wanted to, be together, of course,' he rushed to say.

Oh god, he was seriously messing this up, he thought, scrunching his eyes shut. Would the damn ground come and swallow him whole, please?

The sound of Reilly's footsteps beside him stopped and he felt her cold fingers press into his fisted hand.

'Jacob,' she whispered.

'Yes?'

'Open your eyes?' she asked, still whispering.

'No,' he said. He was too embarrassed.

'Please,' she begged, pulling on his hand slightly.

OK, now he really *did* want to see her.

He prised open one eye and squinted down at her while keeping the other one closed.

'Are *you* with anyone?' she asked and his heart started to pound. Jeez, he felt like he was back in high school.

He shook his head slowly and her smile grew bigger and bigger.

'Can I kiss you?' he asked.

And she shook her head and said no. But she was smiling – so it wasn't a brush off . . . it was more like a tease. A gentle one.

'But I would like to go skiing with you tomorrow,' she said.

'Really?' he blurted. He wanted to ski with her almost as much as he wanted to kiss her again.

'Yes,' she said, laughing, the sound pealing out into the cold night air around them.

'Really, you promise?'

'Yes, Jacob, I promise,' she said as if she was some long-suffering girlfriend. Which, if Jacob had any say in the matter, she might actually get to be.

'Tomorrow?'

'Yes, tomorrow. Now stop pestering me with questions and walk me home.'

And Jacob did just that, grinning the entire way.

CHAPTER FOURTEEN

MINETTE

Minette got out of the car Reilly had called to take her down the hill to the hotel to see her mother. All that morning, Reilly had been quiet and Anike had shot pointed looks at Minette across the table, while trying to make fun, happy conversation involving the three of them.

Minette had thought it was a little unnecessary, but still, she'd followed Reilly back to the kitchen area and tried her best to apologise.

'I really want you to know that I didn't mean what I said yesterday to sound like that,' Minette had tried, when she followed Reilly into the kitchen.

Reilly had smiled at her, and said, 'I know. It's OK. I understand. You don't have anything to apologise for.'

Minette had clung to her smile. She hadn't actually apologised, because she wasn't really sure that she had anything to apologise *for*. It *had* just been a misunderstanding.

But after Reilly had left the club last night, things had been much easier and she, Noah, Hugo and Anike had danced and partied until the very early hours of this morning. There was no way that Anike was going to get any skiing done, so they'd decided to take a 'hangover' day with a list of romantic comedies to watch later on and to order either sushi – which had made Anike turn a little green around the edges – or sloppy burgers from the Vandenburg Hotel chef. Minette's mouth watered just from the idea of it. They'd cured many a past hangover with his triple patty that came with onion coulis, three different types of cheese, peppercorn sauce, pickled cucumber and the crunchiest streaky bacon ever. It would be washed down with a mint-choc-chip milkshake, with a cheeky shot of Kahlúa and whisky, just to help with the 'hair of the dog'.

That was it. Mind made up, she messaged Anike. Sushi was off the menu!

> We're getting the burgers.
> See you after I visit maman.

Anike's reply was near instantaneous.

> Yay!!

Minette pulled her coat around her body and shivered at the blast of ice-cold air that struck her hard as she hurried from the car into the welcoming warmth of the Vandenburg Hotel reception.

She bit her lip as she remembered last night. Noah had managed not to let the whisky go to his head and had asked the car service to take the 'scenic' route back to her chalet, to give them a little time alone. Time that they'd desperately needed.

Minette made her way across the foyer of the Vandenburg Hotel, over to the elevators reserved for the executive guests; ones who had hired entire floors, rather than rooms. She flashed the black key card her mother had given her over the card reader and pressed the button for the Presidential Suite – the Vandenburg's finest accommodation in a hotel already known for its impeccable extravagance. Minette was convinced that it cost just as much as the chalet, but her mother liked lording her wealth over others and she couldn't do that from a private chalet.

She thought of the message she'd received an hour ago from her father.

> Your mother isn't replying to my emails.
> Can you get her to call me?

A part of Minette had wanted to say no. To tell her father that, surely, he knew that she couldn't make Maman do anything she didn't want to do. To ask him to just get *his* assistant to call *her* assistant?

The elevator doors slid open and she entered the mirror-lined gold-tinted lift.

Within seconds she was being whisked upwards to the penthouse and when she arrived, the elevator opened right into the suite that took up the entire floor.

'Maman? I'm here,' she called out.

Minette removed her coat and dropped it over the side of the leather sofa, and walked over to the kitchenette that she doubted her mother had used even once in all the times she'd stayed here. Mientte opened the fridge and pulled out a can of soft drink.

Popping the tab, she frowned, waiting for her mother to appear.

'Maman?' she called again.

Something uncomfortable skittered across Minette's skin. Was her mother out? The space didn't feel empty in the way that some places did when no one else was there. Minette cast a quick glance around the perfectly designed suite. Honey-coloured oak flooring suited the warm, Swiss-style interior design finished with elegant luxury that was so subtle it *had* to cost obscene amounts.

Creams, leathers, furs, velvets and silks. The suite looked cool and sophisticated, just like her mother, Minette thought, as Maman appeared from her room, wearing her dressing gown.

'Are you just back from the spa?' Minette asked as she took a mouthful of drink from the can.

'What are you doing here?' her mother demanded.

Minette clenched her jaw, tensing from the terse tone her mother had adopted. She still, clearly, hadn't been forgiven for eavesdropping outside James Scarisbrick's study on Christmas Day.

'Papa said you haven't been replying to his emails.'

Charlotte sighed impatiently. 'And what has that to do with you?'

Minette ignored the sting and replied, 'Papa asked me to ask you to call him.'

Her mother held her gaze and was about to reply when a figure appeared in the open door to the bedroom.

In the space of a single breath, Minette felt as if she'd been dropped into the ocean from a great height.

James Scarisbrick stood there, towel around his waist, drying his hair and eyeing Minette as if it were the most natural thing in the world for him to be there.

White noise filled her ears and her sight narrowed in on her mother.

'I'll deal with your father. You can go,' Charlotte said.

Minette's body started to vibrate at an invisible, but very painful, level. Her skin flushed, her heart raced and she thought that she might actually be sick. Right there in front of both of them.

Her mother stared at her blankly and Minette wondered why she wasn't reacting. Surely there should be *something*? Some kind of shame, embarrassment, attempt to hide or explain. Some kind of acknowledgement of what Minette had just seen.

'Maman,' Minette whispered.

Charlotte raised a perfectly shaped brow in query.

'Maman!' Minette shouted, the single word echoing around the otherwise silent suite.

Her mother didn't even flinch. Against her will, Minette looked back to James, who levelled her with a bored stare and turned back into the bedroom.

'Don't be such a child, Minette,' her mother said, turning

back towards the same bedroom. 'And next time, message before you decide to come to the suite.'

Minette's eyes were filling with unshed tears, her heart thumping painfully in her chest. Every breath she took was agonising as her head swam in confusion. Numbly she turned back towards the elevator, forgetting her unfinished can of coke. Forgetting even her coat.

Her mother was sleeping with James Scarisbrick.

Did her father know?

Was *that* why he no longer came to the Vandenburg ski resort? Did her father think that *she* knew about whatever it was between her mother and James Scarisbrick?

Did *Noah* know?

Oh god! She pressed a shaking hand against her mouth. Surely he couldn't know. He would have told her, wouldn't he?

Minette's mind raced. How long had her mother and James been . . . ?

Nausea welled in her gut. And betrayal. Betrayal that her mother would do this to her. As if her mother couldn't let her have this one thing. Have Noah. Without some kind of attempt to grab at what should have just been *hers*.

As the elevator brought Minette back down to earth, flashes of the last eight years exploded in her mind. Christmases, parties, gatherings where she and her mother had been with the Scarisbricks. *Janet*. James's wife. Did she know?

Was that why Janet was so miserable and mean? But that couldn't be, because Janet was perfectly civil to her mother. They'd just had Christmas together.

What was she going to tell her dad?

Nothing. Minette wasn't going to tell her dad anything. Not yet.

She swallowed, her throat dry and her heart racing. The questions made her dizzy and the shock made her sick. Noah. She had to find him. She had to tell him.

Oh god, what were they going to do?

REILLY

The clear, cool mountain air filled Reilly's lungs to almost bursting and as she crested the gentle upward peak at the top of the black run and came to a halt, she almost felt like laughing. Unable to hide her grin, she looked across at Jacob, who sliced into a stop, sending a small arc of snow over her skis.

Reilly bit back a comment that would have started off another round of banter. A verbal back and forth between them that was becoming addictive.

It's called flirting.

But she couldn't let herself think that because she didn't have time for flirting. That wasn't what she was here for. Really, she should be—

'You promised me an afternoon,' Jacob chided between heavy breaths. They'd just come off a particularly beautiful – but distinctly difficult – run.

'I'm here,' Reilly replied, confused.

'Most of the time,' he pointed out, showing just how observant 'laidback Jacob' really was. 'But I'll take it,' he added.

'How very generous of you.'

'Oh, Reilly. You have *no* idea,' he said, with a glint in his eye that sent a thrill across her body.

She opened her mouth to reply, but Jacob had already swept off down the black run with the kind of grace that she found irresistible. In front of her a mountain peak pierced the baby-blue sky, a ring of clouds circling it. Overhead shone a sun that bounced off the snow and could burn strange parts of the body, like the underside of a nose, or a chin, if you weren't careful.

The mountain range stretched out before her and with so few people on the slopes, she felt almost as if it were just her and Jacob. And that thought meant more to her than it should have.

Reilly set off down the mountain knowing she could catch up with him easily enough. He was good, but she was better, she thought with no sense of arrogance or ego. And she liked that he saw that too. He seemed a little competitive in other areas – he'd have to be to be on the Harvard lacrosse team. But he didn't try and compete with her here on the mountain.

Reilly narrowed her turns and gathered speed, her heart racing as her skis glided smoothly over the perfect snow. Sleek, focused and alive. That's what she felt like. She'd always felt like that when she skied. And after years of being away from it, she now realised how much she needed this, how much she needed to be doing something she was good at. Something that made her *feel* good.

At the end of the stunning, sweeping run that had brought them only halfway down the mountain, she came to a hard parallel stop, breath punching out of her lungs. Jacob joined her a second later, lifting his sunglasses from his face.

'You OK?' she asked.

'Mm hmm,' Jacob replied, a little out of breath.

'Let's take a beat,' she said, pointing over to a little inlet of trees just off the slope.

'I don't need to,' he said.

'I didn't say that you did. *I* want to take a beat,' she shrugged, pushing off with her poles and lazily snowploughing into the little bay of trees that had crept down the mountainside from the forest. Jacob followed and after clicking out of their skis, they wedged themselves into a snow-bank.

Jacob reached into his rucksack and tossed her a bottle of water and a chocolate bar.

'What else is in there?' she asked, once she'd consumed half of the bottle of water.

'Oh, you know. Just the usual. Crisps, phone, ropes, penknife.'

'That doesn't sound worrying at all,' she replied with easy sarcasm.

'Always be prepared,' he shot back.

'Boy scout, huh?'

He gave her a three-fingered salute and she laughed.

She did that around him. A lot.

'There's a couple of ways back down the mountain,' he said as if she didn't know. 'Some with a few reds, then blues. There's another with a few more blacks, but that one also has some greens in it.'

She nodded. They'd figure it out in a bit.

There was a comfortable silence between them.

Jacob's forearms rested on his knees, the bottle in his hands dangling down as he squinted out over the distance. She knew he had questions. It had been the same last night when he'd walked her home after the club.

Reilly wasn't used to someone trying to look out for her or protect her. Her father's bankruptcy had forced them all into survival mode, doing whatever they had to, to get through the next day. Reilly had kept herself small and quiet, not wanting to rock the boat, because her parents' arguments were bad enough. The only escape she'd had had been vacations with Asma . . . but Reilly didn't want to think about Asma right now. She knew it was bad; she felt guilty for even thinking such a thing. But the way Jacob's attention made her feel was . . . *so good.*

He made her laugh and he made her feel . . . *important* and interesting.

You have things to do here, Reilly. You need proof that Minette was involved in Asma's death. You need to seek justice.

But Reilly ignored her inner voice for now, wanting to have a moment just for herself.

'Where's Hugo?' she asked, taking a sip of her water.

Jacob smiled.

'He's with Mark, having a father-son bonding afternoon.'

They both smiled, happy for Hugo.

'What about your folks?' Jacob asked.

'What about them?'

'They're back home in the States?' he pressed gently.

Reilly nodded.

'Where and doing what?' Jacob asked. 'I mean you don't have to answer if . . .'

Reilly shrugged. 'Dad lost his business a few years back and we had to move and start over.'

'Ouch. That's tough,' he said. 'How old were you?'

'Thirteen,' Reilly said with a flat smile.

'Sucks.'

'Mmm,' Reilly replied, not really wanting to delve into her past. Not really wanting to get into issues that might cause her to have to lie.

I don't like secrets.

Sometimes it felt like those were all she had.

'OK. This is the part of the conversation when you ask me about me,' Jacob said, turning the awkward moment into a joke.

'What if I don't want to know about you?' she teased.

'Ohmygod, whaaat? I'm, like, the best catch around here, babe.'

A laugh burst out of Reilly unbidden. 'Did you just call me babe?'

'Totally, *babe*. And there are, like, soooo many things that you should want to know about me.'

'Give me three,' Reilly commanded, curious as to what he'd reveal.

Jacob opened his mouth and stopped, as if realising the trap he'd set himself.

'I . . . can't dance.'

'No one can dance,' she threw back, a little disappointed.

'No, like, seriously. I can't. It's like awkwardness shuts off the blood supply to my brain and I can't make my body move in the way I think it can.'

'Yeah, OK, Lacrosse,' Reilly replied and he grinned at the fact she'd given him a nickname. The brightness in his eyes, the flush on his cheeks, whether she'd put it there or the slopes had, it didn't really matter. He looked so handsome. And he looked like he wanted her. There it was again. That little spattering of fireworks that spread out from her chest, making her pulse skip and her breath catch.

'I cannot *stand* people that don't return trolleys at the grocery store.' Jacob announced, continuing his list of three things she needed to know about him.

'Really?'

'Like, they deserve corporal-punishment-level shit. Or eternal misery.'

'OK, I think I can get behind that,' Reilly agreed happily.

'And I really want to kiss you again,' he said, without taking his eyes off her.

Reilly opened her mouth to speak before he cut her off.

'But not yet. Because, first,' he said leaning in close, 'I really want to do this . . .'

Reilly went from a near dizzying high to confusion and then to absolute shocked outrage. She screamed as the snowball hit her squarely in the chest, bits breaking off and slipping past her jacket and thermals to melt against her skin leaving an icy cold dribble down her front.

'Oh my—' she cried

'It had to be done. I—'

To be fair, Reilly probably shouldn't have aimed for his face, but his yell of surprise was worth every moment of the sheer terror she felt when he swept up a huge pile of snow and launched himself towards her.

'Noooo, oh god, I'm sorry I didn't mean to—'

Another truncated sentence ended in a high-pitched scream as they leapt across and around the snow-bank, adrenaline zipping through their bloodstreams, shock and laughter on the air, screams and banter hurled as easily as snowballs until, finally, as if tired of letting her get away with it, Jacob rushed her, picking her up and throwing her into the bank. He fell down on top of her, his hands punched into the snow either side of her face.

Reilly looked up at him, breathless and hopeful.

'Can I kiss you, Reilly Clarke?' he asked.

And she felt it. She felt the difference between today and the hot tub. That night they'd been pretending to be anyone other than themselves. But this time? Now? He wanted to kiss *her*.

'I would very much like that, Jacob Arcilla.'

And before the words had even left her mouth, his lips were on hers, and she knew she'd never be the same again.

CHAPTER FIFTEEN
MINETTE

Minette had gone straight to Noah's chalet. Janet Scarisbrick hadn't even bothered to come to the door – which, for the first time ever, Minette was grateful for. She wasn't sure she'd be able to meet the older woman's eye.

Their chalet girl, Tina, had explained that Noah's snowboard was still in the boot room, so he wasn't on the slopes, but that he hadn't ordered the car service to take him anywhere.

Minette looked at her phone again.

> Where are you?
> Please answer your phone.
> I really need to talk to you.

But he'd left every message on read, which had only made her angrier.

Given how much they'd had to drink last night, Minette thought that he might have gone into the village for either something to eat or something more to drink.

She wiped at the angry tears that rolled down her cheeks. Just this once, she really needed him. Really needed to talk to him. And it wasn't that he *wasn't there*. No, he was *actively* ignoring her. She checked her phone again and only just managed to stifle the urge to scream.

As she did, she wobbled and slipped, her feet skidding on the ice. Minette lurched precariously trying not to fall, using every muscle she could to keep herself upright as her body screamed in protest. She managed to regain her feet, but the yank on her pulse and the dump of adrenaline as she caught herself added dangerously to the mix of already heady feelings.

Breath pumping in and out of her lungs, Minette made her way towards the village where tourists were out en masse, getting in her way. She swerved an older German couple and failed to contain her fury when a group of younger teenagers barrelled out of a bar and into her path.

The fact that they reminded Minette of how things had been with Hugo and Noah before life got complicated felt like a particularly cruel twist of fate. She peered into the bar that the teenagers just left and stopped. There was Noah, sitting at a small, tall table, chatting to a blonde waitress. Her hand on his forearm, making Minette see red.

Anger, confusion, frustration whipped around her in a storm that held her in its eye. He'd been here this whole time, ignoring her messages and calls?

Minette pulled open the door to the bar and marched in, the snow falling off her boots in clumps as she made her way towards Noah.

He caught sight of her and for a moment the look in his eyes was utterly blank. Completely devoid of any kind of emotion. A cold shiver that had nothing to do with the rapidly cooling sweat dripping down her spine tripped over her body. And then he blinked.

'Minette! What are you doing here?' he asked with a smile that she couldn't believe.

'What am I . . . ? I've been *calling* you,' she said, trying to keep the hysteria out of her voice. She didn't want to make a scene. Not here, not in public. And, besides, she knew how much Noah hated *scenes*.

'Really?' Noah asked, without even bothering to look at his phone.

'Yes,' she whisper-hissed.

The waitress gave Noah an awkward smile and left them to it.

'Did you want a drink?' Noah asked politely, completely ignoring her obvious upset.

What was going on? Had she walked into a parallel universe?

'Noah, we need to talk.'

'OK,' he said, placing his drink back on the table and giving her his full attention.

'I just . . .' Minette swallowed. *How did she tell him this?* 'I just . . . walked in on my mother and . . . and your father.'

Noah blinked at her.

'And?'

'Noah, did you hear me?' she demanded. 'Your father and my mother. Noah, they're . . . *having sex*.'

Not a muscle on his face moved. No sign of shock, or surprise or horror.

Merde.

Minette wanted to stamp her feet. Why was he being so obtuse? She wanted to strangle him. Actually, genuinely, put her hands on him and gouge at him. She took a breath, trying to calm herself.

'Yes, I know.'

The bottom dropped out of her world, as if everything she thought she knew was being sucked down into a whirlpool.

The way Noah was staring at her as if *she* were the problem made Minette feel as if she *was* going crazy.

'What do you mean?' she asked, hoping she had it all wrong.

'I mean, I *know*. I'm surprised you didn't,' he said, taking a mouthful of his beer as if they were talking about a couple of friends getting together.

'They're our parents, Noah!' she hissed as her mind spun through a thousand imagined scenarios, each one just as horrifying.

'How long?' she demanded.

'Mmm?' he asked, cocking his head to one side.

'How long have they been . . . ?' She couldn't bring herself to say it again. She felt sick and more than a little dizzy.

'Having sex?' he asked. Noah shook his head and shrugged. 'A couple of years?'

What? How had this happened? Why hadn't he told her?

'Did we . . .' She trailed off, not sure how to ask the question, let alone whether she wanted to know or not. 'Was it after we got together?'

Noah pulled a face as if to say, what the hell does it matter. 'I don't know,' he shrugged carelessly, taking another pull on his beer.

'How long have you known?' she asked, her voice trembling.

'That your mother is a whore? Roughly the same amount of time, I'd imagine.'

His words were a sharp slap across her cheek. Cutting, stinging and paralysing.

'*What* did you say?' Minette demanded.

'I'm pretty sure you heard me, but I can repeat myself. Your mother is a whore,' Noah said. There was a flash of that mean glint in his eye that she recognised. The one that scared her. The one she'd convinced herself that she'd forgotten, but hadn't. Something so coldly calculating that she shivered, in spite of the searing heat of shame that burned her cheeks.

'How can you say that? What about your dad!' she demanded.

'Don't you *dare* talk about my father,' he growled, his fury rolling off him in waves.

'So, you can call my mother a whore, but I can't even mention your father? Who *are* you right now?'

'Oh, don't be such a child. You know what this is. *You and me?* It's convenient, it works for our families. It's . . . political. And while that works, I'll take what I can get. But anything else? I'm not here for, Minette. So take your temper tantrum somewhere else until you're ready to be civil again.'

It was as if someone had yanked off the rose tinted glasses she'd been wearing, and Minette's world looked different Meaner. Harsher.

'Oh, Mins. You didn't think it was something else, did you? Come on,' he cajoled. 'You can't have been that naive.' He put down his drink he'd as if disappointed in her.

Instinctively she wanted to reassure him.

No, of course not, darling.

She wanted to be the sophisticated, indifferent person he clearly wanted her to be. Minette thought she *had* been that. She'd thought she was his equal. She thought that, in school, he'd chosen her because she was special – that she wasn't like the others he bitched about. That she wasn't like the people he teased or pranked or shoved.

Just like that she remembered the fall on the ice rink. The way she'd wondered if it had been on purpose. Remembered how Noah had done that to other students in their year or the year below. Minette remembered how he'd laughed at someone just because he didn't like their accent, or how he'd beat someone up if they hadn't given the respect he thought he'd deserved.

She remembered how he would be the first to comment on her posts, which would set the tone for all future comments. She remembered the way he'd bitterly resented her new roommate in the fourth year, Asma Chaudhury, because they'd been looking forward to a whole year of having the dorm to themselves.

And she remembered the way that she'd thought the footage of Asma and the teacher had looked familiar, as if it had been made using the pictures that she'd taken herself.

Minette opened her mouth to speak when the meanness in his gaze returned.

'Now, if you're done, I'd like to finish my drink in peace, please?'

A painful blush stung her cheeks. Embarrassment and humiliation engulfed her like flames. She'd been dismissed and there was nothing left to say.

Minette turned and on unsteady feet made it to the door before looking back at Noah, only to find him talking to the waitress again, who was flirtatiously playing with her hair.

Minette thought she was going to be sick and left, knowing that her life was never going to be the same again.

REILLY

Reilly was putting away her skis in the boot room when her phone buzzed with a message. She was smiling before she even checked it, knowing that it would be Jacob.

> I had fun today.

It was stupid how happy four small words could make her. She liked that Jacob didn't leave her guessing about whether he liked her or not. He felt so clear about it that it made her blush. She typed back her answer.

> So did I.

> Can we do it again tomorrow?

Reilly swallowed. She really needed to get back on track with Minette.

> I have to work. We're taking the snowmobiles out.

> Can't play hooky?

It wasn't his question that made her anxious, but the stress of lying to him – okay, so not strictly *lying* to him, but definitely not telling him the truth of what she was doing here – and the way that time was beginning to run out and she *still* hadn't found proof, was making her freak out.

If she didn't get Minette to reveal herself on this trip and admit what she'd done to Asma – that she had made the fake video of Asma and that teacher and had bullied her, cruelly and mercilessly – she'd never get the chance again. One way or another, by the end of this festive period, she would either have the proof she needed or would have lost her chance for ever.

> Sorry. No can do.

She waited, wondering whether Jacob would leave it at—

> That's OK – I knew it was a long shot.
> Just wanted to ask that's all.
> Let me know when you're free.
> I want to take you out.

> We were out on the slopes today.
>
> I want to take you **out** out.

Reilly smiled. She typed a reply, saying that she was looking forward to it, slipped the phone into her pocket and headed upstairs to the chalet, just in time to see Anike emerging from the kitchen into the living room.

'Oh!' Reilly screamed, which only made Anike scream, dropping the tub of ice cream on the floor and making them both laugh.

'Oh my god, I didn't see you!' Reilly cried.

'That's OK, I feel fairly zombie-like any way. I didn't hear you come in,' Anike said, running across the room to get some kitchen towel.

'Don't do that, I'll get it,' Reilly said.

'Don't be silly, I can clean up my own mess, I promise,' Anike said.

It was a nice gesture, but if Savannah saw it, Reilly would lose her job right then and there.

'Please. Honestly, I'll get this and I'll replace the ice cream,' Reilly insisted, shooing Anike away.

'Urgh. Thank you. I'm just ... soooo hungover,' Anike replied with a grimace.

She did look a *little* worse for wear.

'Have you eaten?' Reilly asked.

'I was supposed to be having burgers from the Vandenburg with Mini, but she's not replying to my messages.'

'Is she OK?'

'I don't know,' Anike replied, tapping on her screen. 'Trying again now.'

The ringtone cut through the quiet chalet but went unanswered.

'Is that unusual?' Reilly asked.

Anike pulled a face. 'I don't know. I . . . think so? It's hard to tell, though. She was going to see her mother, and her mum can be difficult, you know?'

'Yeah, I know,' Reilly replied, thinking of her own mother. 'What is yours like?' she asked, before remembering what the dossier had said about Anike Dossongui and regretted her thoughtlessness.

'I don't know. She died when I was three.'

'I'm so sorry,' Reilly replied.

'That's OK. I didn't really know her; Dad doesn't talk about her much. And whenever we see her side of the family, they always treat me like . . . like they're so sorry for me? And they expect me to miss her like *they* miss her, which is impossible, really, because I don't remember her.'

'That's difficult. That sense of expectation,' Reilly said, finishing clearing up and throwing the towels into the utility room off the kitchen.

'Yeah. But Dad did his best. He may not always get it right . . .'

'Like . . . sending you away after Jacques?' Reilly hedged, as she retrieved another tub of ice cream – this one salted-caramel flavour.

'Like sending me away after Jacques. And insisting on Karel,' Anike said, rolling her eyes.

Reilly offered her the tub of ice cream and a spoon, making Anike cheer and pump her fists in the air.

'Thank you, thank you, thank you.'

'I can make you something if you like?' Reilly offered.

'That's OK, I'll hang on until Minette gets back, just in case. But in the meantime, I will want company while I make a concerted effort to put a dent in this ice cream.' Anike batted her eyelashes and patted the sofa beside her.

'Reilly doesn't quite suit you, do you know that?' Anike observed when Reilly sat down beside her.

'I had a friend who called me RiRi?' Reilly offered.

'That is perfect! I love it.'

Reilly couldn't help it. She laughed and let her head fall back on to the sofa cushion.

'I want gossip!' Anike demanded. 'Hangovers always require sugar, salt, trash TV and gossip.'

'Do they now?'

'Yes! It's practically law!' she announced regally, as she peeled back the plastic lid on the ice cream tub, and dug her spoon into it.

Reilly looked at her, realising that Anike was practically bursting at the seams and she had a pretty good idea that she didn't want to *hear* gossip, she wanted to *share* it.

'Ani . . . ?' she asked.

'RiRi . . . ?' Anike replied in exactly the same tone.

'Is there maybe something you want to—'

'Yes! Oh god, I *so* would have told Mini, but I just can't wait any more. *Hugokissedme*.'

The words rushed out as a single sound, Anike's eyes popping wide open before she grabbed a cushion and buried her face in it and muffled a little scream.

Reilly couldn't help but laugh, Anike was adorable like this.

'And that's a good thing, right?' Reilly replied, pretty sure she knew the answer, but wanting to double check.

'Sooooo good. Like, sooooooooooo good,' she said, face still buried in the cushion. She had drawn the words out longer than Reilly thought humanly possible.

Reilly grinned, knowing the feeling.

Anike finally let the pillow go, threw her head back on the sofa and sighed dramatically before turning to pin her with that rich-espresso gaze of hers.

'You know when it's that good, right? Like, tiptoes good, like . . .'

'Like you just want to curl-up-and-burrow-into-him good?'

'YES! I mean, *weird*, but oddly accurate. Like *that*! Wait, who have *you* been kissing like that?' Anike demanded, sitting bolt upright. '*Youhavetotellme!*'

Reilly was now blushing, laughing and absolutely desperate to tell someone about Jacob, because, yeah, kissing him was like 'tiptoes good'.

'I . . .' And in the back of her mind she heard Savannah. She saw herself being kicked out of the chalet, fired and removed from the only access she'd ever have to Minette ever again.

Reilly let the words trail off, shrugging and shaking her head.

'OK, you keep your secrets, *RiRi*. I'll just have to bore you with all of *my* delicious details.'

'Please. I want to hear everything,' Reilly said sincerely, and not just because she wanted to change the subject. From what she could tell, Hugo and Anike would make a really lovely and very fun couple.

'So after you left last night, we stayed at the club. Noah and Minette were on the dance floor and Hugo asked if he could buy me a drink. I said, of course, you can. But on one condition . . .'

'Which was . . . ?'

'That he told me I was beautiful.'

'Bold!'

'Necessary!' Anike replied lightning quick. 'I think he was a bit in his head about his ex – Minette told me about it, and it sounds like it ended *badly*,' Anike emphasised with a grimace. 'So I figured *that's* why he was taking so long to pick up on, like, *all* the clues I was chucking straight at his head.'

Anike's animation was infectious as she talked ten to the dozen. Reilly could barely keep up.

'So, he reached for my hands, and said, "Anike Dossongui, you are the most beautiful woman in this club, if not on this side of the entire mountain. I have not been able to get you out of my mind since I first saw you. And even if nothing happens between us, it's enough that you know this, and understand it to be true".'

'Cute!' Reilly exclaimed. 'That's . . . yeah. Impressive. Go Hugo!'

'And then, while I was completely and utterly speechless, he kissed me! Hard and fast! And then, like an idiot, he pulled away.'

'What?'

'Yeah, so I grabbed him and pulled him back and *that* kiss, *that* kiss was *the* kiss,' Anike said, stressing all the words, eyes bright with excitement and happiness.

'Aw! That's so—'

Before Reilly could finish her sentence, the front door to the chalet slammed open and Minette came running into the room, looking stricken.

'Minette! Are you OK?' Reilly asked.

'Not now, Reilly!' Minette said, cursing before she ran off upstairs to her room.

Reilly's cheeks pinked from the sharpness in Minette's tone.

'I . . . I'm sorry, Reilly, I'm sure she didn't mean it. Something must have happened,' Anike said, getting up from the sofa and looking torn between staying and needing to see her friend.

'Of course,' Reilly said. 'Please go after her. I don't think she should be alone right now.'

Anike headed up to Minette's room, leaving Reilly on the sofa.

It was clear that things weren't going well for Minette, but it was also clear that there was no way that Reilly would be able to befriend her now. Not in the short time left. Now she had to try something else. And she had to try it fast.

CHAPTER SIXTEEN

MINETTE

Minette adjusted the tightness of her ski gloves around her wrist, looking mutinously out at the crisp frosty snow of the wide trail in front of them.

You have to come. We arranged it as something we could all do together.

It was hard to say no to Anike at the best of times, and this wasn't the best of times.

Come on. Come and show Noah that whatever you've argued about hasn't got to you.

Minette clenched her jaw. *Merde.* Of course it had got to her. And of course she hadn't been able to tell Anike. She'd never be able to tell *anyone*.

Her mother and his father . . .

And Noah had kept that secret from her for years!

He'd lied to her and she'd had no idea.

She must have looked like *such* a fool.

She checked the zip on her snowsuit and bent to make sure that it was secure over her boots.

The boys were huddled around the snowmobiles, checking them out as if they were the latest souped-up motorcycles. Marcus, the chalet host for the Arcillas, was talking them through all the little mechanical details.

Minette rolled her eyes. They'd snowmobiled before. And when it had been suggested that she might like to ride with Noah rather than on her own, she'd simply stared at Marcus until he'd blushed and explained that there was enough for everyone to ride on their own, should they wish.

'I'm going to ride with Hugo,' Anike had announced, completely oblivious to the tension in the small group. Karel's gaze followed her as if this was something he did not approve of, but didn't say anything. He just swung his leg over his snowmobile and manoeuvred himself to the back of the pack.

The crunch of boots on the snow behind her gave her enough warning of Noah's approach.

'Have you got over your temper tantrum yet?' he demanded.

She ground her teeth together in frustration.

'You kept a secret from me for *years*,' she hissed. 'So no, I'm *not* over it yet.'

'That's right, Mins. Now that you're over your wounded routine, you'll get mean. Right on cue.'

'What are you talking about?' Minette demanded.

'Why don't you ask Asma Chaudhury? Oh, that's right. You *can't*.'

Outrage snapped inside her. It was as if she'd felt it physically break. But before she could reply, Noah stormed off, leaving Minette almost apoplectic with rage.

'OK, ladies and gentlemen,' Marcus called, as Reilly passed around steaming hot mugs of coffee or hot chocolate. 'If you'll gather round, I want to talk you through today.'

Minette avoided Reilly as much as humanly possible and it looked as if she had got the message, because *finally* she was keeping her distance.

Anike had told Minette off for being rude. But honestly, Reilly was just the chalet girl! Minette shouldn't have to be nice or worry about Reilly's feelings when she had so much going on. Irritation flared through her, and she tried to fight it, knowing that she was being difficult but feeling unable to control it.

'So, we'll take the tracks out towards the northern part of the mountains – these are private Vandenburg snowmobile tracks so it will just be us.

'Now depending on your comfort level, we can stick to easier routes just to get acquainted with the machines and how they work and, in about an hour, we'll stop and make a decision on the route we'll take towards our destination for lunch. It's a pretty scenic spot and we have a lavish spread planned for you. But if you get hungry in the meantime or want to stop for any reason, just let me know and we'll accommodate that, of course. There are snacks in your packs, a few safety things like flares, ropes, first-aid kits, water and sunscreen et cetera. There are also some energy sachets if needed, but we don't see that being necessary,' he added with a laugh. 'Health and safety notes: You must wear your helmets. We're not messing around. The speeds you can get up to in these babies are over one hundred miles an hour. If you don't wear your helmets, the trip is off.'

The boys all groaned, but reluctantly nodded.

'The views from the lunch location are pretty impressive, so I hope you've all brought your cameras for that Instagram-worthy moment!'

Anike danced over to Minette, her hands pressed together in prayer, as if she were that excited. And then she seemed to remember that her friend had just had a massive argument with her boyfriend.

'How are you doing?' Anike asked.

'Fine,' Minette spat out.

Anike bit her lip. 'If you want, we can call this off and head back down to the chalets and spend the entire day at the spa?'

Minette might have been angry, but she wasn't stupid – she knew that Anike really wanted to do this. She caught Noah's warning glare from across the plateau where all the snowmobiles were lined up.

Don't make a scene. Do as you're told.

You don't have what it takes. Noah does. You've done well to attach yourself to him.

'No, of course, not. This will be fun,' Minette replied, surrendering some of her anger and trying to inject some excitement into her tone.

'Perfect.' Anike all but squealed and skipped off to where Hugo was holding out a helmet for her to put on.

Minette turned away and picked up the pink helmet with the reflective eye screen and pulled it on, tightening the strap beneath her chin. She straddled the leather seat of the snowmobile and put her feet on the rests. She was a little nervous, but as she released the brake and the snowmobile rumbled forward, the familiar thrill shot through her and she struck out in the line, just after Noah, with Hugo and Anike following behind and Jacob at the back.

It took a while, but slowly, mile by mile, the stunning surroundings began to work their magic. The beautiful wide track spread out in front of her, with gentle dips and hills and corners that were smooth and graceful. Not challenging – not yet anyway.

The crisp hard snow of the early morning began to soften as the sun rose higher in the sky. Thinking – or over thinking – was impossible with the stunning backdrop of mountains that stretched out into the distance, and snow-covered forests that reminded Minette of children's fairytales.

Having decided they were all proficient enough with the snowmobiles, Marcus and Reilly led them out through some more challenging trails, and Minette had to concentrate to keep up. Heart pounding and feeling exhilarated for one blissful moment, she let everything drop away and soon it was just her and the high-pitched roar of the snowmobiles zipping and buzzing in her ear.

The freedom, the *control* . . . She increased her speed the more confident she got, overtaking Hugo and Anike, and then Jacob, until only Noah was between her and Marcus, who was in the lead.

She hated the way that Noah wove across the wide lane, as if bored or showing off, but also . . . as if he were trying to purposely get in her way.

Before long, they pulled off the tree-lined track that led further up the mountain and instead followed a smaller path that wound through several twists and turns until they reached a wide plateau.

Without a word, they all came to a stop, hypnotised by the stunning view. Where the ground dropped away, all they could see was the stunning vista of the jagged mountains reaching far into the distance.

Minette was vaguely aware of Marcus and Reilly setting out the things for lunch, the smell of food drifting towards her on the crisp alpine air. But she was lost to the view. The awesomeness of nature.

Reilly came to stand beside her, a steaming cup of thick, delicious-smelling soup in her hands.

'You must have gotten used to this at the Institute,' Reilly observed, making Minette frown.

'Why?'

'Well, Lausanne isn't that far away. I would have thought that you'd have come here all the time?'

Minette pulled a face as she tried to work out why Reilly knew where she'd gone to school. 'Not really. So, I guess you thought wrong,' she replied bitchily. Minette knew she was being mean, but there was something about Reilly that was seriously rubbing her up the wrong way. Overly solicitous, always there, silent, present, watching.

To her credit, Reilly simply smiled. 'I just came to bring you some soup.'

Minette took the soup and left to join the others, wondering what it was that was bugging her, beyond Reilly's slightly presumptuous manner.

She crossed to where Noah was leaning against his snowmobile.

'Have you talked to the chalet girl about the Institute?' she asked, quietly for his ears only.

His gaze flickered from her, to where Reilly stood talking to Marcus over her shoulder, and back again with a slight frown.

'No. Why would I?'

'No reason I guess,' Minette replied.

'You talking to me again, then?' he asked saltily.

'When I have to, yes,' she bit out.

And with that she turned her attention back to the group, realising what had bothered her so much about Reilly's question. The only people that called the exclusive Swiss boarding school by the nickname, the Institute, were the students who had studied there.

REILLY

Up by the edge of the plateau, Marcus was playing photographer for the girls as they took turns throwing handfuls of snow into the air that arched above them in the sky. Reilly didn't need to see them to know that the images would look spectacular. Partly because it had been designed to be by Savannah as part of the 'Vandenburg experience'.

Reilly was at the little prep area that she and Marcus had erected in order to plate up the food and drinks that were part of the special VIP snowmobile tour.

Reilly only had four days left now. She didn't have time to play nice any more. She was going to have to do something drastic to get Minette to confess what she did to drive Asma to take her own life.

Reilly had never considered sharing the letter she'd received from Asma with her parents. Not once. Even if Asma hadn't asked her to show them, there was no way that Reilly wanted the Chaudhurys to know how much Asma had struggled with the merciless bullying.

I can't go anywhere, Reilly. Nowhere is safe.

I get locked out of the dorm room and have to find somewhere else to sleep. And no one will take me in for fear of drawing attention to themselves and end up being treated like me. I eat alone. I study alone. I swear, sometimes it feels like I haven't spoken to another human being in years.

And then, when I hear what they're saying about me, I'm glad that no one is talking to me. All because of that video...

The teacher left. But I don't have that luxury. I ask Mum and Dad, but they won't take me out of the Institute without a reason and I can't tell them, Reilly. I can't. They'll want to talk to the principal; they'll want to try and fix it. And they can't. No one can.

'Penny for them,' Jacob said, his words cutting into Reilly's thoughts and snapping her back to the present.

She forced a smile to her lips.

'They're not worth sharing,' Reilly said with a sad smile.

Something clouded his gaze, but before he could say anything, Hugo and Anike came to join them.

'RiRi,' Anike said, using her nickname, making Reilly smile. 'Are we still on for tomorrow night?' she whispered. Anike had wanted to host a party at the chalet and had been messaging

Reilly about it all of last night. Lists of themes, music, drink options and food.

'Of course. It's going to be the best night ever,' Reilly assured her in the same whispered tone.

'Good,' Anike said, her voice a normal level as she declared, 'I'm staaaaaarving. Oh my god, are those langoustines?'

She went to reach for one and Reilly playfully slapped at her hand, causing Anike to squeal in shock and then dissolve into giggles.

'Please, RiRi,' she begged. 'Please, please, please.'

Reilly looked at Hugo.

'How can you resist?' he said, with a shrug.

'Fine,' Reilly teased. 'But just one. Otherwise there won't be enough to go round.'

'She can have mine,' Hugo told Reilly, before grinning at Anike again in a lovesick way.

'Whipped,' Jacob coughed, unsubtly under his breath.

'Dude, I am one hundred per cent, wholeheartedly whipped and I don't care who knows it,' Hugo proclaimed proudly.

Anike beamed and Jacob laughed.

'Can't argue with that,' Jacob said, rubbing the back of his neck.

'Argue with what?' Noah asked, coming up and stealing a langoustine off the table and popping it into his mouth, before looking up at Reilly and pinning her with his gaze.

Reilly didn't know whether he'd seen what had happened with Anike, but she got the distinct impression that he was testing her to see if she'd stop him.

Perhaps she was imagining things. But she didn't think she was.

'Lunch is ready,' Reilly called, loud enough for the girls and Marcus to hear, without taking her eyes from Noah's.

He grinned back at her, chewing with his mouth slightly open, before turning back to the girls and beckoning them over.

'Come on,' he called loudly. 'The lovely Reilly's laid on a gorgeous spread and we wouldn't want it to go to waste, would we?'

Reilly's heart thudded in her chest. Had Minette said something to him about her she wondered, feeling disconcerted? Until now Noah hadn't really looked her way or even registered her presence.

While Anike and Hugo helped themselves to plates and began to pick and choose their lunch from the platters on the small table, she felt Jacob's gaze fill with curiosity. The others hadn't seemed to notice the odd exchange, but Jacob had.

She bit her lip and turned to play with the urn of hot water behind her that was for tea and coffee. Nothing was wrong with it, but she made enough of a fuss of it so that neither Jacob nor Noah would still be standing there when she turned back.

Thankfully, they'd all gone over to sit on the insulated blanket Marcus had put down on the flat snow. Tina had come up here earlier, with her snowmobile and a sled, to drop off the things they'd needed for lunch. She'd return when they finished lunch to take everything back down, which was how they'd been able to recreate a small paradise out here on the side of the mountain. There were rugs and throws and cushions, as well as a large canvas umbrella that helped keep a little of the wind away from the gathering.

Bottles of champagne chilled in ice buckets, and the sounds of popping corks told Reilly that they were happily getting the party started.

Shaking herself off, Reilly smiled as Minette approached, chatting away animatedly with Marcus as she helped herself to lunch. She barely spared Reilly a glance, which felt more than a little pointed.

Reilly gritted her teeth.

If that's how she wanted to play it, that was fine by Reilly. If the gloves were coming off, they were coming off.

About an hour later, the group had splintered off in different directions, the two couples taking selfies and goofing around, while Marcus checked over each of the snowmobiles, to make sure they were still in top condition and full of petrol.

Reilly was closing down the food area, and wasn't surprised to find Jacob standing over her when she looked up from packing away the cutlery.

'You OK?' he asked.

'Yeah, of course. Why wouldn't I be?'

His gaze was assessing. Instead of answering, he asked the question Reilly had been half expecting.

'What was that about?'

'What was what about?' she evaded, hoping that he might drop it.

'That thing with Noah.'

She sighed. No such luck.

'I don't know,' she hedged. 'I think I might have upset him somehow, but I'm sure it doesn't matter.'

Jacob frowned, as if he wasn't quite sure whether to believe her or not.

Discomfort reached her cheeks in a blush. Asma had always teased her about it.

You always blush when you lie, Reilly. It's why you're so terrible at it.

'I can give you a hand clearing up if you like,' he offered.

'Please don't,' Reilly said, worried and looking over his shoulder in case Marcus or any of the others had seen.

'Reilly—'

'Jacob, if anyone sees or suspects anything I could lose my job. You know that.'

'Fair enough, but . . .'

'But what?'

He hesitated as if torn. He looked over his shoulder and – satisfied everyone else was busy or distracted – he turned back to her.

'I can't shake the feeling that there's something you're not telling me.'

'I'm not seeing anyone else, Jacob. I—'

'No, it's not that. But it's *something*. And,' he pressed on before she could argue, 'and I don't know if I can let that go. My mom . . .' He inhaled deeply. 'She has a drug problem. It's shit. It sucks. It's made a lot of things horrible in her life and ours – me and my father's. But by far the worst is having to pretend to everyone that everything's fine. And we have to because if we don't, she'll lose her job, and we can't afford that right now. Not with college, and not with . . . paying for what my mom needs.'

The words rushed out of him, pulling Reilly into a world she'd heard of time and time again.

Her heart went out to him. She remembered seeing his mother at the party. A little too bright-eyed, laughing a little too hard. She'd just thought Mary Arcilla had been drunk.

'What kind of drugs?' she asked.

'Opioids.' The word punched out of him on an exhale.

'Jacob, I'm so sorry.'

'Me too. But see, I needed to explain, I needed you to know. I . . . I can't have any more secrets in my life.'

There was frustration and upset in his gaze. It was tearing him up and she could see it. She hated that she'd even been a little part of whatever had put that in his eyes.

Reilly wanted to beg him not to do this. Not to ask her. But she knew she didn't have that right. And . . . perhaps this was for the best. Hadn't he been enough of a distraction? She had such a short amount of time left.

He looked pained. As if he knew already which way she'd go.

'So you'll need to choose, Reilly. It doesn't have to be now. But when you're ready, you can either tell me, or this . . . whatever it is . . . is over.'

'You don't know what you're asking,' she said miserably.

'Because you won't tell me,' he whispered, frustrated.

But she *couldn't* tell him. Because he might want to stop her and she couldn't do that. She'd come so far and was determined to get what she needed; for Minette to admit what she'd done.

Telling him simply wasn't an option. But before she could answer, he walked away.

CHAPTER SEVENTEEN

JACOB

To say that he didn't want to be here was a bit of an understatement. The girls' chalet was almost exactly like the one he and his parents were staying in. Only the decor was slightly different. His, thankfully, felt homely. This one was sleeker. A little more . . . *monied*.

He figured that if he and his folks had been given this chalet, they might have felt uncomfortable. But it seemed to suit Minette and Anike.

Jacob shot a glance across the room to where Reilly was pouring champagne into glasses. There was music streaming through speakers and the girls had clearly been drinking for a while. He wasn't sure if Reilly had – she looked happy enough, but there was a tension about her that was slightly unusual. But he didn't think she'd be so reckless as to drink while she was working.

He was half regretting what he'd said to her yesterday out on the snowmobile tour. He rubbed the back of his neck in frustration. Only half, because he'd been honest at least. He really did hate secrets.

Was he being a fool? They only had three days left. He wasn't sure what would happen between them after the end of the vacation. He wasn't sure what Reilly had planned, and he'd head back to Harvard, he supposed, but ... things just felt ... too unfinished. He didn't want things to end. It had felt like the beginning of something special. Something important.

Jacob looked up and caught her eye – but Reilly turned away before he could read anything into it. He *wanted* it to continue. Hell, it was only a six-hour flight to California from Boston, and that was even if he went back to college. If his family could even afford it. He thought about the argument he'd overheard before coming out that night.

'It'll be different. I promise. Your brother doesn't need to help us out. I'm fine. Done. It won't happen again.'

'You say that every time.'

'I know. But it's different this time. It really is.'

'Even if that's the case, we barely have enough for the rest of the school year. What about next year and the year after?'

'I'll ... I don't ... I don't know, but we'll make it work. I can cash out my private—'

'For fuck sake, Mary. You cashed that out last year.'

Maybe he should just drop out. That would take the pressure off at least. And he'd meant what he'd said. He'd rather his mom got into a decent rehab centre than him staying on at Harvard. He could transfer somewhere else. Somewhere cheaper. Christ, he could probably come to university in Europe at half the price of what it cost in the States.

Distracted by the idea forming in his mind, he didn't notice Hugo approaching and startled when Hugo slapped him on the back.

'Jesus, sorry, bro. I didn't mean to scare you.'

'No worries. Sorry, I was miles away.'

'Clearly,' Hugo said with a small smile.

'Everything OK?' Jacob asked, realising he hadn't been paying much attention that evening.

Hugo scrunched his nose. 'Yeah. Kinda. The girls are getting pretty drunk, though.'

As if to punctuate that thought, on the other side of the room Anike and Minette screamed at something and then descended into rounds of hysterical laughter as Minette pushed Anike over the back of the sofa and fell down on top of her.

'Pretty early start to the festivities,' Jacob commented.

'Yeah,' replied Hugo, as if he wasn't entirely happy about it.

'Come on, Noah, don't be such a spoilsport,' Anike whined, trying to pull on his arm.

'I'm not letting you anywhere near me with that thing,' Noah grinned, pointing at the mascara wand Anike inexplicably held in her hand.

'But you have such pretty eyelashes, it'll make them even *better*.'

'Do you need to go and ... like ... check on her?' Jacob asked Hugo.

'Not yet. I've got my eye on it, though.'

'Where's Karel tonight?' Jacob asked.

Hugo shook his head. 'Anike gave him the night off because we're staying in.'

'He buy that?' Jacob asked, frowning.

'I doubt it,' Hugo replied. 'He's probably parked right outside.'

Jacob let out a laugh in agreement.

'Don't bother,' they heard Minette complain as Anike approached Noah. 'He's no fun at all.'

Jacob pulled a face at Hugo. 'They're still arguing?'

'Apparently. I have no idea what it's about, though. I thought they might have made up during the snowmobile tour. But it seems that alcohol has caused the hostilities to resume.'

Jacob turned to watch them settle on the floor next to the sofa in front of the wood burner. Anike was vaping and Noah was spinning an empty wine bottle in his hands. Something about the sight made Jacob a little uncomfortable.

'Spin the Bottle, anyone?' Noah winked.

'There's an uneven amount of boys to girls,' Hugo pointed out.

'Not if Reilly joins in,' Noah pointed out.

Absolutely not.

Jacob opened his mouth to object, but Hugo got there first.

'Reilly, no matter how cool you are,' he said, 'I don't want a member of staff involved in anything remotely—'

'No worries, honestly. I would have politely declined anyway,' Reilly insisted.

'Booorrring,' Noah whined.

Jacob took a pull of his beer. Perhaps he should nurse this one for a while. Things were getting a little out of hand. But he couldn't quite tell why. He'd been around these guys for nearly ten days now and he knew that they could all pretty much hold their alcohol. Yes, tempers had been high and tensions had been building, but even so . . .

He watched Reilly head back to the table and prepare some more drinks.

'I know, how about Truth or Dare!' Anike called.

'Oh, *absolutement*,' Minette added with a glimmer of something Jacob couldn't quite put his finger on.

'I'm sooo in,' Noah replied with a smile. 'How's that, boss?' he asked Hugo. 'Surely Reilly can join in with *that*?'

'Her call, dude,' Hugo said, washing his hands of it.

But Jacob was distracted as he realised that Reilly was pouring something into the champagne glasses. Was that a vodka bottle?

'What about you two? We can't play without you,' Anike called over.

'I'm pretty sure you can,' Hugo said, shooting Jacob a wry glance, before heading over to where Anike sat, catching her hand and letting her draw him into a kiss that got heated pretty quickly.

The music was beginning to grate on Jacob's nerves.

'Come on, Arcilla,' Noah called. 'Don't be a spoilsport.'

He didn't like the idea that he was being cajoled into it, but he didn't want to derail everyone's evening so he threw his hands in the air and joined them, receiving a round of applause from the group.

He caught Reilly's gaze as he sat down on the plush carpet, his nose wrinkling at the blueberry vape Anike streamed into the air above them.

From where she stood at the table preparing the drinks, Reilly gestured to a glass of champagne and he shook his head. She pointed at a beer and he nodded, just to have an excuse for her to come within touching distance of him. They'd been circling each other awkwardly all night.

And he was half convinced that Minette had been sending them suspicious looks, so he'd been trying really damn hard to make sure he didn't get Reilly into trouble.

Reilly came over from the table with two trays of fancy-ass canapés. One tray had folds of smoked salmon and shrimp with some kind of dill pickle on crispbread and, swear to god, edible gold leaf on the top. The other tray looked like some kind of roast beef and horseradish inside the world's smallest Yorkshire pudding.

Anike snatched the crispbread from the platter and moaned in orgasmic bliss.

'RiRi, these are di-*vine*.'

'You made these?' Jacob asked, surprised.

'Yes. I *can* cook,' Reilly replied with a laugh.

Of course she could. She's a damn chalet host, you idiot.

'These are amazing,' Hugo said around a mouthful of beef. 'But don't tell Tina I said that or she'll get jealous.'

'I won't. Promise!'

Reilly placed the trays on the coffee table behind them and went back for the drinks.

'Hey, Reilly, change the music, will you?' Minette called.

'Jeez, Mins. She's not an Alexa. If you want the music changed, go change it,' Noah replied snippily.

Minette blushed angrily, clearly embarrassed by Noah's

put-down, and Jacob caught the glare she cut Reilly's way as if it were her fault.

Minette got her phone out and clicked on whatever app she was using to control the music, which made it even weirder to Jacob that she'd asked Reilly to do it, unless it was a power trip of some kind. He swore the French girl he'd met at the beginning of this vacation wouldn't have done something so obviously rude, but maybe he'd had her all wrong.

Or was this what happened when the rich found their beds weren't turned down correctly?

Jacob frowned and shot a glance at Hugo, who wasn't like that in the slightest, but he didn't really know the others. That much was becoming painfully clear.

When Reilly returned there was nothing about her to suggest she'd been upset or offended by Minette's demand.

There was a space in the small circle for Reilly to sit next to him, but she looked at it as if it were the *last* place she wanted to be. Then Anike patted the floor beside her.

'Move up, Noah, RiRi can sit here,' Anike commanded regally, leaving Jacob dissatisfied, and more than a little concerned about how the evening was going to end.

REILLY

It had taken Anike *ages* to suggest they play Truth or Dare. Reilly had mentioned it a few times in the lead-up to the party in various different ways, but hadn't want to go in with a sledgehammer. In the end it had worked out perfectly.

As for the alcohol, she hadn't had to *force* anyone to drink it. And so far no one had noticed the extra shot of vodka in the champagne, other than to say it was the best they'd ever had.

Of course it was.

Did she feel bad about making their drinks stronger? A little. But she'd seen how they all drank over the last ten days. Tomorrow was New Year's Eve. Time had run out and Reilly had no other choice. She had to kick this plan into gear or she'd lose the opportunity forever. And she couldn't let that happen. She owed it to Asma to get Minette to confess to what she'd done.

In her mind's eye, Reilly saw Minette at the memorial the Institute held, accepting the condolences of the staff, of other students ... of Asma's *parents*. They'd hugged her. They'd told her that they were glad she'd been there for their daughter.

Acid and bile crawled up her throat causing her to cough a little.

'Do you want some water?' Jacob asked from across the circle. His eyes had barely left her the entire evening.

She was shaking her head when Noah answered for her.

'She doesn't need water, she needs a *drink*!'

Anike and Minette cheered. Hugo laughed.

'I don't want to intrude,' she hedged.

'Intrude? You're integral to the game. We need even numbers.'

'I thought that was just for Spin the Bottle,' Minette said cattily, but no one listened.

Settling into the seat on the floor in between Anike and Noah, Reilly avoided Jacob's heavy gaze. She didn't think anyone else had noticed, but that was only because they were involved in their own dramas. Hugo and Anike were unable to keep their hands off each other – which was cute and made Reilly smile in spite of herself. Minette? Well, she was in a mood. A mood that had been growing steadily worse and worse ever since she stood Anike up for burgers the day after the night at the club. No matter how many times Reilly had asked, Anike didn't know what was wrong either. She was, from what Reilly could tell, steadily losing her patience too.

Noah was either blissfully ignorant, or had chosen to ignore his girlfriend's crappy behaviour. He also seemed to have shrugged off whatever had passed between Reilly and him on the mountain yesterday and gone back to being affable. Even friendly.

Reilly wondered whether he knew how mean his girlfriend could be. Whether he knew that she'd driven Asma to her death – and then collected some kind of social cachet from it. Everything she did, everything these people did, was about how it benefited them. Either what they could get out of it or what they could get away with.

And she wouldn't blame the money. *She'd* had money once. *The Chaudhurys* had money. And it hadn't made *them* monsters. It hadn't twisted them up into arrogance and outrageousness, or made them insatiable for things that would never satisfy them.

'OK,' Noah began. 'So, I'll spin the bottle and whoever it lands on will have to choose truth or dare. We'll decide the dare together and the dare must be performed!'

'Do we get to hear the question first or do we have to decide beforehand?' Anike asked.

'Question first,' Noah explained, placing the empty champagne bottle on the floor.

'Isn't this all a bit childish?' Minette complained.

'What are you worried about, Mins? Afraid that the truth will come out?' Noah teased, taking the words right out of Reilly's thoughts.

The first few rounds passed easily enough, Hugo choosing a dare and having to do a tequila shot from Anike's body – licking the salt from her chest and taking the shot glass from her mouth with his. Neither of them were complaining.

Next Anike had to answer the truth: had she really not known that Jacques was such a dick, or had it been a publicity stunt?

'A publicity stunt for who? Him? My dad?'

'All publicity is good publicity!' Noah had parroted.

'Not at all. I hadn't a clue,' Anike confirmed, the 'truth' being far more boring than Noah's imagined reality.

They were each taking it in turns to spin the bottle and when Reilly set the bottle free she could have cursed when it landed on Jacob. She hadn't intended it to at all, but the faint blush on his cheeks suggested that he thought she had.

'Ohhh! I know!' Noah cried. 'Shag, marry, kill. Minette, Reilly and Ani. Which one?'

'Shag?' Jacob repeated, with a raised brow.

'It means have sex with,' Noah said.

'I know what it means,' Jacob shot back. 'I'm not touching that question! And I'd never kill anyone.'

'It's a game, mate,' Noah added.

Instead of replying, Jacob simply held his gaze. 'Dare.'

'Fine. Strip off your clothing and run around in the snow for one whole minute.'

'What?' Jacob demanded as Hugo burst into a fit of giggles. 'I'm not doing that. Hugo only had to do a shot!'

'Thems da rules,' Noah replied nonchalantly.

'I don't—'

'Do it, do it, do it,' Noah chanted, which was soon picked up by the others.

Reilly felt a twist of discomfort. It was extreme in comparison to the other dares, but no one seemed to notice.

'We won't look. Promise!' Hugo claimed.

Downing the rest of his beer, Jacob shot them all a glare and disappeared into the bathroom to change. He came back out, wrapped in a towel, the planes of his body on display – impressive enough to stop the words on Anike and Minette's lips for a moment, which seemed only to annoy Noah more.

'You been hiding your light under a bushel, Arcilla,' Noah bit out.

'No, you just weren't paying attention,' Jacob shot back. Without another glance, he let himself out on to the deck and, barefoot, walked into the snow. Keeping his back to the gang watching from inside, Jacob dropped his towel and started counting down from sixty out loud.

The girls squealed with laughter and the boys howled. Reilly tried really hard to keep control of herself. His body was . . . It was . . . incredible.

Anike shot her a look and they both started to laugh.

'Harvard lacrosse players; made of strong stuff,' Hugo said approvingly as Jacob counted down from ten.

'I'll say,' Anike commented and then asked 'what?' when Hugo shot her an amused look.

Jacob picked up the towel, wrapped it round his waist and slowly made his way back inside, walking straight past them and back in to the bathroom. He emerged a few minutes later fully dressed, but flushed with a healthy glow.

'OK, Wim Hof, we get the idea,' Noah complained, and Jacob just smiled, satisfied he'd won the point.

Noah spun the bottle next and it landed on Reilly. Her pulse jerked as nervous energy dumped into her bloodstream.

'Where did you go to school?' Noah asked.

Reilly bit her lip and cocked her head. Everyone round the circle seemed confused by the question, but the way that Noah held her gaze, that penetrating stare, cut right through her. She shrugged, pretending to be just as confused by the question as everyone else.

'St Michaels, Des Moins, Missouri.'

'You can prove that?' he asked, ignoring the reactions from the group.

'Graduation photos OK for you? I don't have my transcripts with me,' she replied, forcing a laugh. She wasn't lying. She had gone there. *After* leaving the Institute.

'You don't sound like you're from Missouri.'

'I'm not. But you'd need another spin for that question,' Reilly replied, teasing.

He nodded as if to say touché.

Jacob shot her another look but she ignored it as the game continued. But Reilly was unsettled.

Why had Noah asked her that question? She might have expected it from Minette, but not Noah. Why would he care where she went to school . . . ?

The bottle came back round to her and, finally, when she spun it, it landed exactly where she needed it to.

'Minette.'

'*Oui?*' she replied, as if bored.

'Truth or dare?' she asked.

Minette met her eyes for the first time that evening. 'Truth.'

Reilly's pulse thundered in her chest and the roaring of blood in her veins blocked out all rational thought.

'Have you ever hurt anyone before? Like *really* hurt them?'

CHAPTER EIGHTEEN
MINETTE

The breath shot out from Minette's lungs in white streams as she marched down the hill.

How dare she? How fucking *dare* she?

Minette pulled her coat tighter around her, anger burning away some of the alcohol fogging her brain, before she stumbled on a rock beneath the snow.

Merde.

Managing to regain her footing she carried on, stomping towards the spa centre. Minette didn't care about their stupid party any more. She wanted to be warm. She was so tired of being cold.

It's just a question, Minette.

It's just a game.

But that was bullshit. There had been nothing playful about the question that Reilly had asked. Minette hadn't even wanted to play the stupid game anyway.

After asking that ridiculous question, Reilly had just sat there, staring at her, as if she actually expected her to answer.

In the morning she'd speak to Maman. No, not Maman. She hadn't spoken to her mother since she'd seen her at the hotel with James Scarisbrick.

No, Minette would speak to Mr Vandenburg. Make a complaint about Reilly and get her fired. Minette didn't know what Reilly was after, but that girl was after *something*.

Yes. That's what she'd do.

Feeling a hundred times better than she had just moments before, she stamped her way towards the spa, uncaring how the ground beneath her lurched from one side to another.

Minette knew she was drunk. Very drunk. But she was beyond caring.

The lights in the spa were sensor activated and as soon as she turned down the path towards the low-slung wooden building that sprawled luxuriously to one side of the private road, they grew to full brightness and walking became a little easier.

She shivered in anticipation of the warmth of the spa.

It didn't matter that no one had come with her, Minette told herself with a sniff. Noah had crossed too many lines. She was done with him. *So* done.

She wondered what her parents would say. Her father would only want to know that she was OK, but her mother? She was beginning to realise that her mother had been using her daughter's relationship with Noah as an excuse to access her lover.

Minette scoffed, creating a hot stream of vapour in the cold night air as she stalked up the stairs of the spa centre.

She pushed through the doors, immediately engulfed by a wall of warmth so sweet it made her want to cry.

Minette peeled off the jacket she'd thrown on before storming out of the chalet. Her hands went to the zip on her trousers as she toed off her boots and kicked them to the side. Of course she'd not had time to go back to her room and pick up her swimming costume – that would have ruined the effect. So she'd just go in in her underwear. It wasn't as if there was anyone here to see her. She shucked the trousers off and tossed them over her shoulder.

Hopping from one foot to another, she peeled off her socks and stripped off her top, carelessly dropping it just outside the door of the steam room – Minette's *favourite* part of any spa.

The hot damp heat was the only thing that would take the edge off the cold that had haunted her for years.

Ever since . . .

No. Minette jerked her mind back from the painful thought, yanking on the door a little too hard and wincing when it struck her on the shoulder.

'Ouch!' she whined, rubbing her shoulder as she slipped into the steam room. She stood there for a blessed few seconds, letting her head drop back as she welcomed the heat that burned so deliciously after the frigid cold of the night.

Have you ever hurt anyone? Like really hurt them?

Yes. The answer heaved out of Minette on a sob.

But how did Reilly know? What was she after?

Moments from the last ten days filtered through her mind. Reilly in her room. Reilly asking about the Institute. Something niggling in the back of her mind. Something off about her.

The only people who called the Swiss boarding school 'the Institute' had been there.

Where did you go to school, Reilly?

The sound of the door clinking in the frame of the steam room made Minette open her eyes. She turned around and gasped, almost choking on the thick damp air that filled her lungs.

'What are you doing here?' Minette demanded, her pulse thudding sluggishly in her chest.

'The others were worried. I told them I'd make sure you were OK,' Reilly replied, her gaze unreadable through the heavy steam between them.

'And they believed that, did they?' Minette scoffed as Reilly stared back at her from the open doorway.

The blonde chalet girl shrugged. 'I'm not sure it matters any more. It's not like you'll let me keep my job now, will you?'

Minette worked her jaw, before shaking her head. '*Non.*'

Reilly tutted. Minette could finally see a mean glint in Reilly's eye as the steam swirled around her.

'What do you want? What did I do to you?' Minette asked, her words muffled by the thick air.

'Oh, no. Mins. Not *me*. You didn't do anything to *me*,' Reilly said in a strange sing-song voice. 'I mean, you were a bitch, even back then, but I was so far below your attention it didn't matter. No wonder you didn't recognise me or remember my name.'

Back then? School. So she *had* been at the Institute. Minette searched her features trying to remember her. There was something about her eyes. The hair . . . it was wrong, dyed. It should have been . . . *brown*.

Minette looked again and this time she remembered.

Reilly Clarke. RiRi. It wasn't Anike's nickname. Someone else had called her that. Asma. Asma Chaudhury.

Minette felt the blood drain from her face.

'Ahhh. There it is,' Reilly said, as if she'd been waiting for Minette to catch up. 'It's taken you long enough.'

'You were at school with us. You were friends with her,' Minette said, her voice shaking, not able to say Asma's name. She hadn't said it since the summer she took the boat out on the water and died.

'Yes. She was my friend. My *best* friend,' Reilly said. 'And you made her life a living hell!' The accusation had been shouted, Reilly's face distorted by the steam.

'I don't know what you're talking about,' Minette denied, her heart pounding and a cold sweat breaking out beneath the sheen of wetness that already covered her skin. Minette felt impossibly vulnerable, standing there in a near-dizzying heat, in her bra and knickers. Her legs began to shake.

'Yes, you do,' Reilly said. 'You know exactly what I'm talking about.'

'I—'

'The Instagram posts? The bullying. The whispers and the rumours. The exclusion. Making her sit alone. Locking her out of her room at night. Stealing her things and mocking her for being even remotely different to you.'

'I know that things were hard for her—'

'No!' Reilly cried, slamming her palm on the glass door, making Minette jump. 'They weren't hard. They were *impossible*. And it was *your* fault,' she said, banging on the door again.

Fear was making Minette angry. It *wasn't* her fault. OK, so they hadn't exactly been best friends, but so what? Sweat gathered in her hair and dripped down her back. It was getting too hot in here and she needed to get out.

'Look, I'm sorry your friend had a hard time at school, but really? It's not my problem, Reilly. Now let me out,' Minette demanded.

'No,' Reilly said, shaking her head and pulling the door closed between them.

Minette cursed and walked across the hot, wet floor and grabbed the door handle, her hands slipping from the sweat that covered her palms. She pulled on the handle, but Reilly held the other side of it shut.

'Reilly!' Minette yelled, yanking on the door but it wouldn't budge. 'Don't be stupid, Reilly, this is crazy. Let me out.'

'Do you know what tomorrow is, *Mini*?' Reilly asked.

'New Year's Eve? I don't know! Let me out, Reilly.'

'It's Asma's birthday.'

Minette stopped pulling on the door and despite the heat, goosebumps pebbled her skin.

'What do you want?' Minette asked, a strange cold dread filling her veins.

'I want you to admit what you did.'

'I didn't do anything, Reilly. *Merde*. Seriously. This is getting dangerous,' Minette insisted, her head feeling more than a little dizzy thanks to the heat and the alcohol.

'That's not true, though, is it?'

'OK, I was a bitch. I posted some stupid stuff on Instagram and I locked her out of the room a few times, just so that I could spend some alone time with my boyfriend.

So what, Reilly? I'm sorry, OK? Really sorry, now let me out.'

'No.'

'Reilly!'

'No. There was more.'

'I don't know what you're talking about.'

'The video?'

'What video?' Minette asked, even though she knew exactly what Reilly was talking about.

'The fake video of Asma and the teacher.'

'That wasn't me,' Minette insisted, getting even more dizzy now, her legs trembling so badly that she was going to fall down if she didn't get out soon.

'Really? Footage that was clearly taken in your dorm room? Was somehow miraculously taken by someone else bullying her?'

'Reilly, it's getting hard to breathe, I don't think I can be in here much longer,' she pleaded.

'I'm not letting you out until you admit what you did.'

'But I didn't have anything to do with that!' Minette cried, pulling on the door handle to no avail. 'Honestly, Reilly, you have to believe me.'

'Like everyone believed Asma when she denied sleeping with a teacher?'

'That's not my fault, Reilly. I can't control what people think.'

'No? You did so well on the comments that she was tagged in.'

Minette's brain, working sluggishly now, began to realise just how much Reilly had invaded her life.

'Oh my god. It was you,' she released.

'What was me?'

'The messages. To the group chat. The picture of the girl and Noah. It was *you*,' Minette accused, dropping to the floor.

'No,' Reilly said, shaking her head. 'Not me. You must have pissed off someone *else*, Minette.'

'I don't believe you. Please, Reilly, you have to let me out.'

'You haven't admitted it yet,' Reilly spat.

'I can't admit to what I didn't do . . .'

'You *killed* her,' Reilly hissed.

'She died in a boat accident,' Minette shouted.

'No, she didn't. She killed herself. Because of you.'

Shock sliced deep into Minette's chest and she sucked in a lungful of hot steam that scoured her insides and, in that moment, she would have sworn she was in hell.

JACOB

Jacob couldn't make sense of what he was seeing. He'd had to wait a few minutes after Reilly had left the chalet before following her, to try and at least make it look like he wasn't chasing her down. He'd told the others that he had to get back to his folks and he took the not-so-gentle piss taking about it from Noah with grace. He wasn't sure what particular bug had crawled up *his* ass that evening, but Jacob hadn't liked it one bit.

He'd hurried down the track to see where she was going, half tempted to message her and tell her to wait up. But she'd been acting kind of strange, and something, some kind of warning instinct, told him that he'd be better off waiting. Waiting to see what she did.

Only now he wished he hadn't.

'Reilly?' he called across the spa centre.

She was holding the door to prevent Minette – who had collapsed against the glass – from getting out.

'Reilly!' he yelled, finally getting her attention. The look on her face when she saw him nearly stopped him in his tracks.

She looked devastated. Almost unrecognisable from the girl he'd had a snowball fight with a few days ago. Her crystal blue eyes were wild, her hair dishevelled and her cheeks flushed to such a hot red, he imagined he'd feel the burn if he were to cup her jaw right now.

Whatever fight, whatever tension had been gripping every muscle in her body so tight, seemed to leave at once and – strangely mirroring Minette – she collapsed to the floor, her back against the glass.

Minette pushed the door open and crawled out in a plume of steam. Jacob rushed over to her, grabbing a towel from the shelves on the wall, and wrapped it around Minette, who lay panting on the floor.

'Are you OK?' he asked her gently, pushing back the wet strands of hair that had fallen over her face.

'Mmm,' Minette said, eyes closed but head shaking side to side.

'Minette, look at me,' he ordered, needing to make sure she was OK. 'What the hell is going on, Reilly?' he demanded.

But Reilly just stared back at him, tears gathering in her eyes.

OK, he had to get control of the situation. Whatever was going on could be figured out later.

'Minette, I need you to open your eyes,' he said loudly, his hand on her forehead. Shit, her temperature was high. Too high.

He fumbled for his phone in his trousers, but when he raised it to his ear, Minette pushed it out of his hands.

'No.'

'Minette, seriously, you need a doctor.'

Her eyes rolled over to where Reilly sat staring at them.

'*Non. Non*,' she said, shaking her head, and then wincing as if in pain.

Jacob bit back a growl of frustration.

'OK then, we're going to have to cool you down. I'm going to pick you up and take you over to the showers.'

Minette moaned as if she didn't want that either, but he couldn't do *nothing*.

He'd found his mother in enough terrible states to know how to cajole someone into letting him help and he hated that he was having to rely on that knowledge now.

He wrapped Minette tightly in the towel, to cover her and make her feel safe, and then picked her up and took her over to the showers, feeling Reilly's eyes on them the whole time.

But he couldn't worry about her right now.

He turned on the shower and made sure that it wasn't too cold. He didn't want to put her into shock; they'd have to bring down her temperature slowly. He was barely aware of getting soaked himself, his focus was on Minette.

Degree by degree, he brought the temperature of the water down, relieved to see Minette begin to come back to herself.

Eventually she was sitting up against the back of the shower and feeling strong enough to glare furiously at Reilly. Whatever Minette had to say, she was keeping to herself. Either she didn't want to, or wasn't sure about, sharing it in front of him.

'What do you need?' he asked her.

'To get the hell out of here,' Minette hissed, still glaring at Reilly. 'I want my clothes,' she all but growled at Jacob.

'OK,' he said, backing away and raising his hands in the air. The last thing he wanted was to get mixed up in this.

He found a trail of her clothing that she must have dropped on the way to the steam room.

Minette reached up to turn the shower off, fisting the towel around her chest.

'Look, I don't want you to think that I—'

'I couldn't care less, Jacob. Just give me my clothes.'

He passed them to her and she stared up at him.

'Turn around.'

'Of course,' he said, doing as she'd asked. 'Do you want me to call Noah?' he offered.

'No!'

He heard the sound of the wet towel hitting the floor and took a few steps away before looking over to Reilly, who was trying very hard to pretend that she wasn't crying.

What the hell had happened here?

He heard the zip of Minette's jeans and the sound of material getting caught and stretching.

'She's not who you think she is,' Minette called out from behind him. It was clear she was talking about Reilly.

'That's rich coming from you,' Reilly threw back.

'You know what, I don't care!' Jacob yelled. 'Whatever this is? It's got nothing to do with me, so take it somewhere else,' he commanded.

Minette came round from behind him, shoving her feet into her boots, the look on her face thunderous.

'She's a lying scheming bitch who's been keeping secrets from all of us!'

Jacob hated the way that word rang an alarm bell that couldn't be unheard. He'd known Reilly was keeping secrets. Hell, he'd asked her to choose and clearly she had chosen. She'd chosen this, whatever *this* was.

Minette stormed past him, shoving her arm into her ski jacket as she went, and left the spa centre at a run. Leaving him and Reilly with a silence that bounced off every surface in the spa.

'Jacob . . .'

His name on her lips was desperate. It was a plea. But when he turned to face Reilly, he hated what he saw there.

Regret, hurt, anger . . . desperation.

All the things he'd seen over and over and over again in his mother's eyes as she'd torn through the house looking for pills. Or money to buy pills. Or anything she could sell.

He couldn't, wouldn't, tie himself to another person like that. Not again.

He turned away, but what he heard next stopped him in his tracks.

'She killed my best friend.'

Shock short-circuited his brain, so it took him a moment to really appreciate what Reilly had just said.

'What?'

Reilly swallowed and used the back of her hand to wipe away the tears that had fallen down her cheek.

'She killed my best friend,' Reilly repeated, her words a whisper that exploded like a bomb.

Then Jacob remembered what he'd heard the first night they'd arrived in Val D'Amer Doux at the Vandenburg welcome party.

Yes, it was terrible business. Minette was roommates with her that last year. She handled it in her stride, obviously. But it made a pretty big impact on the school. They held a memorial for the girl.

There'd been something else. Something about bullying.

He looked up at Reilly, who was staring at him hard.

'All I wanted to do was make her admit it,' Reilly said helplessly. 'I wanted Minette to understand what she'd done. To know that she was responsible for Asma's death. To *know* and be punished for it. Minette Aillet is a bully. A bully and a coward who ruined my best friend's life, and then got to stand there and pretend like she was devastated. As if she had no idea what had driven Asma to her death.'

'I heard the police declared it an accident,' Jacob said.

'Yeah. They did. Asma's parents wanted to believe that. *Asma* wanted her parents to believe it. *Everyone* wanted it that way. The school. The students. Their very rich families. "It's in everyone's interest." Everyone's apart from Asma's. Everyone apart from anyone else who gets in Minette's way.'

'Reilly—'

'Don't "Reilly" me. I know. I know what you walked in on,' Reilly said, the sob in her voice cutting him deep. 'I know what that looked like. And I know that it was too far. I'm sorry. I'm so sorry. I swear, sometimes I don't even recognise what I'm doing any more.'

Reilly was shaking, but she managed to haul herself up to standing.

'I couldn't help her, Jacob. I wasn't there for her. I wasn't there to stop her from being picked on, from being tormented. And you can shrug it off and say that she should have just ignored it. But I wish you could read the comments on the posts that they all deleted from Instagram. I wish you could see what Asma had to see and read. Hear the things they called her, see the way they treated her. Like she was worth nothing but their contempt and their derision. They spat in her food, locked her out of the gym without her clothes. They locked her out of her room and they made a fake a sex tape of her and a teacher that every single person in the entire damn school saw. So yeah. I *am* sorry. I *did* go too far. But I don't regret it.'

And before Jacob could stop her, she'd raced out of the spa centre, leaving him alone and utterly stunned.

CHAPTER NINETEEN

REILLY

She didn't know how long she'd been running. Reilly's cheeks were numb, the ice-cold wind freezing wet trails on her skin and cutting her lungs every time she tried to take a breath.

She couldn't go back to the chalet. She knew that. She just couldn't.

What had she done?

Oh god. Pressing a shaking hand to her mouth, she pulled to a stop. Reilly wouldn't have hurt her. She *wouldn't* have. Because that would make her like Minette. Like the people who had hounded Asma to her death. And she wasn't anything like that.

Stifling a sob at the memory of the look Jacob had given her, she forced herself to get a hold of herself. She *really* couldn't go back to the chalet. But where could she go? She could probably call Lisolette, but Reilly couldn't face her. Couldn't explain how she'd let Minette slip through her fingers ... How she'd screwed up so badly that she'd never get Minette to admit what she'd done now.

There was only one other person she could turn to.

Can I come over? I need somewhere to stay.

Are you OK?

Gustav's reply was instantaneous.

Not really.

Where are you?

She looked around and realised that she was in the middle of the village.

She dropped a pin on Google maps and sent it to Gustav.

Within minutes he'd come out to find her and pulled her into a hug.

'What have you gotten yourself in to?' he asked, framing her face with his hands.

All she could do was shake her head before she started crying again.

'Was it that boy?' he demanded.

'No,' Reilly quickly replied.

'One of the guests? Did they—'

'No. It's my ... it's my stuff,' Reilly said, her breath shuddering in her lungs.

He raised a sceptical brow at her, but tucked her into his side anyway and walked her back towards his chalet.

Reilly looked around as he walked her into a little block of apartments just off the main road.

'The Vandenburgs put you here?' she asked as he led her into the space.

'God no. This is mine. I have it so I can be in Val D'a D whenever I want. You know I don't like being beholden to the whims of others.'

She surprised herself by smiling a little at his nickname for the town, tugged off her snow boots and walked into an apartment that was by no means anything like as grand as the Vandenburgs', but it was beautiful nonetheless. It too boasted a beautiful view out over the mountains, and a large fireplace.

'I'm going to put the kettle on and make us some tea,' Gustav nodded, his phone beeping with an incoming message.

'I'm sorry if I ruined your night,' Reilly called regretfully over her shoulder.

Gustav waved her away and disappeared behind a door.

Reilly peeled off her jacket and collapsed on to the large L-shaped sofa that made the most of the small but perfectly formed space of the living area, her heart feeling vulnerable and her body feeling weak.

Reilly heard the low rumble of Gustav speaking to someone and felt bad all over again. She pulled her knees up to her chest. She couldn't believe she'd done that to Minette. She'd meant what she'd said to Jacob. She was sorry, and she hated herself for going that far. But she also didn't regret it. She'd wanted, needed, Minette to know that *someone* knew what she'd done. And the fear in Minette's gaze, the moment Reilly had told her that Asma had killed herself . . . Reilly knew that had landed.

And it would have to be enough, because Reilly's time here was done now. There was no way Minette would let her keep her job. And it wouldn't matter what Reilly said, it was Minette's word against hers. Just like it had been for Asma.

Gustav emerged with a cup of tea and pressed it into her hands.

'Drink that,' he ordered. 'I'm going to set up the spare room for you.'

Reilly lost the next half an hour to the view out the window. Gustav had the lights on low in the living area, making it easy to see the snow that had begun to fall and the moon that shone down on flat snowy planes of the mountain. The skiing would be perfect tomorrow, she absently noticed.

The doorbell rang and Reilly turned around with a frown.

'I'll get it,' Gustav called and moments later, he ushered a worried-looking Jacob into the living room.

Reilly's heart bobbed, veering in her chest between sinking and rising just at the sight of him.

'I'm going to head out for the night,' Gustav said, keys in hand.

'But—' Reilly started.

'Don't you worry about me, I've enough to keep me occupied,' Gustav said, sending her a wink. 'Have fun, kids, and don't do anything I wouldn't!'

They both watched Gustav leave before Jacob came further into the living room. 'How did you find me?' Reilly asked, over the beating of her heart.

Jacob shrugged, his cheeks hollow, dark smudges under his eyes. He looked worried. *She'd* done that. She'd put that worry there.

'Are you OK?' he asked, slowly crossing the room to where she'd come to a stand.

'Jacob—'

'Are you OK? That's all I need to know,' he stressed, reaching for her and pulling her gently towards him.

'I don't know,' Reilly said helplessly, fighting off the need to cry again.

'Please don't cry, I don't want you to be sad, Reilly. I want you to know that you can trust me,' he said, his voice a whisper.

She looked into his eyes. Gold swirls in a bitter-chocolate gaze that promised sweetness and sincerity.

'I'd like you to tell me everything, from the beginning. Not now, but when you're ready. When you're able to. I'd like to hear about your friend. About Asma. But all you need to know *now*, is that I get it. I understand – mostly,' he said, with a small smile. 'But I accept it. I accept what you felt you needed to do to get answers. I don't know if it's over—'

'It's over,' Reilly rushed to say. Because it was. There was nothing left for her there. The breath shuddered in her chest with the realisation that what she'd said was the truth. It was over.

'But even if it's not. I want you to know that you can trust me. You're *safe* with me.'

The thing was, Reilly didn't need him to say it. She'd known that already. She knew it from the moment she'd agreed to get into the hot tub with him. She'd known it from the time they'd spent on the slopes and from the way he'd told her that he needed there to be no secrets. And now ... there were no secrets left. There would be no job for her in the morning, not when Minette was through with her.

'Reilly . . .'

The plea in his voice reminded her of the look in his eyes and she was unable to help herself. His chest rose and fell in a staccato motion along with the punch of his breath. Knowing that he was feeling this as much as she was was a blessing and a curse as it soothed as much as it inflamed whatever this was between them. She let her forehead rest slightly against his chest, wondering whether this small act of surrender would just pave the way to a bigger one.

Jacob leaned back, his finger hooking gently under her chin and lifting her face to his. His gaze was intense as it scanned her features, as if he were recording them, as if he *needed* to.

She would never know if it was her or him, or whether they both came together in that moment, but the next thing Reilly knew was the press of his lips against hers. And it was . . . *oh*. Her mouth parted in a little gasp of surprise.

Her hands rose to frame his face, as his arm swept around her, drawing her against him, drawing her deeper into the kiss.

After a delicious eternity, Jacob pulled back, breathing harsh, forehead pressed against hers. And then, as if he couldn't help himself, he stole another quick kiss from her lips.

'I'm sorry,' he said and she wondered what he was sorry for. That was the most magical experience of her life. As if he'd read the confusion in her gaze, he smiled softly and it was the most beautiful thing she'd ever seen.

'I'm not sorry for *that*,' he stressed. 'I just . . . I don't want to . . . if you don't . . .' He stopped, took a breath and seemed to gather himself. 'I don't want you to think that I came here with expectations. I don't want you to think even for a second that—'

'No!' she rushed to assure him. Not for one minute did she think that Jacob would try to coerce her into this, or into anything. 'I don't. Truly, I don't. You're not like that,' she said.

'You haven't known me for long. You don't really know that,' he tried to warn.

No, she hadn't known him for long, but she *did* know that. She couldn't explain why, but she knew, with every fibre of her being, in the same way that she knew she could trust him.

She wanted this more than she'd wanted anything in her entire life. Because she knew that she'd found something precious in him. That he would be important to her. That he already was.

This time she cupped his jaw, drawing his gaze to hers.

'I do know that,' she whispered as she rose to her toes and pressed a delicate kiss against lips that had touched her more deeply than he'd ever know. 'So, please? Will you stay?'

JACOB

'Will you stay?'

Jacob had never wanted to say yes to anything more in his entire life.

Just moments after Reilly had left the spa centre, he'd had this absolutely terrible feeling that he'd let the most special thing that had ever happened to him slip through his fingers.

And he'd not been able to shake the feeling that something awful was going to happen to her, which was why he'd messaged Gustav, thinking that he'd be the person she'd reach out to in that moment.

> Please. I need to find her.

Jacob had been so damn relieved when Gustav had called him back. He'd given the Swiss ski instructor the least information possible while trying to convince him to tell him where Reilly was.

After a few minutes of back and forth, Gustav had sent him his address and, thankfully, answered the door when he'd rung.

And now, standing here, with Reilly in the middle of Gustav's living room, with her crystal blue eyes on his, there was only one possible answer.

'Yes,' he whispered against her mouth as he kissed her.

And it was all he wanted. To kiss her over and over and over again. To chase this impossible high that he got from being anywhere near her.

Jacob pulled Reilly to him, deepening the kiss. He couldn't get enough of her, his hands shaping every curve and dip and hollow he could find, as if memorising her. He cupped her jaw with his hand.

'Are you sure this is OK?' he asked, staring deep into her eyes. 'I need to hear it. Is this what you want?'

'Yes, Jacob. This is what I want,' she said, not questioning his need for reassurance, for confirmation. Not belittling it or dismissing it, but understanding that he needed to know. Understanding that her consent was not only important to him, but respectful of her.

Her gaze was steady, clear of the powerful emotions that had ridden her so hard earlier in the evening. That felt like a lifetime ago. And this? This was something completely separate.

'We can stop at any time. You can change your mind at any time,' he whispered. Of course he hoped that she wouldn't, but his hopes meant nothing. Her comfort meant *everything*.

Reilly looked up at him and smiled. 'OK.'

'I'm serious, Reilly,' he said, worried that her smile was skating over things.

'I know,' Reilly repeated, the smile still there.

'It's just that you're smiling . . .'

Her smile grew even wider and it was beautiful but—

'I'm smiling because I like that you're taking care of me. I'm smiling because I want this, I want *you*. I'm smiling because I've not felt like this before and I'm excited,' she ended on a whisper and a small shrug as if she was embarrassed by her excitement. It was the first moment of vulnerability he'd seen and it was because of how much she liked him and that made him feel . . . everything.

'Tell me what you want, and I'll give it to you,' he whispered.

'I want you to kiss me,' she said, rising to her tiptoes and winding her hands in his hair at the back of his neck, gently pulling him towards her.

He kissed her the moment her lips came close enough for him to claim. Kissing was interspersed with giggles as if neither of them could quite believe that anything could feel this amazing.

When Reilly's hands slipped beneath his jacket and jumper, her cold palms on his abdomen made him shake. Pulling back, he undid the zip and slipped out of his jacket, reaching for the sides of his jumper and pulling it over his head in one swift movement.

He returned to her, kissing her, once, twice, until she chased his lips when they left hers.

'You have me at a disadvantage, Ms Clarke,' Jacob complained. 'And that simply won't do.'

'Won't it?' Reilly asked, with a soft tease in her eyes.

They fell to the floor, where the light from the fire danced shadows over their skin.

Afterwards, with the glow of the fire burning more softly, yet still giving out a beautiful warmth, he stroked his fingers up and down her arm, where she lay with her head on his chest.

'I don't want this to end,' Jacob admitted. 'I don't mean that in a wishful way,' he explained. 'I mean it in a, I really want to keep seeing you way.'

Reilly bit her lip. 'Me too. It's just . . .'

Jacob tried to keep hold of himself, despite the fact that his stomach lurched at her hesitation.

'It's just that I don't know what happens now. I mean, I have college – Berkeley, which starts in the fall, but it all feels a little weird now. I've spent the last few years putting so much effort into . . . Asma, Minette, I . . . I'm not quite sure where that leaves me.'

'I know what you mean. I . . .' Jacob inhaled deeply. He'd not told anyone about his parents' money troubles, but he knew that Reilly would understand. 'I might have to drop out.'

'Why?' Reilly asked, placing a hand on his chest and lifting herself up to look at him.

'One of the only ways we've been able to keep Mom out of trouble is by buying her the drugs she needs.'

He hated it. The words were sticking on his insides and speaking them hurt and took effort. The confession. The revelation of it all. Nothing wanted to come out. But he *needed* it to come out. He wanted it expunged from his system, his body, his soul.

'We thought we'd been managing it, Dad and me, until Dad realised that the account for my college fees was empty. She'd drained it ages ago, hoping to somehow find a way to fill it back up before we noticed.'

'Oh, Jake, I'm so sorry,' she said, her hand on his face, soothing and comforting. He leaned into her palm.

'It's not as bad as it could be. Some people don't have savings. Some people lose their homes, and worse. At least . . .'

He wanted to say that it wasn't that bad yet, but it wasn't far off. It had been a surprisingly shocking realisation how close they were – anyone was – to completely life-changing circumstances.

'It might just be easier for me to drop out.'

'Is that what you want?'

'What I want is for my mom to get help.'

'I'm not sure you can do that for her,' Reilly suggested softly.

He looked into her eyes, hoping that she would understand his next words, to take them in the way he meant them.

'I think that might have been the same for you and Asma,' he whispered, hoping he wasn't pushing her away.

Reilly's eyes glistened with unshed tears, and although her lip wobbled and she bit down on it, she nodded.

'Yeah. I think you might be right,' she said, and he pressed kisses everywhere he could see hurt or sadness, offering comfort and acceptance in its place.

CHAPTER TWENTY
MINETTE

Minette's feet slipped in the dirty snow and she swore out loud, grabbing on to the rail at the side of the road as she struggled to make her way back up to the chalet. She might have been drunk before, but she was stone cold sober now. Sober and shocked and miserable. She stopped to catch the breath that jerked in and out of her lungs from the sharp incline.

When they'd first arrived at Val D'Amer Doux, everything had looked pristine, perfect white inches of snow, almost chocolate-box pretty. But now, ten days later, the snow had mixed with grit and mud and boot prints from tourists and locals alike. Everything that had once been crisp, sharp and brilliant now felt like sludge, as if the shine had worn off, and reality was trying to seep through.

Minette was furious . . . furious and nauseous and . . .

She killed herself. She killed herself because of you.

A sob built in her chest, but it just wouldn't come out. It was as if all the emotions, all the anger, fear, misery, *guilt* had got blocked up inside her, filling her until she was ready to burst, but she just couldn't.

She *wanted* it out of her. She wanted it all gone. But the tears wouldn't come.

She threw her head back and growled into the night, the noise inhuman as it emerged from her throat. Disgust and shame were toxic in her bloodstream.

Minette wasn't stupid, she'd known what people had said after Asma's accident. She'd heard and felt the rumours turn against her. She knew that everyone thought she had been the one to make and share the 'sex tape', even though she hadn't.

'Don't worry about it, love,' Noah had said. 'They'll forget it soon enough.'

And he'd been right. Mostly. Because while things had eventually got back to normal, *she* hadn't forgotten it.

Because she'd seen it. How the tide had turned, quickly and without warning, dragging her under for a few terrifying months. *She'd* been the one that people had whispered about, *she'd* been the one that people had wanted to distance themselves from. Until the school's 'investigation' into the bullying had come back with no evidence to prove one way or another that Asma had been bullied.

She killed herself because of you.

Reilly was lying. She had to be. Asma had died in a terrible accident, that was all. The police had said as such. Reilly was lying, she had to be.

Only, it hadn't sounded like a lie. It had sounded horribly like the truth.

The cry of a bird somewhere in the forest cut in to Minette's thoughts, dragging her attention away from the road and into the darkness of the mountain. She was too far from the village below to hear the sounds of music and karaoke from some of the more crowded bars. No, up here, things were quiet. So very quiet.

A crunch from deeper in the tree-line and the snap of a twig. The flutter of wings as a bird took off – all noises that were recognisable. So why did her heart start to pound? Why did the hairs on the back of her arms begin to stand?

She frowned, catching sight of something yellow and was convinced that someone was watching her. There, the flash of yellow again. A pair of eyes.

Just some dumb fox, she dismissed and looked back to the string of lights lining the edge of slopes that looked like silvery blue strips poured down the side of the mountain.

Minette felt a shove to her back and screamed. A hand clamped down over her mouth and her heart catapulted forward in her chest, her legs kicking out behind her.

'Oh, Mins, you'll have to stop that. You're turning me on,' Noah growled into her ear.

'*Merde*, Noah,' Minette cursed, as relief replaced fear, even though her pulse still raged out of control. He'd scared the crap out of her.

She turned and glared at him.

'Oh my god, did you think I was actually serious?' Noah joked, only the humour didn't quite reach his eyes.

'No, but you don't have to be a dick about it,' she replied, trying to hide her feelings – feelings that he'd take advantage of.

'Where did you go?' Noah demanded, rocking back on his heels.

Minette bit her lip. She knew she should tell him about Reilly ... but something told her that it would be a mistake. That it would make things worse.

'I just wanted to go for a walk.'

'Yeah? So why's your hair wet?' Noah asked.

Minette blinked, reaching up to touch a damp tendril of hair. She'd been so angry, so furious, that she hadn't even realised.

'What affects you affects me, Mins, and I can't help if you won't let me,' he pressed in a sing-song voice that grated on her last nerves.

'I had a fight with Reilly,' she bit out.

'Now, that I would have paid to see,' Noah replied with wide eyes and a grin.

'It's not like that, Noah. It's ... It's between me and Reilly,' she insisted.

'*Uh ugh*,' he exclaimed like a buzzer. 'Try again.'

She stopped struggling and stood her ground. 'It's nothing. So just go away.'

He leaned into her face, locking his gaze with hers. She could smell the alcohol on his breath and see the brown flecks in his grey eyes, reminding her of the sludgy snow.

'I'm not even going to count to five, Mins. You know I'll make good on it,' Noah warned.

She went to turn away, but his other hand came to grip her chin, hard, to hold her in place. She tried to yank out of his hold but it didn't help. Anger and fear were hot and heavy in her chest. Minette swallowed, wondering why she was protecting Reilly anyway? Why not just let them at each other and leave her the hell out of it?

'Mins—'

'She went to the Institute. She was in our year. She left but she was Asma's best friend.'

Noah blinked in shock. It was almost satisfying to see. It was the first time she'd ever really seen him appear anything other than supremely and arrogantly in control.

'What is she doing here?' Noah asked, his voice perilously tight.

Minette huffed out an incredulous breath. 'What do you think she's doing here? It's not a damn coincidence, Noah.'

'What does she want?' he demanded, pinching her chin tighter.

'I don't know, Noah. She wants to tell the world that Asma's death wasn't an accident. At least that was what she said, before her boyfriend showed up.'

'Boyfriend?'

'Jacob. Her and Jacob. I'm pretty sure they're a thing.'

Noah's gaze pressed her to continue.

'I don't know,' Minette said, shrugging. 'She wanted me to admit what I did.'

'Which was?' he demanded.

'Bullying? She wanted me to tell her that I made the sex tape.'

'Jesus, that sex tape,' Noah said, releasing her chin and fisting his hands. 'Did she have any proof?'

'Proof of what, Noah?'

'That the sex tape was fake!' Noah roared.

'I don't know,' Minette replied, confused by his reaction. 'Does it matter?'

'Of course it matters, Minette. I can't afford to be involved in any scandals right now. Not with the internship. It's too public.'

Minette's mind was spinning. Noah was too angry about it. Too worried...

'Wait, that was *you*?' Minette asked, incredulous. '*You* did that?' she demanded.

'Well, I couldn't have done it without *you*, Mins.'

Noah's reply filled her with confused horror.

'What do you mean?'

'Where do you think I got the footage from?' he asked as if she was stupid.

'Noah—'

'What? *You* took a video of her.'

Shock hit hard as Reilly's words echoed in her mind.

Footage that was clearly taken in your dorm room? Was somehow miraculously taken by someone else bullying her?

'But that was just for a prank, some silly reel about her clothes. And I decided not to use it...' Minette said, realising that Noah had not only accessed her phone, but had used the footage for something so much worse than she'd originally intended.

Noah glared at her. 'So?'

'*I'm* the one that got blamed for it, Noah!' she yelled. '*I'm* the one that people gossiped about and treated like... like...'

'Like Asma?' he pointed out cruelly and she felt as if she'd been slapped. 'Do you still have that footage, Minette?'

'What?' she asked, the thoughts in her mind pouring through her fingers like sand.

'Do you still have that footage,' Noah demanded, peering into her face.

'I don't . . . I don't know, why?' she asked.

'Because if they can find that footage then they can link it back to us. To *you*,' he stressed, and when she realised what he was saying, she thought she might actually be sick.

'You delete it and I'll handle the rest,' he said, sucking in a breath through his teeth, his eyes going so cold she shivered.

'The rest? What are you going to do?' Minette called out as he turned away from her and back towards the path that would take him to his chalet.

'You'll find out soon enough,' he warned and disappeared into the night, leaving Minette alone in the dark. More scared than she had been before.

JACOB

Jacob walked back from the village, trying really hard to keep the smile from his face. He was just . . . He shook his head as if that might help put his thoughts together better.

Amazing. Incredible. Sad. Shocking. Hard. Easy. Touching. Meaningful.

And then he rolled his eyes at himself for waxing lyrical about a girl. And then smiled again because that was actually OK, really.

He hadn't expected it. What they'd shared. It had hit him like lightning. Oh, sure, Jacob liked her. Really, really liked her. As in *don't-look-at-it-too-hard-or-you'll-get-scared* kind of like.

Flashes of the time they'd spent together burst into his mind like fireworks. Her fingers on the button of his shirt, her shoulder as he smoothed aside the strap of her vest, a kiss, a gasp.

He bit his lip and when his foot slipped on a patch of ice, his teeth drew blood. Shoving his arms out to balance his weight and keep himself upright, he couldn't tell whether the jerk in his heartbeat was because of Reilly or his near fall.

Jacob hadn't wanted to leave her alone at Gustav's. He hadn't wanted to sneak out while it was still dark. He'd wanted to stay with her, find out more about her. What she liked, what she wanted, what they might possibly have in the future.

He rounded the corner to the little cul-de-sac that his chalet was in, and frowned when he saw the light on in the living area. His stomach dropped and he instantly worried, before it turned to irritation. Before it turned to frustration. He swept a hand around the back of his neck, biting back a curse, and braced himself for what he would find when he opened the door.

He kicked the snow off his boots and typed in the key code for the door, weary already. A tiredness that had nothing to do with lack of sleep and everything to do with the last three years.

He paused on the threshold, not knowing what he'd find. Would his mother be high? Would she be passed out on the sofa? Would she have been sick, smashed something, broken something? What would he have to clear up this time?

He didn't want this. Didn't want this for her, not for his father or himself, he realised with the kind of finality that felt like the end of something. That felt like a line drawn in the sand.

Jacob pushed open the chalet door and followed the thin strip of light down the hallway and out into the open living area.

His gaze took everything in instantly. The standing lamp by the sofa was on, the soft yellow glow illuminating what could have been a peaceful scene. A mother asleep on the sofa waiting for her son to come up.

Only she wasn't asleep. And she hadn't been waiting for him.

Shit.

'Dad!' he yelled, as loudly as possible as he rushed over to his mother.

There was sick on the cushion and her breathing was shallow.

Jacob checked her airway, dimly registering that this was the second time in the same night that he'd been genuinely concerned about the consciousness of a woman in front of him.

'Dad!' he yelled again, as he made sure that his mother wasn't choking on anything.

He shook her gently.

'Mom, can you open your eyes for me? Mom, come on,' he cajoled. 'I need you to wake up,' he pressed gently, shoving aside his emotions.

He couldn't panic. He couldn't feel. It was as if something in him was being severed. Cut off. Cauterised. He dimly recognised that it wasn't a good thing, either.

Jacob gently thumbed back her eyelids, her pupils reacting at least to the light in the room, and her shoulders shifted on the sofa.

He fisted his hand and pressed his knuckles into her sternum, rubbing the surprisingly sensitive spot on the human body hard in order to bring her back round.

Her body responded, trying to shake him off, and the groggy groan was enough to make him do it all over again. She was in that grey area now, and he didn't want her slipping back.

Marcus came into the living room in T-shirt and boxers, staring at the scene with sleep-filled eyes, until they cleared with shock and burst into horror.

'Ambulance?' he asked as Jacob's father came into the room, pushing past Marcus and coming to kneel beside Jacob and the sofa.

'Christ, I'm sorry, I fell asleep,' his father said. 'Is she OK?'

'I think so,' Jacob said as his mother's eyes opened and closed again, her face scrunched in annoyance and anger.

'Get off me,' she slurred, trying to bat Jacob's hands away.

He clenched his jaw and released her.

Now that she was regaining consciousness, everything else finally rushed in and he realised that his heart was pounding furiously in his veins. And he was angry. Really, really angry. But beneath all that? He'd been really, really scared.

Scared that this time, *this* time, she might have been too far gone to come back. That this time she might have died.

His father looked up at him and his expression fell. 'Son—'

'No,' Jacob said, holding up a hand to ward off whatever damn excuse he was going to make this time.

'She told me she didn't have anything left,' his father said miserably.

'And since when can you believe a word that comes out of her mouth? Hey?' Jacob demanded.

'I'm going to put the kettle on,' Marcus said and backed away from the living area.

Jacob collapsed into a chair on the other side of the room.

He watched his father remove the vomit-covered cushion from the sofa and replace it with a clean one, taking the long throw from the back of the sofa and covering his wife with it, tucking her in as if she were a sick child.

'I'm done,' Jacob announced, his mother's face turning to his, her eyes pleading.

'Son—' Sandro said, clearly trying to stop him before he went too far, but Jacob couldn't stop.

'No. It's not OK. What she is,' he said of his mother, 'and what she's doing, it's not OK, Dad. We can't tiptoe around it any more. We're enabling her. She's not well.' He turned back to face his mother.

'You're not well and you need help. And it's help that we can't give you.'

His mother's face was ashen, her eyes barely able to focus on him, let alone what he was saying.

'You're drowning, Mom. You're drowning beneath the weight of your addiction. You're not *living*. You're dying, Mom,' he said, trying really hard to supress the sob of hurt and anguish that completely took him by surprise. 'And I don't want to die with you,' he said, the words scratching and kicking their way out from the depths of his soul.

She looked utterly stunned as she started up at him, and then he saw it happen. And he hated her for it. He saw her switch off.

'Don't. Don't do that,' he begged, but she pulled out of his hold and turned her back on him. 'You need to do something. You need help. You need to do it properly. Not just pretend to. Because I won't let you pretend any more. I won't let *us* pretend any more.'

Breath shuddering in his lungs, he turned to his father, the understanding in his father's gaze doing nothing to soothe the devastating betrayal he felt from his mother's rejection.

'She'll fight it, Jake. She's a fighter. She'll be OK.'

'You've been saying that for three years,' Jacob accused quietly. He shook his head. 'Get her help. Don't get her help. Do whatever you have to do. But I'm getting my stuff and I'm going to stay with Hugo. And if not there, then the hotel, or somewhere else,' he said, thinking of the room he'd left Reilly in just a short while ago. 'But I won't stay here,' he said.

'You don't need to do that, Son,' his father said. 'It's New Year's Eve tomorrow. Why don't you stay until then? Just . . . give us some time?'

'We've had three years, Dad. And it's not changed a single thing. So yes. I really do need to go,' Jacob replied and left his father standing in the living space with the kind of silence they had both come to hate.

CHAPTER TWENTY-ONE

JACOB

Jacob laughed at something Hugo said but his friend didn't notice that his heart wasn't in it. He checked his watch. 4.30 p.m. on New Year's Eve and all he could think about was Reilly.

He'd messaged her after leaving the chalet to ask if Gustav would mind if he also took refuge in his apartment, only to learn that Gustav had apparently been whisked off to Paris by the billionaire uncle of one of his ski students for New Year's Eve and wouldn't be back until the 2 January.

He'd apparently told Reilly to treat the place like hers and they were damn thankful for it. Neither of them wanted to involve Hugo and with little money, and almost every room in Val D'Amer Doux booked out for New Year's Eve, they'd have been in trouble without Gustav's kind offer.

But Jacob was worried about Reilly. She had gone back to the girls' chalet to get her things. She didn't really care that much about the job, in part because she'd only needed it for access to Minette. So, she wasn't too devasted by the thought of losing it. But still, she couldn't exactly leave her stuff – including her passport – behind. So they'd left Gustav's apartment at the same time, Jacob heading to the bar to meet Hugo and Anike, and Reilly heading back to the chalet.

Was she in danger?

It was alarming how easily he thought these things. He'd only just met her, and now he'd push everyone off a mountain if she needed him to.

Anike's giggle brought him out of his thoughts. Hugo and Anike were about as loved up as he wanted to be with Reilly. Hugo had his arm slung around Anike's shoulders and they were kissing in such a way that would probably get them into trouble if it wasn't for the fact that Hugo's last name was Vandenburg.

Jacob averted his eyes so that he wasn't completely nauseated by the PDA.

His phone vibrated and he checked it immediately in case it was Reilly.

> Happy New Year, Son.
> I hope you're out celebrating and being safe.
> We love you. Xx

Jacob swallowed. It had been terrifying to confront his parents like that. Terrifying in case his mother did something, or if something happened to her. But he couldn't be responsible for that. He couldn't be responsible for *her*.

He could lie and say he didn't know what it was about Reilly Clarke that made him see that properly for the first time, but he didn't want to. Reilly made him want something more for himself. She made him want to be everything for her.

Jacob typed his reply.

Love you too. Xx

And he meant it. He *did* love his parents, but he couldn't keep secrets for them anymore. And he couldn't, *wouldn't*, be the one to pick up the pieces for them.

'Everything OK?'

He looked up to find Hugo staring at him and no sign of Anike.

'Bathroom,' Hugo explained.

'Dude, I wasn't sure you were ever going to come up for air,' Jacob teased.

Hugo hid behind a hand, a blush of both embarrassment and pure joy on his features, his blue eyes sparkling in a way that Jacob hadn't seen before.

'She's amazing,' he whispered across the table, making Jacob both laugh and feel just a little bit envious. He wanted to be able to do the same, to tell Hugo about Reilly, but he was still the boss's son. Even if Reilly was about leave the Vandenburg's employment.

Hugo's hands cupped the back of his neck and he pressed his forehead to the table and groaned. 'I'm so screwed.'

Jacob was genuinely pleased for Hugo. There was a silly kind of giddy excitement about him that was stupidly good to see. It was so easy to get bogged down by the hardness, the grief and the guilt of life. But this? Seeing Hugo happy? Priceless.

'So, are you, like, girlfriend and boyfriend now?' Jacob asked in a girly pop way.

Hugo laughed and chucked a peanut at him from across the table. Jacob dodged it, but got smacked in the forehead by a second volley.

'Christ, Vandenburg, your aim is too good,' Jacob complained.

'Still got it!' Hugo laughed, punching the air in victory.

Anike came back to the table looking at her phone.

'Is everything OK?' Hugo asked, reaching out to rub her hip, their easy affection enviable.

'I think so. It's just that Minette isn't replying to my messages,' Anike said, sounding concerned.

'Did something happen? I've never seen her like that before,' Hugo asked.

'Last night?' Jacob asked.

'Yeah,' Hugo nodded.

'I don't know,' Anike said, sliding on to the bench seat beside Hugo. 'This morning, she was being very—'

Anike's words cut off midsentence as she looked across the bar in horror.

'Oh my god, shit, shit, shit!'

Jacob turned around, craning his neck to see what had made Anike react like that, but couldn't catch sight of much over the small groups of people. Until he spotted Karel, Anike's bodyguard, coming towards them, grim faced, beside a very tall, broad man who bore a striking resemblance to Anike. Just looking at the man made Jacob feel like he was in trouble.

'Hugo, whatever you do, just don't talk back,' she warned. 'And I'm sorry. In advance.'

'Sorry for what?' Hugo asked not having seen what Jacob had seen.

'Anike Dossongui,' the man announced as he approached the table, other patrons making way for him like the parting of the sea.

'Papa,' Anike greeted, not making eye contact and very much looking like a naughty schoolgirl caught with her hand in the cookie jar.

Jacob didn't have a hope in hell of keeping up with the furious French that passed between father and daughter. But when he glanced at Hugo, wincing guiltily, he could hazard a guess that it wasn't good. Jacob was struggling to contain his laughter when he felt a very steely glare from Karel, which had Jacob clearing his throat and sitting straighter in his chair.

His phone vibrated on the table and he checked the screen. Just another NYE message from a friend. After the initial buzz of interest from the arrival of Anike's impressive father, most of the other customers went back to their business while the intense, angry-sounding back-and-forth continued.

Jacob's phone buzzed again with another message, *not* from Reilly.

Anike's father placed a single, pointed finger firmly down on the table next to his phone.

'Are you going to answer that?' he demanded of Jacob.

'No, sir.'

'Silence it or turn it off,' he commanded.

'No, sir,' he said apologetically and Hugo looked like he was going to bug out. 'I'm waiting for a very important message, I'm sorry. I will put it away, though,' he conceded. Anike's father eyed him suspiciously and eventually returned his attention to the table.

'You are Hugo Vandenburg?'

'Yes, sir,' Hugo replied, looking half terrified.

'OK. Let's go. We're to meet with your father,' he announced.

Hugo bit back a groan, and Anike punched his thigh lightly under the table.

'Yes, sir,' Hugo said, before shooting a panicked look across the table at Jacob.

Jacob mouthed 'good luck', before losing the fight against the laughter locked in his chest. Hugo glared at him but shot a smile at Anike's father, though he seemed impervious to it. But that didn't stop Hugo from helping Anike into her coat and defiantly taking her hand in his.

'I'll message when we're done,' Hugo said to Jacob as he passed.

'I doubt you'll be done before midnight, *if* you survive,' Jacob teased. 'But no worries. This is important.'

'Yeah, it is. Thanks, bro,' Hugo said, slapping Jacob on the shoulder.

Jacob grinned and reached for the beer he'd barely drunk half of, as Hugo, Anike, Karel and N'Guessan Dossongui – one of the world's richest men – made their way out of the small Swiss pub.

Jacob's phone vibrated in his pocket and he pulled it out, checking the screen to see a massage from the the last person he expected to hear from. Noah Scarisbrick.

Jacob's heart thudded painfully in his chest. Once. Twice. As if he knew something was wrong before he even read the message.

> Something's happened to Reilly.
> She's hurt. You need to come to
> the meet point at the top of the main ski lift.

What?

Jacob pressed the call button against Noah's name, but the call didn't even go through. He looked around and realised that the entire world was trying to call or message their friends and families with new year's wishes right now.

You need to come now.

Jacob frowned and typed furiously on his phone.

What is she doing up there?

Her and Mins went up there to talk.

Jacob's mind scattered as he grabbed his things. He knew that Reilly had wanted to talk to Minette. To try one last time. Had Minette somehow convinced her to go out on to the slopes alone with her on New Year's Eve? And if so, how did Noah know about it?

He tried to call Reilly as he left the bar at a run, but just like before it didn't even connect.

Shit. Hurry. She's not doing so good.

REILLY

Reilly folded up the last of her jumpers and put it into her suitcase. She'd sneaked into the chalet earlier, slipping in through the boot-room entrance. She was pretty sure that the girls would have noticed that their usual breakfast feast hadn't been served. Or their rooms hadn't been tidied, and the mess from the party hadn't magically disappeared.

She'd called Lisolette to tell her everything that had happened to prepare her for any negative fall-out from being the person to recommend Reilly for the job that she'd just royally messed up. Reilly should never have worried that the Chaudhurys' ex-housekeeper would be anything but supportive and understanding. Lisolette had always known that Reilly's plan could impact her and had been willing to take the hit. Lisolette's one request had been for Reilly to visit before she left – a request that Reilly was more than happy to fulfil.

But Reilly still felt bad. Bad for letting the Vandenburgs down. Bad that she'd left Anike without a goodbye or an explanation. Reilly had really liked her. Anike was everything she appeared to be – lovely, bubbly and fun, with a little bit of sass thrown into the mix to make things interesting. And Hugo genuinely seemed like a decent guy. They'd be nice to have as friends . . . which was probably unlikely now.

She couldn't even begin to imagine what story Minette would tell about what had happened. With no one to contradict her, Minette could say anything she wanted.

But Jacob knew the truth. He'd seen it, he'd stayed. They'd . . .

Reilly felt the heat rise to her cheeks from the memories of what they'd shared last night. She hadn't expected to meet someone who would make her laugh, who would matter so much to her. She never thought that she'd be able to share the hurt and anger over what happened to Asma and to not have that destroy whatever was in its path. But he'd stood there and listened. He'd held her as she'd told him everything and he hadn't run away. He hadn't ignored her or laughed at her.

Her bruised and battered heart beat a few times experimentally – as if to ask, *is it safe? To love him, is it safe?*

I think so, she replied to herself.

And then she smiled at her foolishness.

Reilly didn't really have the luxury of wasting time. She had to get her stuff and leave. With Jacob's help, she'd composed an email to Savannah earlier citing a family emergency and would send it later.

She packed away the toiletries she'd retrieved from the little en suite bathroom. When she'd got Gustav's message about going away and offering up his apartment, his only request had been to stay in touch whatever happened and she'd wondered how she'd got so lucky.

She'd lost so much to her anger and grief over Asma. Her friends, two years of her life. She'd delayed her university education for this.

I didn't ask you to do that.

I know you didn't. But I didn't have a choice. I had to.

Silence met her imaginary conversation with the girl who'd been like a sister to her.

I think you'd like him, Reilly hedged, leaning her head back, trying to stop the tears escaping.

Of course I'd like him, you idiot. He likes you.

And Reilly's heart crumpled.

I'm sorry I couldn't show the world what happened to you.

And this time she let the tears fall, releasing all the emotions she'd locked down during the months of planning, the school investigation, the police search for Asma and then ruling Asma's death an accident. The grief, the loss, the hurt and the anger, Reilly let it all go.

Eventually she collected herself and packed away the last of the things, looking around her little room to make sure she'd not left anything behind. She'd almost come to like it. Would she come back to Val D'Amer Doux, after this? Not for a while, Reilly thought. But maybe she'd come back here eventually . . . *with Jacob.*

Was that crazy? They'd spent one night together, but he had an entire life in Boston. Would she be able to fit into his life? With his friends like Hugo? With his lacrosse games?

She heard the door to the chalet slam and checked her watch. It was 4.30 p.m. It was probably the girls, expecting high tea. Reilly pulled her suitcase to the doorway and removed her coat from where it hung on the back of the door, placing it on top of the case and braced herself.

She walked out into the living area and came face to face with Minette.

Minette looked terrible. The dark smudges under her eyes were enough to let Reilly know that at least she'd had a sleepless night. But it was as if the fight had gone out of her as much as it had gone out of Reilly.

'I don't want to fight, Minette. I don't want to go over it again. I just want to leave.'

Minette just stared at her for a moment, before looking down at the floor, her hands twisting in front of her.

'I . . .' She shook her head as the words trailed off, the messy strands of a usually sleek bob brushing her shoulders. 'I'm sorry.'

Reilly tensed, Anger flashed over her burning away just as quickly, leaving her almost weak from an exertion that hadn't really happened.

'I didn't realise how bad things had got until it was too late,' Minette tried to explain.

'Really? You didn't read the comments under your posts? The hatred? You didn't wonder what the other school kids would do after that *tape*?' Reilly demanded. She hadn't wanted to get drawn into this again.

'I didn't make the video tape,' Minette whispered. 'I couldn't have done that.'

Reilly laughed. 'I don't believe you.'

Minette paled. 'I *didn't*.'

Reilly stared at her, trying to work out what she stood to gain from this. *Was* she telling the truth?

'If it wasn't you, then who was it?' Reilly asked.

Minette shivered. It was a ripple across her whole body. But she didn't open her mouth to speak.

'Why are you even telling me this?' Reilly demanded. 'Trying to clear your conscience?'

'No, I'm telling you this because . . . Because I think you might be in trouble,' Minette said, the words rushing out of her mouth on a single, helpless breath.

Reilly laughed. 'From who? *You?*'

Reilly didn't have time for this. She wanted out of this entire drama. She wanted to go back to Gustav's little apartment and wait for Jacob so she could put this behind her. All of it.

'No, not me . . .' Minette said quietly. 'Noah.'

'Noah?' Reilly asked.

Minette looked torn, and . . . *scared*, Reilly realised.

'Look, Noah isn't . . . He's not as easy going as he seems.'

'I mean, I hate to break it to you, but I kind of guessed that, Minette,' Reilly replied, pushing past her.

But Minette's hand snuck out and grasped her arm.

'You don't understand. He's . . .' Minette swallowed. '*He's* the one that made the tape, Reilly. He's the one that started this whole thing.'

'What? I . . . Wait, you *knew* that he was the one who did that, and you stayed with him?'

'No, I didn't know. Not until last night,' she explained.

'You spoke to him last night?' Reilly asked, trying to wrap her head around things.

'Yes, that's why I wanted to warn you. He knows who you are.'

'Because you told him?'

'Yes! Reilly, you tried to kill me!' Minette yelled.

'I didn't try to kill you, I just wanted you to tell the truth!' Reilly yelled back.

'By trapping me in a steam room?' Minette demanded.

Reilly grit her teeth together. 'I didn't . . . I wasn't . . .'

'Whatever, I don't care. I just wanted you to know. Noah, he's . . . just be careful, OK?'

A message alert chimed on Reilly's phone but she ignored it.

'And for what it's worth,' Minette said. 'I really am sorry about Asma. I didn't . . . I'm just sorry. Truly.'

Reilly wanted to believe her. So badly. She wanted to put this whole sorry thing behind her once and for all.

Her phone buzzed again and, frustrated with the interruptions, she went to swipe away the alerts. That's when she saw the first message.

Reilly's heart began to pound.

> Reilly, Reilly, Reilly.
> You did a bad thing. You had a secret.
> But I know what it is.

'What is it?' Minette asked.

Reilly unlocked her screen and scanned the messages, before holding up the phone so that Minette could see.

Minette came closer and was reading the messages when the next one came through.

> Does Jacob know?
> Know who you really are?
> I doubt he would have rushed up
> here to your rescue if he did.

Heart pounding, Reilly watched as a picture dropped into the conversation. It was a screen grab of a message exchange that didn't take long for Reilly to unravel. Noah had lured Jacob to the slopes by telling him that she'd been hurt.

'*Merde*,' Minette said.

> Be at the top of the red slope by
> the main ski lift in twenty minutes
> and don't be late.

CHAPTER TWENTY-TWO

MINETTE

Minette snow ploughed to a stop, panicking at the sight of so many people gathered on the slopes in the darkness, until she remembered that they were there for the New Year's Eve Night Ski.

Was that why Noah had chosen to meet there? Near witnesses?

Reilly pulled up beside her, her eyes scanning the faces of the people by the ski lift.

'The red run is over there,' she told Minette, still scanning the crowds.

Heart racing, Minette couldn't see either Noah or Jacob. There were so many people, decked out in ski gear and hats and sunglasses. Although it was dark outside, the floodlights that illuminated the slopes and the wind coming down the mountain required them.

Noah could be anywhere.

Anike had sent some message about her father and Hugo, but Minette had barely glanced at it as she'd hurried into the only ski suit in her wardrobe. She'd found everything she needed in the boot room, skis almost brand new and boots that were too tight, but she didn't have time to worry about that.

In silence, Reilly had done the same, thrusting her feet into her boots and skis.

Reilly had no idea what she was up against.
And you do?

In the last twenty-four hours Minette felt as if the world had turned on its head and everything she thought she knew, everything she'd thought she *had*, was slipping through her fingers.

Reilly, Noah, Asma, her.

The four of them were locked in some horrible version of the present, defined by a past she'd never really known. The shock of realising that Asma had taken her own life fisted her stomach and filled her chest with sand.

Just the thought that she'd had something to do with that was so awful, Minette was convinced she'd be sick. She shoved the urge to cry aside. She didn't have time for guilt or self-recrimination. She had to make this right. *Had* to. Whatever Noah planned to do, she had to stop him. It was the only way she could even hope to make up for her mistakes,

Reilly turned to her.

'Will you be able to keep up?' she asked briskly.

'Yes,' Minette replied, trying to sweep aside the critical sting.

'I haven't seen you ski. Can you?'

'Yes.'

'Runs?' Reilly demanded, clearly expecting a detailed answer.

'Blues, reds – fine. Blacks are a little tricker, but I'll manage.'

'He's got Jacob. I'm not stopping for you,' she warned.

'I'm ready,' Minette said, not needing to argue or defend herself. She'd be able to keep up.

Minette scanned the crowds once more; most were focused on either the busy on-piste or the floodlit slope leading down the side of the mountain towards the heart of the village.

Was Noah watching them?

What had he done to Jacob?

What would he do to *them*?

Whatever he had to, Minette realised. She'd seen how desperate he could be. Knew how dangerous his father could be when he wanted something. The cold, dead-eyed way that he'd looked at her in her mother's suite at the hotel had turned her stomach, but the way he'd struck Noah across the face . . . Just how much of his father did Noah have in him?

'Do you have a plan?' Minette asked Reilly.

Reilly tucked her hair up into a ponytail.

'Stop him.'

'That's it?' Minette asked.

'That's it,' Reilly replied, and without another word, hauled herself forward with the poles, leaving Minette scrambling to follow, leaving crowds behind them. It wasn't entirely unusual for skiers to head off on their own and make a different way down the mountain, so it was unlikely that anyone would notice them splintering off from the group gathered for the night ski.

Minette shifted her weight from ski to ski, her quads already screaming, but more from protest rather than fatigue. At this point, at least. The cold air bit into her cheeks, but the sweat that had come, first from fear and now from exertion, slid across her skin uncomfortably beneath the layers that were there to keep her warm in the minus temperatures.

As they drew further and further away from the revellers, the silent swish of skis on snow filled her ears and for the first time, to Minette's ears it sounded like a knife scraping against meat.

Reilly seemed to know where she was going, leading them along a path bordered by the jagged shapes of trees in the night. Moonbeams punched through gaps in the branches, casting shards of light across the track that looked as if it had been barely used.

They were alone, out here, far from anyone else. Far from help . . .

And for the first time since she'd seen the messages on Reilly's phone, Minette wondered if maybe she'd got it all wrong.

The powerful single thud in her chest nearly caused her to fall.

What if Reilly had lured her out here, not to confront Noah, but instead to trap *her*? To punish *her*? Like she'd failed to do in the steam room?

Merde. Had she been that stupid?

Had their whole interaction been some kind of set-up to get her out here alone?

The thought made Minette slow to a stop.

Further up ahead, Reilly realised and swept into a sharp parallel stop.

'What are you doing?' Reilly hissed, her voice sounding like a scream in the silence.

'That's a really good question. What *am* I doing here, Reilly? Why did you ask me to come?'

Minette's breath punched out into the night in bursts of smoke, vapours dissolving in the wind. Dread built in her gut, making her shake, twisting her thoughts until she was so confused, she didn't know what was going on.

'What?' Reilly demanded. 'Minette, we don't have time for—'

'What am I doing here!' Minette yelled at her.

Oh god, she'd lost her mind coming out here on her own with the friend of a girl who had killed herself because of her. Noah probably wasn't even here. He was probably back down in the village, getting drunk with Hugo. And Minette was here with a girl she barely knew, who had already tried to hurt her once, only just last night.

A twig crunched to her left and Minette started.

'What do you mean?' Reilly asked, as if confused.

Was she really confused? Or was she just that good an actress.

'Is this . . . some part of your revenge? Against *me*?' Minette asked, her voice breaking with fear.

'I don't have time for this,' Reilly said, pulling out her phone and swiping at her screen, before putting it back in her pocket. 'You can come or you can stay here or you can turn around and go back,' she said between her own panted breaths. 'I really don't care. I'm going after Jacob.'

Don't leave me out here!

It was what Asma had begged her when Minette had locked the door to their dorm room. The sounds of Asma's fists against it, louder than the punch of Minette's heartbeat in her ears.

Don't leave me out here.
Please, Minette.

And now Minette was saying exactly the same words.

Nausea, acrid and bitter, stuck in her throat.

Oh god, what had she done?

She looked up to find Reilly, turning back around and using the poles to haul herself forward.

'Wait!' Minette called.

But Reilly didn't answer.

A bird cried out in the night, and Minette felt eyes on the back of her head. To her left, she could have sworn that she saw a fox again, eyes mean, hungry and *ready*.

Minette had to choose. She couldn't stay here. She couldn't do nothing. She either had to trust Reilly and follow her, or head back down the mountain alone in the dark.

Minette looked up to see that Reilly was getting further and further away.

Merde.

Before she could change her mind, Minette plunged her poles into the icy snow and hauled herself forward. Reilly glanced over her shoulder, but didn't slow down.

The end of the track was coming up, the opening illuminated by the moon. Reilly emerged first, where the track approached the top of the red run from the left, with Minette not that far behind.

The light out here was eerie. The moon bright in a cloudless sky gave the slope an otherworldly feel. Minette swallowed as she followed Reilly towards the upper part of the slope that would, she imagined, drop down from a sharp incline.

Minette almost missed them – the two figures standing perilously close to the edge, silhouetted against the night sky.

It had been the raised voices that drew her attention. Looked like Reilly wasn't tricking her after all.

The moment Reilly saw them, she yelled. The figures stopped and looked their way. When Jacob recognised Reilly, he turned to Noah, shouting something at him.

Jacob took a swing at Noah, striking him across the jaw. Noah fell to the ground and Reilly gasped. She went to go to Jacob, but Minette reached out to grab her arm to hold her back.

'What the—'

But before either of the girls could do anything, Noah scrambled back up, his snowboard in his hand and whacked Jacob around the head with it, sending him falling backwards over the top of the run.

REILLY

A scream tore through the air and it took Reilly a moment to realise that the blood-curdling sound came from her. It echoed around the silent mountain top, drowning out the pounding in her head.

Reilly launched herself towards the lip of the slope that made this particular run so treacherous. The top of it was actually a black run. The red run swept off on the right-hand side and took a slower circuitous path down the mountain. But this section was a near twenty-foot steep drop, down to the bottom where Jacob now lay, unmoving.

'Jacob!' she screamed, but there was no response.

Minette appeared by her side, eyes wide with horror. Behind them Noah laughed like what he'd just done was some frat-boy prank.

'What can I do?' Minette asked, shaking, but determined.

'Take the red, down to Jacob. You have your phone?'

'*Oui.*'

'Call emergency services when you get down there.'

Minette looked back at her, worried – as if she wasn't sure she wanted to involve them.

'Leave him, Mins,' Noah ordered.

'Don't be stupid, call them!' Reilly said, grabbing Minette's shoulders and giving her a shake.

'Mountain rescue?'

'And the police,' Reilly ordered. 'Now go!'

'I don't think you want to do that, Mins. Your mother wouldn't approve,' Noah taunted.

Minette cast a nervous glance down the slope.

'Go!' Reilly yelled.

Minette backed away from the edge of the black run and, giving Noah a wide berth, made her way to the start of the red run.

Reilly was shaking. Trembling. Not with fear but fury. She'd never, *ever* been so angry before. She'd been terrified and devastated for Asma, furious that it had come to this, but what Noah had just done . . . And he found this *funny*?

The anger seemed ravenous, unending, insatiable and she saw it; how easy it would be to kill. How utterly reasonable it could seem.

'Why did you do that?' she screamed at Noah.

He looked at her and stopped laughing. His eyes boring into hers. 'Because I need you to take this seriously.'

'He did *nothing*,' Reilly cried, clicking out of her skis and, closing the distance between them, her boots crunching in the icy snow. It wasn't the thick, fluffy snow of the afternoon she'd spent out on the mountain with Jacob. No, this was *hard* snow. Dangerous snow.

'No, he didn't. So, imagine what I'm going to do to you.'

She felt the threat down to her very soul.

In his eyes she saw how deadly serious he was. That he'd permit nothing and no one to put him, his name or his family in jeopardy.

Noah thought he'd get away with this, but he was wrong. So wrong.

She shoved at him with both her hands, the power of it taking Noah a little by surprise. He slapped at her arms, and she shoved him again.

'Noah, I'm surprised at you. Letting a girl push you around,' she said, shoving at him once more. 'Then again, you're not really used to doing your own dirty work. You prefer to get someone else to do it for you, don't you?' she challenged.

Noah dug his heel in and held his ground. She'd either have to stop, or let him have his way a little.

Which would give her what she needed anyway.

'I don't know what you're talking about.'

'No? It's just you and me here, Noah. There's no one to perform to. There's no one else to threaten, so you can admit it now. That you made Asma's life a living hell. That you made a fake sex tape of her and a teacher. *You* did these crimes, Noah.'

'So what?' Noah replied with a careless shrug.

'You don't care? You don't care that you made it impossible for her to live?'

'Why should I? Asma was just an irritant in our lives. Jacob? Just another bloody hanger-on. You . . . ? Just a bit of unfinished business to clean up before I get back to uni.'

Reilly shook her head and smiled sadly. It was done. She'd got what she needed. He'd never be able to squirm his way out of this one. No matter what happened now, the phone in her ski-suit pocket had caught everything. His attack on Jacob, and enough of a confession for the sex tape to be linked back to him.

Justice at last.

Reilly turned to go, but his arm whipped out and grabbed her by the throat. Shock and fear struck, quicker than he had. She choked, her fingers scratching at his wrists, but he held on tight. Until his gaze flickered from her to her pocket.

'You little bitch!' he screamed, letting go of her throat to snatch the phone from the front pocket of her ski suit.

'No!' she yelled, grabbing at his hands, but he held the phone away from her. He shoved her hard and she fell back, giving him the time to click his boots into the snaps of his snowboard.

In a sudden rush, she realised his plan. He'd head down the mountain with her phone, the only evidence that she had of what he'd done. To Asma. To others. It was her only chance to make him pay.

Kicking out with one foot, he edged his way towards the red run Minette had gone down. If Reilly tried to do the same she'd never catch up, he'd have far too much of a head start.

Her only chance was the terrifying drop at the top the run, with limited visibility.

She clicked her boots into the skis and pushed towards the edge. Heart in her mouth, stomach in her throat, she didn't have a choice. She took a shuddering breath as she looked out over the near sheer drop. Even during the day, in the full light of sun, this would have been damn difficult. To get down it, she couldn't second-guess herself. She had to trust that she could do this. Hesitation would break her. There wouldn't be time or space to turn into the run. She'd just have to go straight down.

Go.

Ankles loose, knees slightly bent, stomach crunched, she launched herself over the edge, careening into the darkness. Just as the ground fell away from her, a firework exploded in the night sky. She had to let go and let gravity take her and trust her body to ride out the movement through her skis.

The out-of-body experience that swept her soul up as her body fell down lasted for a few terrifying moments before the bottom curve of the slope came rushing towards her, and if she didn't nail the landing, the least she would do was break something.

Reilly's skis sliced into the curve, sliding in directions she couldn't physically go. She nearly pulled a muscle trying to keep control of her skis and almost broke something when her pole yanked hard on the strap around her wrist, having got caught in the snow.

She pulled to a messy, terrifying stop; legs shaking, body trembling, bent double just trying to catch her breath.

'Reilly!' Minette cried, running towards her from where she'd been with Jacob. 'What's wrong with you?'

'Jacob?' Reilly managed to ask, the taste of blood in her mouth from where she must have bit her tongue. Her head ached and her eyes burned, just from staying open and terrified for the whole of that section of the run.

Minette shook her head and instead asked, 'Where's Noah?'

'He's coming down. He's got my phone,' Reilly said between gasps.

'Your phone?'

'It was recording. When he attacked Jacob. And then when we were talking. I got him to admit it. What he'd done. I got the evidence. But we need that phone!'

Shock and surprise registered in Minette's gaze but Reilly didn't care. She made her way over to Jacob on shaking legs, collapsing by his side. Red stained the side of his head, by his hair line, and bled into the snow.

Hands trembling, she was almost too scared to touch him.

'Jacob. Please, be OK. You have to be OK.'

Minette shifted her weight from foot to foot, behind her.

'Mountain Rescue are coming.'

He stirred.

'Oh my god, Jake, are you OK? Jacob? Can you hear me?'

His eyes fluttered.

She pressed her hands to either side of his face, careful not to move his neck. She might have just skied down that incline, but he'd *fallen*. He could have broken a hundred bones.

'Jacob,' she whispered, and his eyes opened, taking a heartbreakingly long time to focus.

'You . . . OK?' he asked, as relief broke through the lock on Reilly's lungs, and she wanted to curse.

Her head fell back and she blinked away the tears, before turning back to press a gentle kiss on his forehead.

'Don't worry about me. Are you OK?' Reilly asked.

Jacob let out a groan.

'He said you were hurt,' Jacob tried to explain through clenched teeth.

'Reilly,' Minette called, her voice urgent and worried.

'I'm OK,' Reilly told him.

'Where is he?' Jacob asked.

'Coming.'

'He's dangerous, Reilly.'

'I know.'

Jacob swallowed.

'Reilly,' Minette whined again.

'We need that phone,' Reilly said, turning to her. 'We need to get it back.'

Minette bit her cheek, and then braced herself, nodding finally.

'Can you do it?' Reilly asked.

'Yes,' Minette said, clipping into her skis.

'If you go now, you can get ahead and hide in the tree-line.'

She nodded again.

'All I need is for you to distract him enough to make him fall.' Minette stared at her with dull eyes. 'Minette!'

'I've got this,' she insisted, shaking herself alert and starting down the slope and into the run.

Reilly was torn, but not because she didn't trust Minette.

'You should go with her, it's not safe,' Jacob managed.

'I don't want to leave you,' she said, being pulled in two different directions.

He raised his hand to cup her cheek.

'Go. Rescue are on their way,' he insisted. 'She can't do this alone. She'll need you.'

The sound of board against snow from above was enough to warn them of Noah's presence, passing them from the upper slope of the red run.

'Go,' Noah commanded.

'I lost my pole,' she replied weakly.

'Take mine. Take mine, Reilly, and go. Minette's in danger. And so are you.'

CHAPTER TWENTY-THREE

MINETTE

Minette swept to a sharp stop and looked over her shoulder, her breath catching in her lungs. All she could see was the pale light of the moon bouncing off the hard icy snow of the slope dotted with the shadowy silhouettes of trees.

She'd found the narrowest part of the red run before it merged with an easier blue a little further down the mountain. If Noah reached that, he'd be free.

On the other side of the mountain was the New Year's Eve Night Ski route and she was sure that if her heart wasn't thundering in her ears, it might have been possible to make out the sounds of their celebrations.

Minette felt as if she were living a parallel life to those people. The people who had come to celebrate, to ski, to have fun. The people that didn't know about scouring guilt or hatred so powerful it stole your breath. She could blame Reilly. She could blame Asma. But really it had always been about her and Noah.

Minette strained to hear any kind of sound that would tell

her where or when Noah would come. Just the thought of it fisted an icy hand around her throat.

How was she supposed to get Reilly's phone from him?

She wasn't. She was just supposed to scare him enough to fall.

She could do that. She *could* do that.

But a part of her – a new part, shocking and powerful – wanted to do more than that . . . She wanted to end it. She didn't want this hanging over their heads any more. He had betrayed her; he had lied to her. She would forever be tainted by the guilt of what happened to Asma. She would never be clean and he would never let her forget it. She'd never escape him. Unless . . .

Minette flinched at the sound of fibreglass and wood on snow – a sleek, swishing noise that would haunt her for the rest of her life. Almost like the swish of a blade being sharpened on leather.

She needed that phone. It was her only redemption, the only way she could even begin to make up for what she had done in the past. She clicked out of her skis, picked them up and stepped back off the slope into the tree-line, so that he wouldn't see her. She had to time it perfectly, or he'd fly right past her.

She forced herself to imagine it. Jumping out wouldn't be enough. He'd be going at speed, he could easily slip around her. She could throw a branch across the run, forcing him to navigate around it, but that wouldn't stop him.

The swish came again. She was running out of time. She had to do something and quick.

She picked up the long ski by the back end and tested the weight in her hands. It was doable, she realised, with sickening clarity. Very doable.

Minette made her way to the edge of the tree-line, the swoosh coming for her like an anxiety dream, closer and closer and closer.

The boots made standing awkward, and she had to bend at the knee to maintain her balance. She'd have to step out on to the run and she'd have to do it quickly or—

'Mins?' Noah's nickname for her sent shivers down her spine. 'Where are you, love?'

They'd done this once. At the Institute. A whole group of them had snuck out at midnight and fled the campus grounds, scattering into the woods that surrounded the school, and played *la partie du touché*, or 'it', as Noah had called it. Only if you were caught . . . you were made to do whatever the person who caught you wanted.

Some had made it sexual, some had made it punishing. Noah had made it mean.

'Mins,' he roared.

She clenched her teeth together. She was supposed to be the one catching him this time, not the other way round.

Expectation wrapped around her fear. A visceral need for this confrontation. A knowing that it needed to be this way settled around her and she slunk back into the trees.

'Why did you take her side?' he called out. 'You know I wouldn't allow that,' he taunted sickeningly.

She heard the crunch of his boots – softer than the ski boots she wore – on the snow very close by.

He'd be expecting her to do nothing. To run away and hide.

Well, this time she wasn't hiding. Not from herself and not from him.

Minette saw Noah's shadow to the right of her and tightened her grip.

A second before he stepped into view, she let the long ski swing, twisting her hips for momentum and not stopping to brace for impact.

But he saw her a second after she moved, and Noah managed to shift so that the side of his arm took the brunt of the hit.

'Fuck,' he yelled, just managing to hold himself upright, while the force of her motion twisted her around into a fall.

'*Merde*,' she cursed, struggling to keep her balance.

Noah recovered more quickly than she did and he glared down at her. There was no way she could run, not in these boots.

She could take them off, but then she'd only be in her socks, in the snow.

But while she was thinking, he gathered himself and slapped her hard across the face.

Noah had never once hit her. The shock of it blanketed her, tuning her out of the present and wrapping her in cotton wool as she fell to the hard snow.

Ears ringing and face throbbing painfully, she looked up to find Noah standing over her, looking like he was *excited* by what he'd just done.

He grabbed her by the neck of her ski suit, shaking her as her boots scrabbled for purchase on the ground.

'Do you really think that you're anything without me?' he yelled in her face. 'You're just the same as them. Asma, Reilly, Jacob. You're *nothing* without me. Just the daughter of a whore.'

'I should never have let you have power over me. I should never have let you do what you did,' Minette spat at him.

'Let me? Let me? You *started* it, Mins. You enjoyed every minute of it. The power, the thrill of being able to turn a whole school against someone. You wanted it as much as me,' he whispered sickeningly into her ear.

Minette clenched her jaw. Yes, there had been times when she'd relished the power of it. And she would *never* forgive herself for that. But this time she *was* going to do something.

'Do you think that Reilly's only looking to punish *me*, Mins? Do you not think that she's got something against you too?' Noah half screamed at her.

Minette frowned. 'What are you talking about?'

'The messages and the picture? They were for you, Mins. *You* were the who she went after. You think she's just going to let you get away with it?'

Minette paused, looking back up the track to where she saw Reilly in the far distance coming towards them.

She shouldn't listen to him, but could she afford not to?

Noah's eyes glinted in the night and she didn't know whether he was lying or telling the truth.

'She said she didn't send the messages,' Minette whispered.

'She lied! You need to listen to me. She's not just after me,' he insisted.

Minette shook her head and he tightened his hold around her.

'You have to believe me,' he said, sounding almost as if he was begging.

But she didn't. She didn't have to listen to him ever again.

She struggled in his hold a little more frantically, waiting until he felt confident, until he thought he'd won, and then let herself just *drop* – her entire weight, utterly dead in his arms – pulling him down with her. Before they hit the ground she twisted out from under him and scrabbled up, her boots slamming down awkwardly on the hard snow.

Noah grunted in shock as she slammed a boot down on his back, relishing the way that he collapsed to the ground. His arms thrust out at his sides, one hand clutching Reilly's phone.

Evidence.

You think she's going to let you get away with it?

Before she could question herself, she stamped down on the hand holding the phone, smashing the screen and probably the bones in his hand at the same time. Noah howled in agony and it was as if the dam had burst. All that hatred, all that resentment came loose, pouring out of her like an avalanche.

Never again. She would never again let him threaten her or anyone else. Never let him bully her or anyone else. Legs trembling, she went to retrieve the snowboard that he'd left on the ground beside the tree-line. It didn't matter that her hands were shaking and her fingers were half frozen and numb. All she needed was the grip on his board.

'Mins—'

'No, Noah. Just . . . fuck off.' And with that, Minette swung the board down hard, meeting the back of his head with all her force and a sickening thud.

She dropped the snowboard and braced herself on her knees, body shaking from fear or exertion, she wasn't quite sure any more. Minette sucked huge mouthfuls of frigid air into her lungs, but it didn't feel like enough. As if she'd never be able to breathe properly again. Hands covered in sweat, she tore her gloves off with her teeth and grabbed a handful of snow and washed the stinging heat from her face with it.

Pulling her hands back, she caught sight of the streaks of red merging with the snow melting on her skin and she screamed, realising that she was covered in Noah's blood. She shook her hands to get it off, but it was everywhere. Her hands, her skin, her coat.

The swish, swish of skis cut over the sound of the unholy cries she was making as she tugged at the zip, trying to get her jacket off. Someone was coming, and when Minette looked up, she found Reilly staring at her in horror.

'What have you done?'

REILLY

Reilly couldn't believe what she'd seen. Minette ... the board ... Noah.

Minette staggered back from Noah's body as Reilly clicked out of her skis and stumbled towards them, gorge rising as she caught sight of the blood pooling from his head.

'I didn't ... I didn't ...' Minette stuttered.

'Shhh.'

'I—'

'Minette!' Reilly yelled, cutting her off before she could say anything incriminating just as the sound of voices came from further up the mountain.

Minette looked wide-eyed in shock back to the run Reilly had just skied down, finally noticing the flashlights of the search and rescue team who had come for Jacob. And that's when Minette started to really shake.

'Is he ... ?' Minette asked from behind the hand pressed against her mouth as if she hadn't realised what she'd done.

Reilly frowned. Did Minette really have to ask?

Reilly looked down at Noah's body, saw the crumpled mess of his hand wrapped around her phone.

Her phone. The evidence.

She looked back up at Minette, who was watching her from hooded eyes.

Reilly reached over Noah's body and pulled her phone out of his rapidly cooling hands.

Then suddenly they were surrounded by red-suited skiers, lighting up the run with hand-held torches, shouting at them in a mixture of French and German.

A tall man clicked out of his skis and rushed over to take Noah's pulse, while at the same time shouting into the radio clipped to his ski jacket.

Reilly slipped her broken phone into her pocket and glared at Minette, hoping she'd understand the warning to keep her mouth shut.

'What happened here?' he demanded in English.

Reilly opened her mouth, but Minette answered before she could.

'We were just supposed to go night skiing. We wanted more of a challenge than the organised route. We were just trying to have some fun.'

The desperate pleading in her tone almost had Reilly convinced.

'We got to the top of the run and we,' Minette said, gesturing to Reilly, 'wanted to go down the red run, but the boys were arguing about going down the black. Noah went first and we thought we heard him fall, but we couldn't be sure. So, Jacob went straight down after him, but got hurt too.'

'How did he get down here?' the man asked, feeling around the side of Noah's head and grimacing. The blood pooling around his body looked devastating and Reilly couldn't be sure she hadn't seen brain matter.

She turned away before she could be sick.

When one of the other men approached, Reilly reached out a hand to his arm. 'Jacob? The other boy? Is he . . . Is he going to . . .'

The man pressed his hand over hers, understanding shining in his gaze.

'They're bringing him down the mountain in a rescue sled. Can you give us his parents' details?'

'Yes, I can find them,' Reilly said, turning back to Minette, who nodded at her to go with the ski patrol guy.

Once again, Reilly was torn. She wanted to go with Jacob, but she wasn't entirely sure it was a good idea to leave Minette either.

'Go, I'll wait here,' Minette urged her.

Reilly gave Noah one last look, just as the man trying to assess him on the ground shook his head at his colleague.

Dead.

Noah was dead.

Reilly met Minette's eyes one final time, her expression unreadable, before turning away to follow the two-man crew taking Jacob down the mountain to the medical centre.

She refused the offer of help from ski patrol, perfectly capable of getting down the easy blue and green runs that led back to the heart of the village.

She kept the orange sled on which Jacob had been secured in her line of sight the entire time and the moment they reached the hospital she used the phone to call Savannah Coates, the Vandenburg manager who would no doubt get in touch with Mark Vandenburg and Jacob's parents. Beyond that, her only focus was Jacob.

Reilly waited in a white, sterile hallway, not seeing anything other than the doors that separated her from Jacob. She stared at them with one single thought in her mind.

He had to be OK. He *had* to be.

She barely even stirred when Hugo came rushing in with Anike by his side. With them came the adults – Mark, Jacob's parents . . . Reilly pushed herself into a corner, feeling strangely separate from them and, despite what had passed between her and Jacob, unsure as to whether she should even be there?

Reilly tried to peer through the frosted glass of the doors to the treatment rooms, but all she could see was the curtain that had been drawn around Jacob's bed. She bit her lip until the sharp sting and metallic taste warned her to let it go.

That was when the team that had been up on the mountain brought in a sled carrying a black body bag. Everyone came to a slow stop, the mounting horror of a death on the slope was something no one wanted to imagine, let alone see. Minette followed behind the sled, her every step slow and dragging.

But before Reilly could catch her attention, James Scarisbrick came bursting through the double doors, demanding to see his son.

Whatever James had done, whatever part he'd had to play in covering up his son's behaviour – which he surely must have done – wouldn't come close to justifying the look of anguish across the man's face as he was told of his son's death.

Reilly turned away. James's face merged with Asma's father's face – the same look of grief across them both, the same shock and disbelief as if what they were being told was inconceivable.

She'd never imagined that this was how it would end. All she'd wanted was the truth to come out, for justice to be served. But not like this.

Reilly gripped the broken phone in her pocket with shaking fingers.

Hugo and Anike made their way over to Reilly, hand in hand, inseparable.

'What happened?' Hugo asked, wide-eyed and shocked.

'I don't know, Hugo. He went down a run he shouldn't have,' Reilly said, picking her words from what Minette had said earlier. 'He just . . . disappeared.'

'What were you all doing out there?' Anike asked.

Reilly didn't even know how to answer that question. If she said as little as possible, then perhaps it would be OK.

Anike turned to find Minette coming towards them and broke away from Hugo to take her in her arms.

Hugo met Reilly's gaze. 'Is there something I should know? It's OK, if there is . . .' he let dangle. 'You can tell me.'

Reilly swallowed. Absurdly she *did* want to tell him. She wanted to tell Hugo everything, but just then Jacob's father appeared in the open doors to the treatment room, his gaze roaming the corridor until it landed on her.

'Reilly?' he asked.

She nodded, not quite trusting herself to speak. Jacob's father beckoned her back through the doors to where they had been treating Jacob.

Jacob looked very much like his father. Tall, lean, high cheekbones. Steady. Dependable. Trustworthy.

Reilly looked back to Hugo who shooed her away and she all but ran to where Mr Arcilla stood holding the door open for her. He greeted her with a tired smile and ushered her, heart pounding, through to the curtained room where Jacob lay on the gurney. Everything in her wanted to just collapse at the sight of him. Bruises marked his torso; his ribs had been bandaged and his leg was in a splint.

Oh god.

Reilly started to shake.

'He's going to be OK,' Mr Arcilla said, placing a gentle reassuring hand on her shoulder and Reilly forced a nod, pulling herself together. Until Jacob prised his eyes open, and the look in them made her want to cry all over again.

His gaze was fierce, protective, full of questions that she couldn't answer in that moment.

It was done. Noah was no longer a threat. He was no longer anything.

Jacob raised his good hand from the bed and she went to take it, pressing kisses across knuckles that had somehow remained miraculously unmarred by damage from the fall.

She opened her mouth to apologise. To tell him how awful it had been, but with his parents just behind her she couldn't.

'It's OK,' Jacob said, reassuring her and this time she did cry. 'It's all going to be OK,' he said, smoothing her hair and she laid her head on his shoulder as he drew her to him and knew that she would stay right there until he said he didn't want or need her.

It's done, Asma.

I'm done.

CHAPTER TWENTY-FOUR

JACOB

Reilly fluffed the pillow behind his head and Jacob made a grab for her, pulling her into a kiss. There was something in her eyes now . . . or perhaps just something *gone* from her eyes and she seemed lighter, happier and quicker to laugh. Things that made his heart sing to see.

She groaned lightly and tapped him gently on the arm.

'I have to go,' she complained against his lips.

'Just a few more minutes,' he begged.

She laughed, the curve of her lips pressed against his making him wonder how he'd got so lucky to have met her. And Jacob then inwardly rolled his eyes at himself. Cool bro, play it cool. But when she looked at him with that glitter in her eyes, he pulled her back to him for another kiss.

'OK, you two, parent present.'

They sprang apart quicker than he thought himself capable of moving, just as his father came into the bedroom.

He looked around at the hotel suite Mark Vandenburg had

put Jacob up in to recover. 'You know, I think I like this more than the chalet,' he said. 'It's not so . . .'

'Money?'

'It's still money, Jacob,' his father replied, reminding him just how indebted they were to the Vandenburgs.

Jacob nodded, wanting his father to understand that he wasn't taking this for granted. He wasn't taking *anything* for granted any more.

Reilly kissed him on his forehead and whispered goodbye before giving his father a shy smile and heading back to the chalet. The girls were leaving and she wanted to see them before they left.

Mark Vandenburg had released her from her contract, which Reilly had accepted without saying a word about the draft resignation letter in her emails. But she wanted to say goodbye to Anike and Minette.

Just the thought of her seeing the French girl again made Jacob uncomfortable, but Reilly had assured him that things were fine through a combination of acceptance and mutually assured destruction. But there were worse ways to make sure she was safe, Jacob told himself.

'How're you doing?' his father asked.

'Sore,' Jacob admitted, wincing as he shifted, the fracture in his ribs making itself known every time he laughed, coughed, tried to move or tried to kiss Reilly, which was just plain annoying.

'Do you think they let you out too soon?'

'No, they wouldn't have dared risk it for a guest of the Vandenburgs. If anything, they probably kept me in longer for it. Were work mad that you had to delay your return?'

His father pulled a face. 'You come first. They can wait.'

It was the 4th January. Four days since the events on the mountain on New Year's Eve. Jacob had been set free from the treatment centre forty-eight hours ago and been brought straight to the Vandenburg Hotel. And Reilly hadn't once left his side.

'I like her,' his father said happily, as if divining his thoughts.

'I do too,' Jacob added, scrunching his face at the realisation of just how much.

His father laughed. 'I think I made that face when I met your mother.'

'What face?' Jacob asked.

'The kind of "oh shit, I think I need to keep her" face?'

Jacob bit his lips, trying hard not to smile.

'Yeah, that one,' his father confirmed before the humour died away a little.

Jacob felt the shift in the room and knew what was coming.

'I'm going to take your Mom home. I think it's time that she got some proper help.'

Jacob nodded, his throat thick with emotion. Guilt, at forcing the issue, but also relief and hope.

'I'm sorry I didn't do it sooner. I . . . just kept hoping and hoping,' his father said, looking at the floor.

'Me too, Dad. Me too,' Jacob admitted.

'Call me when you know what your plans are. I'll do the same. But we'll figure it out. Your uncle has offered to lend us some money. It might not cover everything, but at least it means you can stay on at Harvard. But whatever happens, we'll – *I'll*' – he hastily corrected – 'make sure that it's OK.' His father had a determined look in his eye and Jacob believed him. Jacob knew that he was right.

And for the first time in a really long time, Jacob felt a damp heat press against the backs of his eyes.

'I love you,' his father said.

'Love you too, Dad,' Jacob said breathing through a strange kind of tightness in his chest.

He watched his father go and pressed his head back against the pillow. His mother had been in a state when she'd met him at the medical treatment centre, her withdrawals making her probably worse than him. And he'd seen it. How hard she was fighting her addiction to be there for him, to make sure that he was OK. For that moment, she'd been his mother again. And though he'd never have wanted to go to such extreme lengths to see it, it had given him hope that she was still in there somewhere.

'Knock, knock,' Hugo said from the doorway. 'Nice digs,' he added without looking around the room.

'I mean, some cheap prick couldn't be bothered to get me an upgrade,' Jacob whined.

'Ha ha,' Hugo said with an easy grin, but Jacob could still see the smudged shadows beneath his eyes.

'How's it going?' Jacob asked.

'I should be asking *you* that,' Hugo said, coming to stand at the end of Jacob's bed.

Jacob shrugged, purposefully not wincing as the crack in his ribs pinched his side. 'Humour me.'

'Ani's father let her stay, despite wanting to drag her back home,' Hugo offered.

'Now that *is* impressive,' Jacob acknowledged, happy to hear it.

Hugo rubbed his chin with the heel of his hand, grinning. 'Yeah. Well, I'm not saying it's going to be easy. I've had lighter interrogations from the Caribbean police.'

And Jacob knew he wasn't joking.

'And while I don't have a green light, I don't have a red light either,' Hugo shared.

'You'll get there,' Jacob assured him.

'Of course I will. Fathers love me,' Hugo said with unabashed confidence. There was an easy pause before Hugo pressed on. 'So, Reilly, huh?'

'Yup,' Jacob replied, popping the 'p'.

'She's cool,' Hugo said with a smile.

'She is,' Jacob replied with a grin.

'You guys are going to stay on for a bit?'

Jacob nodded. They'd discussed it briefly over the last few days.

He couldn't really go that far with the leg splint which would need to stay on for a few more days. And then he'd have to work around the cast for a bit. Jacob certainly wasn't going to be running marathons any time soon, let alone playing lacrosse. Hugo had to be thinking about Jacob's place on the team. Maybe Coach would finally give Hugo a second chance.

It had taken Jacob a little by surprise. He thought he'd have been devastated at not being able to play, but after the last few heart-stopping weeks, Jacob realised that he just wanted to rest. He hadn't shared it with Reilly yet, but he was thinking about pausing his academic year. Taking the next couple of terms off and perhaps looking for somewhere else to finish college.

Whatever future he had coming to him, it wasn't worth bankrupting his family, certainly not just for some fancy college name. And having seen what some people would do just to keep their hands on their wealth, to hide their depravity and desperation behind money and corruption ... No. Jacob needed a break from people like that. Hugo excluded, but still ...

'I reckon I won't be heading back for at least a few weeks,' Jacob said, answering Hugo's question. 'I need a holiday. And not at your expense!' he rushed to say.

Hugo let out a laugh.

'Don't be silly, bro. You're here for as long as you need. For *anything* you need, OK?'

'Appreciate it,' Jacob replied.

'Have the police been by?' Hugo asked.

Jacob nodded. 'Yeah.'

'What did they say?'

Jacob still felt a little sick when he thought of the interview with the police, James Scarisbrick standing behind them, glaring at him as if he knew Jacob was lying. But he hadn't. He'd answered every single question they'd asked, truthfully. But he hadn't offered them anything more. His conscience was clean. As was Reilly's. But Minette? That was a different matter.

Jacob hadn't liked leaving Reilly alone with the police. He'd had his parents, Minette had her mother, but Reilly had looked almost vulnerable standing there by herself. Until an older

Swiss woman had arrived and had used a grim-faced stoicism to protect Reilly better than any high-paid lawyer. Even Jacob's father had been impressed. Reilly had later introduced her to them as Lisolette Keller and it was clear that they'd known each other for a long time.

Now, Jacob remembered how before the police had questioned him, his father had looked at him. 'Is there anything I need to know?'

No judgement, no fear, just honest-to-god acceptance, and it had been close to the most pure, exquisite thing that Jacob had ever experienced between him and his father.

And that's when Jacob realised what he felt for Reilly wasn't so different. Call it love, loyalty, devotion . . .

'You thinking about Reilly again?' Hugo asked, pulling him back to the present. 'You look whipped,' Hugo observed with a grin.

'A lot can happen in twelve days,' Jacob replied.

It can and it had.

'Yeah, well you can invite me to the wedding,' Hugo quipped.

'You'll be the first on the invite list,' Jacob assured him.

Hugo held his gaze, and Jacob saw it sober, as a furrow appeared across his brow.

'What happened out there?' Hugo asked.

Jacob inhaled slowly and sighed. He'd thought about how to answer this. For the most part, he didn't actually know. Reilly had told him what she'd seen, what she'd heard. But it didn't change a thing.

'A terrible accident,' Jacob replied. 'Nothing more.'

REILLY

Reilly pulled a tissue from the box on the sideboard and passed it to Anike.

'I'm sorry, it's just . . . it's all a little much,' Anike tried to explain with a watery smile.

'Don't be silly,' Reilly assured her. 'It's been a lot.'

'But the thought of the two of you, out on the mountain, with Jacob hurt and Noah . . .'

Reilly flicked her gaze to where Minette was hugging her coffee to her with both hands, staring down at the table.

'It just, doesn't bear thinking about,' Anike said, shooting Minette a miserable look and flapping the tissue in her hand at her eyes rather than dabbing it.

Anike's bags were by the door and her father and Karel were in the car waiting for her to say her goodbyes.

'I think we're going to be OK,' Reilly said, daring to answer for Minette, who had been quiet all morning. With Reilly not actually working at the chalet as host any more, her presence had disrupted whatever hierarchy had been in place before.

Anike nodded and swept Reilly up into a quick, firm hug that made her smile. She liked Anike. She'd never be able to say the same of Minette, but she had genuinely liked Anike and maybe one day in the not too distant future, they might even become friends. But really, the only future Reilly could picture at the moment was with Jacob.

Finally letting Reilly go, Anike went around behind the chair that Minette was sitting on and hugged her from behind.

Minette smiled and rubbed a hand over Anike's where they met just above her heart.

'*Merci*, Minette.'

'*Au revoir*, Ani,' Minette said, turning her face to press a kiss against Anike's cheek.

If Minette noticed the sense of deflation in her friend's demeanour, she didn't respond to it. So Anike swept out of the chalet with her handbag in one hand and her rolling suitcase in another; a positively chic exit anyone would be proud to make.

Reilly let the smile slowly drop from her lips as she turned back to Minette, who was staring up at her with solemn eyes. Reilly took a seat at the table.

'When do you head out?' Reilly asked.

'Soon,' Minette replied. 'Papa is coming to pick us up.'

'Your mother?' Reilly asked.

'She's fine.'

Personally, Reilly wondered if there was something wrong with the woman who had not once displayed a single drop of emotion. Not even when she finally turned up at the medical centre to pick up her daughter. Reilly might have been fluent in French, but it was completely unnecessary to translate the few short, clipped words shared between mother and daughter.

And maybe for the first time, Reilly realised how alone Minette had been. Her parents, uninterested or absent; her friends, interchangeable. Her boyfriend, emotionally toxic and coercive at best.

The thought must have reflected in some way on her face, because Minette asked, 'What?'

'Nothing,' Reilly replied.

'So . . . I guess we just . . . go back to normal? Pretend like none of this happened?' Minette asked and Reilly wondered if she saw hope in the other girl's eyes.

Reilly took her smashed phone from her back pocket and laid it on the table in between them.

Minette stared at it, her face an indifferent mask and for the first time Reilly saw the resemblance between Minette and her mother.

'Does it work?' Minette asked eventually.

Reilly shook her head.

'Can you fix it?'

'Maybe.'

Minette looked away. 'Are you going to?'

Reilly sighed. 'I'm not sure yet.'

The silence between them wasn't tense. It wasn't comfortable, but more resigned, as if too much had happened for them to ever be anything other than wary of each other.

'Do you think it would do any good? For any of it to come out?' Minette asked.

'That's the question, I suppose.'

Reilly hadn't yet watched the footage. She'd been too wrapped up in making sure that Jacob was OK. She wasn't even sure she ever wanted to watch it. She was pretty sure it had caught the moment that Noah had attacked Jacob. She didn't think that he'd had enough time to stop the recording or even delete it. It wouldn't be that hard to check. She was also pretty sure that both Noah and Minette had thought the footage was only stored on the phone, and not on the private server she'd been live streaming it to. Not that Reilly had any intention of letting Minette know that.

'How did you send the messages?' Minette asked, and Reilly blinked.

'I told you. I didn't send those messages, Minette,' Reilly said gently.

Minette stared at her a little bit longer before nodding and taking a sip of her coffee.

Minette's phone vibrated on the table with a message from her mother.

'And that's me,' Minette said after a beat, pushing her chair back and coming to stand.

Reilly mirrored her movement and the two of them faced each other in the living area of the chalet.

'Forgive me for saying this, but I hope I don't ever see you again,' Minette replied with a brutal honesty that, of all that Reilly had seen of her, she respected.

'I understand,' Reilly said truthfully.

Minette walked past her to get to the front door. Just like Anike, Minette's cases were waiting at the entrance.

There was both so much more and very little left to say. A very strange feeling filled Reilly. As if she was losing something. As if, when Minette walked out that door, she'd have lost the last little piece of her best friend, Reilly thought as her heart thudded painfully in her chest.

Minette's steps slowed as she reached the door.

'I . . .' Minette swallowed, before trying again. 'I really am sorry for what happened with Asma. I'll never regret anything in my life as much as what happened to her. She was a good person, filled with a kindness that was beyond me, and I am so very sorry for the part I had to play in her death,' Minette added.

Reilly struggled with her temper. There was a bit of her that still wanted to hiss and bite and snarl.

'I wish she'd never met me,' Minette confessed. 'I wish she'd never moved into my room. But there's nothing more I can do than say I'm truly sorry for what happened.'

Reilly held Minette's steady gaze, wishing so very badly that she could trust what she was saying.

Was she telling the truth? Did it really matter?

The questions lasted long after Minette had left the chalet.

It was almost dusk when Reilly realised that she'd been standing in the middle of the chalet's living area for at least an hour, her cheeks damp and her tears run dry.

She'd come her for revenge, for her best friend, to make the person responsible for her death pay for it. And in doing so, she'd got closure for herself. She'd done everything she said she would, everything she'd promised herself she'd do.

Asma could rest in peace now.

And Reilly? She would leave this all behind and never think about it again.

Instead, she would think about a future with Jacob. She was wondering whether he might be interested in deferring his university year. Perhaps they could spend some time together. Reilly didn't even want to travel. She just wanted to get to know him. All of him. This guy who had captured her heart.

She wanted to make decisions based on *her* wants and needs now.

The sun was setting behind the mountains and it was dark as she made her way back down the hill to the Vandenburg Hotel for the last time.

Out on the slopes, two skiers were making their way down pristine white slopes, looping gracefully across the width of the run.

In her head, Reilly heard the sound of Asma's laughter, remembering the way that they had done the same, the last time they went out skiing.

The last time that they had felt truly free.

And in her mind and her heart, that's how Reilly wanted to remember Asma.

Free. Happy. Laughing.

Reilly thought she might have finally got that for Asma. And maybe, just maybe, she could get that for herself with Jacob.

EPILOGUE

SIX MONTHS LATER...

The bright sun beamed down on the little café in Paris. Summer was truly in full swing now and, for Minette, it felt as if the events of six months earlier were a whole world away. She leaned back in her chair, the large, oversized sunglasses allowing her to people watch without getting caught.

Sometimes something reminded her of what had happened. It could be the sound of someone's laugh, perhaps a little too similar to Hugo's, or a flash of blonde hair like Reilly's, or maybe even just the occasional message from Anike.

They'd tried to stay in touch when they'd come back to college, but Anike's father had moved her out of the halls of residence and into an apartment in the heart of Paris where he could keep a better eye on her. And . . . it had been hard. Anike had got caught up in her relationship with Hugo, which the press had absolutely adored. Headlines had proclaimed the Vandenburgs 'cursed', but despite that, the relationship had survived. Anike's father's company shares had wobbled a little, but money begat money, and within a month both the Vandenburgs and the Dossongui empire, were doing just fine.

Still, the messages between Minette and Anike had become less and less frequent, which had suited Minette just fine. Coming back to university, she'd finally been able to put the past behind her, and as Anike was now linked to that past, she'd had to go.

It was a shame, but *c'est la vie*, Minette thought with an elegant shrug of her shoulder.

She took a sip of her cappuccino, her tongue slipping out to sweep away the scattering of ground cinnamon and nutmeg that clung to her Chanel lipstick. She put the cup down and, for a second, the kiss of rouge on the lip of the white cup reminded her of the blood pooling around Noah's head and bleeding into the snow.

Minette let the ebb and flow of tourists and pedestrians distract her as she waited. She'd made a new friend. Her name was Annabelle, and she was studying languages as well and was not being as subtle as she thought she was being about wanting to do some work experience with Minette's mother. Not that it really bothered Minette that much.

She turned her face to the sun and felt the delicious warmth heat her skin. Never again would she go back to Val D'Amer Doux. Never again would she go skiing.

Never again would she be that cold.

She'd put everything behind her.

Everything, she thought, as she smiled at the waiter who asked if there was anything he could get her. Anything at all.

Minette smiled at the flirtation and thought that perhaps it was time to dip her toe back into the dating pool. She was just about to ask for his number, when she thought she felt someone's gaze on her. She looked up and her eyes snagged on a woman across the street.

Asma.

Minette blinked and sat up, knocking the cup and spilling coffee into the saucer.

It couldn't have been, could it?

They never found a body.

She was still there, the woman staring at her from across the road – long dark hair and brown eyes just like Asma's and—

The waiter came to mop up the spilt coffee, promising her a fresh cappuccino. She waved him away, but by the time he moved, whoever had been standing across the street from her had gone.

Minette's heart pounded in her chest, and she tried to dismiss the encounter as something silly brought on by the reminder of Noah.

Annabelle arrived shortly after and they caught up over croissants and more coffee, complaining about parents and the lack of boyfriends. Minette politely offered to introduce Annabelle to her mother, and the girl seemed so happy and so thankful, Minette wondered why she'd waited so long. They finally bid each other farewell and just as she paid the bill her phone chimed.

She checked the message and dropped her phone in shock. Hands shaking, legs trembling, Minette bent down to the floor and swept up her phone before the waiter could see the message she'd just read.

Her head whipped around, looking to see if someone was watching her, feeling sick and feeling scared. No, no, no, no. This couldn't be happening.

She glanced back at the phone.

UNKNOWN NUMBER
Someone's been naughty.
You've been keeping secrets.
But don't worry. I'll be there for you.
See you soon.

ACKNOWLEDGEMENTS

A small army went into the making of this book and it's only right that they are thanked – profusely – for the heavy lifting that allowed *How The Other Half Kill* to go from their incredibly capable hands into yours. Every single person in the team at Hachette Children's is fabulous, deserves a huge raise and epic holidays – just maybe not at a Vandenburg resort! My enormous thanks goes (in no particular order) to Anne Marie Ryan, Katie Levy, Laura Pritchard, Naomi Greenwood, Emma Zipfel, Victoria Ing, Valentina Fazio, Kirsty Moore, Nils Jones, Inka Melson and Katie Maxwell.

This book was planned, discussed, thought about, written, revised, and completed across dinner tables, ferry trips, glasses of wine, drives up and down the country, memories of family holidays, walks in Wales, lazy mornings and late nights with friends, family and loved ones. So here are the people that took care of *me* while I wrote the book . . . My deep and fervent thanks go to Carrie Nichols, Rachael Thomas and Katy Watson for keeping me on track so I hit my deadlines; to Nic Caws, Joanne Grant and Laurie Johnson for keeping me (mostly!) sane along the way; and to Rani Jenz, Stella Giatrakou and Hannah Cowley for supporting me long before I began writing this book.

ALSO AVAILABLE

Photo credit: © Richard Bloom

P. C. ROSCOE

has sold cheese in Borough Market, scrubbed pans in a canteen, poured more pints of beer than is strictly necessary, processed invoices for a multinational, researched TV scripts, and edited romance. But her favourite job, by far, is writing, where she gets to immerse herself in tension-filled, high-stakes stories. She grew up in London and recently moved to a cottage in Norfolk where she splits her time between writing, cooking disasters and half-finished DIY projects, and she honestly couldn't be happier.